SPQR XII

ORACLE OF THE DEAD

Also by
JOHN MADDOX ROBERTS

SPQR XII

ORACLE OF THE DEAD

JOHN MADDOX ROBERTS

THOMAS DUNNE BOOKS
ST. MARTIN'S MINOTAUR ☙ NEW YORK

This is a work of fiction. All of the characters, organizations, and events portrayed in this novel are either products of the author's imagination or are used fictitiously.

THOMAS DUNNE BOOKS.

An imprint of St. Martin's Press.

SPQR XII: ORACLE OF THE DEAD. Copyright © 2008 by John Maddox Roberts. All rights reserved. Printed in the United States of America. For information, address St. Martin's Press, 175 Fifth Avenue, New York, N.Y. 10010.

www.thomasdunnebooks.com

www.minotaurbooks.com

Library of Congress Cataloging-in-Publication Data

Roberts, John Maddox.

Oracle of the Dead / John Maddox Roberts.—1st ed.

p. cm.

ISBN-13: 978-0-312-38093-9

ISBN-10: 0-312-38093-3

1. Metellus, Decius Caecilius (Fictitious character)—Fiction. 2. Private investigators—Rome—Fiction. 3. Priests—Rome—History—Republic, 265–30 B.C.—Fiction.

PS3568.O23874 O73 2008

813'.54—dc22

2008030117

First Edition: December 2008

10 9 8 7 6 5 4 3 2 1

This book is dedicated to the Albuquerque
First Friday Writer's Group,
with special affection for Tony Hillerman,
an inspiration and encouragement
for writers everywhere

SPQR XII

ORACLE OF THE DEAD

1

I FIRST HEARD OF THE ORACLE OF THE Dead during the year of my praetorship. I was *praetor peregrinus*, traveling all over Italy and hearing cases that involved foreigners. It was an extremely agreeable way to spend a year in office and it kept me out of Rome, where things were getting very ugly that year. I spent much of the year in and around Baiae, partly because I had the use of a villa near there and partly because it was a very pleasant place and I could do pretty much as I liked.

"It's not far from here," Sextus Plotius told me. He was a director of the bronze founder's syndicate, a very prominent local *eques* and, most importantly, he served the best Chian vintage I ever tasted. "Been here forever, maybe from the time of the Aborigines. It's said that Odysseus and Aeneas both consulted the Oracle there."

Baiae is, of course, named for its founder Baios, the steersman of Odysseus. Half the towns I have been in, including Rome, claim to have been founded by a Trojan War veteran or a near descendant of one. This is odd since, if you credit Homer, so many people were killed there that it's hard to believe so many town founders could have survived.

"How wonderful!" Julia gushed. "Can we see it?" My wife was much more interested in religious matters than I. I had already visited the far more famous Cumaean Sibyl, also nearby, and had not been impressed.

"Actually," I said, "we have a perfectly good *mundus* in Rome, my dear."

"It's not the same thing at all," she insisted. "The *mundus* just gives us access to the souls of our dead in the underworld. There's no oracle."

"And the dead know the answers to all things," our host added.

I knew that I would end up going to see this marvel. I have never understood why people attribute such omniscience to the dead. Nobody thought most of them were knowledgeable while they were alive and I don't anticipate a postmortem education. Even if they want to contact us, why expect them to tell the truth? Most people are liars while alive, so why shouldn't they continue as such after death? People have such unrealistic expectations.

So, the next morning, I found myself occupying a monstrous litter on its way to the Oracle. Besides myself, my wife, and Plotius, the litter held Julia's cousin, also Julia but nicknamed Circe, and Antonia, a sister of Marcus Antonius, the famous one, Caesar's loyal supporter, soon to be Master of Horse and, in time, triumvir. Behind us in another litter were a few others of our party: my freedman Hermes, a kinsman named Marcus Caecilius Metellus, and a few others whose names escape me now. Being a praetor and holding imperium, I traveled in considerable state in those days, with a whole gaggle of attendants. I'd left my lictors at my villa, since it was a day on which official business was forbidden.

It was an enjoyable trip, because traveling through the Campanian countryside is always enjoyable. Campania holds some of the fairest land in all of Italy. It was once held most unreasonably by a pack of

Campanians and Samnites and Greeks and such before we conquered it and settled a lot of good, dependable Roman citizens there to keep the natives in their place. In time we came to a temple on the beautiful bay, with a fine view of the water and the island of Capreae beyond. At the moment we arrived, a fleet of galleys set out from the nearby naval harbor, walking across the water on their oars like aquatic centipedes, adding to the picturesque aspect of the scene, like a fresco come to life.

The ladies made the usual delighted noises as we disembarked from our prodigious transports. Looking around, I gave the temple some attention. It was a strange one, even for southern Campania, where many odd gods are worshipped. It had recently been refurbished to traditional Greek taste, in the Doric style like most Greek temples in Italy. But I could see that it was far older and had been built on a plan I had seen only in certain very ancient ruins, most of them in Marsian territory.

Even odder than the temple were the priests waiting to greet us. Atop the steps were six men in white robes wearing laurel chaplets, clearly devotees of Apollo and quite conventional, but at the bottom were six more robed in black, three men and three women. They wore wreaths of asphodel, a funerary plant, and the priestesses held a number of black dogs on leashes.

"Is there one temple here or two?" I asked Plotius.

"Two, really. The upper temple is dedicated to Apollo, as you can see. The cave of the Oracle of the Dead lies beneath it."

"Those look like priests of Hecate," Circe said. "The asphodel is sacred to her."

"And the black bitch is her tutelary animal," Antonia added. Like many other aristocratic Roman ladies, they knew far too much about foreign cults, especially the less reputable ones. Hecate is Thracian in origin, though she used to be worshipped widely in southern Italy.

"How fitting," Julia said. "Ulysses and Aeneas both invoked Hecate before entering the underworld." She caught my look. "Well, after all, Aeneas was an ancestor of my family." Sometimes I wondered about Julia.

3

Plotius made the introductions. The chief priest of Apollo was named Eugaeon, and I have forgotten the others. They extended the customary welcome, all the more enthusiastically because I was a Roman praetor. While they did this, they ignored their black-robed colleagues. It was as if these people did not exist. I refrained from asking, willing to go along with whatever local custom prevailed.

Then we got the tour of the temple. As I had thought, the interior revealed far greater antiquity than the exterior with its veneer of white marble and its new, Doric columns. It was murky inside, despite the coating of white paint, which covered what appeared to be older paintings and low-relief carvings. The statue of Apollo was pretty but looked out of place in this gloomy setting. He was in his rarely depicted aspect as Apollo the Far-Shooter, holding a bow with a quiver of arrows by his thigh. This is Apollo in his aspect as avenger. I was certain that one of the old terra-cotta images had once occupied its plinth, or perhaps one of wood. There were rude Italian gods in this place for many centuries before the Greeks came with their graceful deities.

Back outside, we were turned over to the other lot for the real purpose of our visit. They stood where we had first seen them. None of them had as much as touched the lowest temple step. To my surprise, the first to greet us was one of the women.

"Does the praetor seek wisdom?" she asked, oddly.

"Well, I have a fair store of it already," I began. Julia hit me in the ribs with an elbow. "I can always use more, of course."

"Praetor," Plotius said, "this is Iola, chief priestess of the Oracle."

"The Oracle is the source of all knowledge," she said in that thrillingly portentous voice employed by religious charlatans everywhere.

"Then it has some competition," I observed. "The Sibylline Books, the various prophetesses situated here and there—" another elbow from Julia.

"Frauds," Iola said succinctly.

"How so?" I asked.

"They claim to speak for gods. Our Oracle communicates with the dead. Have you ever known a god personally?"

"Well, they've only come to me in dreams," I admitted.

"But I will wager you have known a great many dead people."

"Um, never thought of it that way," I said, flustered as always when some total loon employs good logic.

She nodded. "Just so. Come with me." She turned and led us around to the rear of the temple, with the other sacerdotes and bitches in attendance.

"Why is the entrance around the back?" I wanted to know.

"To face the sunrise," the priestess explained. "At sunrise on Midsummer Day, the sun is positioned precisely in the center of the doorway and shines straight down the shaft."

"That must be impressive," I said. Roman religion does not make a great thing of the solstices and equinoxes, except to have festivals in their general vicinity, such as Saturnalia. This may have been because, prior to Caesar's reform of the calendar, it was so difficult to predict when they would fall.

The ground fell away behind the temple, so that the cave entrance was situated in the center of a middling hillside. The area around it was positively overgrown with vegetation associated with death, funerals, and graves: asphodel and hemlock, myrtle, cornel, towering cedar, and other, equally evocative plants.

"It's a gloomy gardener that planted this place," I said.

"Nothing was planted here, Praetor," said Iola. "All is as it has always been. The growth here obeys the will of the gods we serve."

"Don't be such a Skeptic, dear," said my ever supportive wife.

The entrance was smaller than I had pictured, and less rugged. It was a tall, narrow doorway surrounded by facing stones carved in a peculiar and antiquated fashion, the designs being similar to the ancient figures and patterns I had seen plastered over in the temple. The stone was deeply weathered and stained and bore no writing in any language. It looked older than the Lapis Niger and I suspected that it predated the appearance of writing in Italy. For the first time I began to take seriously the suggestion that this shrine was indeed Aboriginal. Just before the entrance, instead of the usual altar, there stood a broad stone table laden with cult objects: more chaplets of asphodel, miniature *thyrsi* or wands of cornel wood tipped with small pinecones, amulets depicting a tripartite woman's face, caps of dogskin, and so forth. There was also a tray of cups and a pitcher, all carved from wood and blackened with age.

"First," Iola said, "you must be purified and protected by the apotropaic rites." This involved a great deal of chanting and fumigation with incense, sprinkling with water from a holy spring, followed by more chanting, and culminating with the sacrifice of a black dog. Iola broke a sprig from one of the cedars, dipped it in the dog's blood, and painted our foreheads, our feet, and our hands with it.

It was all very conventional. I had been hoping for something more exotic.

Iola poured the cups full of something from the pitcher. Like just about everything else in the vicinity, the liquid was black. I knew that she expected us to drink the stuff. Sure enough, each of us was handed a cup and watched expectantly. Julia and the other women knocked theirs back as if they'd never heard of Socrates. I eyed my cup dubiously and the men of the party watched me.

For a while I toyed with the idea of throwing the cup away and going back to the villa. I reflected, however, this was some sort of religious charade, not a likely assassination plot. You don't murder somebody you intend to fleece. So I swallowed the vile liquid and the rest did the same. It was predictably bitter and I was pretty sure I detected oil of wormwood among the ingredients.

We were draped and garlanded with leaves and hung with amulets. Fortunately, only the freedmen of the party were required to wear the dogskin caps, which they accepted with poor grace, Hermes in particular. He had been getting arrogant since I freed him, so perhaps this little humiliation was beneficial.

One of the still-speechless priests or acolytes or whatever brought a flaming torch and the others produced small torches from someplace and ignited them. The flames were streaked with green, a bit of mummery I recognized: certain preparations of copper, mixed with firewood or any other burning medium, will produce green flame. The black-robed torchbearers filed into the cave entrance and we followed.

My first impression of the cavern was one of disappointment. In the first place, it was not a natural cavern at all, but a man-made tunnel, and not a very big one at that. Its roof was so low that the taller members of the party had to duck their heads somewhat. It was so narrow that the walls brushed the shoulders of the men of the party. The closeness was quite oppressive, though from the giggles I heard behind me, the younger men and women were enjoying it. The smoke from the torches may have contributed to the carefree mood of the young people. Besides the acrid copper scent, I detected a smell of burning hemp. I had encountered this in Egypt and it is known to encourage merriment.

Soon the giggling stopped as the pervasive gloom affected everyone. Every few steps a small niche was cut into the wall, in which burned the flame of a small lamp. With this bit of light added to that of the torches and my improving night vision, I could discern the tool marks on the walls. Every bit of this tunnel had been cut from solid rock, and as we progressed along the down-sloping passage, I was struck by the incredible amount of labor and time that must have been expended in its carving, for surely only a single man could have worked on the rock face at one time; perhaps two if one worked crouching while a second leaned over him, standing. All the same, it seemed an unreasonable way to carve a tunnel. A small gang of miners could have made a wider tunnel in much less time.

Still, there it was. It had been cut with great care, the walls perfectly plumb, the floor smooth and sloping with great regularity. The ceiling was somewhat of a mystery, for what appeared to be centuries' worth of torch soot obscured it. It seemed more like something Egyptians would do than Italians. We are no slouches at stonework, as witness the wonderful masonry of our Cloaca Maxima, built when Rome had kings, and still as sound and perfect as the day the stones were first set in their courses. We carve away whole hillsides and tunnel through mountains to build our roads and aqueducts, but these projects are sensibly planned and carried out for practical purposes: to facilitate transport or carry water or conduct sewage away from a city.

This tunnel to Hell was something else. It was an uncanny work, produced at an immense cost in time and labor for purely occult purposes. My mood seemed to grip the others as well. They became very silent except for occasional shudders and gasps. I do not know whether it was the effects of the smoke or that drink or the stupefying monotony of the priestly chant, but we began to see and hear things (I questioned everyone later and confirmed that we had all experienced the same thing). Streaks of colored light began to dart among us and we heard whispering voices. I could not make out what they were saying, but they had that maddening quality so common to half-overheard conversations that if they were a tiny bit louder we might understand them.

The women became truly frightened, even Julia. We men maintained our stout Roman facade of Stoic impassivity to hide the quaking of our bowels. For make no mistake about it, we were all frightened. The hazards of battle and politics, the terrors of the natural world, these things may be dealt with employing one's physical bravery, strength, and resources. But what may a mortal man do in the face of the supernatural?

Not that I truly believed that these people could take us to the underworld and communicate with the dead, but those feelings of dread are easily aroused under the right circumstances, and they had the circumstances in the form of that tunnel. Thoughts flitted through my mind like those flickering lights, of cleverly manipulated mirrors and hidden holes to bear the voices of whispering confederates. At the Museum in Alexandria I had seen many wonders, all of them performed openly by philosophers without the slightest recourse to supernatural means, but that had not been amid such surroundings.

The tunnel still took us down. It may be that the smoke and drink distorted our sense of time and distance. Sometimes the flames of the torches seemed to draw far ahead of us and every word spoken or chanted seemed to echo endlessly. As always when venturing underground, I found that the weight of earth and stone above me seemed to press down and I had to slow my breathing, knowing that it would take little for me to burst into panic, a state far too undignified for a praetor.

Just when I thought the whole ordeal had become unbearable, the air grew humid and there was a smell of sulfurous water. The tunnel opened somewhat and divided, one way sloping up, the other downward. We came to a room that would have seemed intolerably small for a proper shrine, but after the suffocatingly cramped tunnel it was almost like emerging into open air, though the light was still dim and the air full of smoke and mist.

In the center of the chamber was an altar decked with dead foliage and covered with innumerable bones that piled high and spilled onto the floor. Some of the bones were human, among them the skeletons of infants. Julia and Circe turned away in horror, but Antonia stared in fascination. She was as demented as the rest of her family.

"Here we pay tribute to the shades of the dead," intoned Iola, "and to their queen, Hecate." At that, one of the priests walked to the back of the chamber and thrust his torch into a bowl that contained twigs and brush. The flames rose, revealing an image of the goddess, hewn from the same stone as the surrounding walls. The women gasped, though it was only an archaic carving. The goddess was depicted holding her leashed hounds and she was three-faced, with the face on one side that of a young woman, that on the other an old hag, and the one in the center that of a mature matron, all of it done so crudely that it must have been made long before people in these parts knew anything about Greek sculpture.

The priest, if that was what he was, cast a handful of incense upon the fire and we were wreathed in fragrant smoke. Iola shouted what sounded like a prayer in some incomprehensible language, although I thought I caught a Marsic word or two.

Circe gasped. "The goddess moved!"

"Just the flickering light," I muttered. Julia turned and glared at me.

9

"The goddess grants us permission to approach the Styx and summon her subjects for questioning," Iola said.

The Styx? I thought. It was a long walk, but surely we haven't come that far!

Now Iola took us down a side passage that descended just a short way and the smell of sulfur water grew more pronounced and the mist more dense. This time the other black-robed figures did not accompany us. There was a sound of rushing water and even my hardened, Skeptical faculties deserted me. We were headed for the Styx, and I wasn't ready to cross it yet. I didn't even have a coin beneath my tongue.

At last we came to a chamber full of steam and there before us was a rushing stream of water, literally boiling as if it had run through Vulcan's forge before entering the chamber. We could not see the far side of the stream, for the fog obscured it. I had the impression that the distance was not great. In an odd way this was of some comfort to me. I had always heard that the Styx was a wide, slow-moving, black river, but if this was not the true Styx, it was certainly something uncanny.

I could see that most of my party were quite convinced that they were standing beside the river over which the gods swore their most solemn oaths, but their minds did not work like mine. I was puzzled by something else, something to me as strange as any supernatural manifestation: Somebody, long ago, had driven this tunnel, at the cost of great difficulty, straight down to this underground river, with absolute sureness and no hesitation. In the entrance tunnel I had seen no side shafts or exploratory excavations, as you see when miners search for metal-bearing ore. Whoever cut the tunnel knew exactly where he was going, and accomplished it in such a fashion that the doorway was precisely aligned with the sunrise on Midsummer Day.

Everyone jumped when we heard a hoarse, croaking voice from the river.

"Who seeks the wisdom of the Oracle?" I have heard ravens with more melodious voices.

"A praetor of Rome," Iola said.

"Approach."

"What?" I said. "I'm already here."

"Praetor," Iola said. "You must stand so that you actually touch the water."

"But it's boiling!" I protested.

"Wisdom does not come without cost," she informed me.

"Go ahead," said my beloved wife. "Don't be so timid." I heard chuckles from behind me. My loyal entourage, no doubt.

So, much against my better judgment, I stepped to the edge of the stream and just let the tips of my toes touch the water. To my surprise, while quite warm it was not truly boiling, despite the turbulence and foaming bubbles. Reassured, I went out ankle-deep. The bottom was perfectly smooth rock, not a trace of sand or gravel.

"What would the praetor know?" croaked the goddess or whatever it was.

Might as well ask something of consequence, I thought. "What will be the outcome of the current strife between Caesar and the Senate?" This was the great question on everyone's mind, and a source of great dread.

"Caesar is doomed," Hecate said baldly.

"Well, that's plain enough," I said. "Not like that old hag at Cumae who only babbles gibberish."

"Decius!" Julia hissed. She suspected me of disrespect, no doubt.

"Well, then, will the Senate prevail, and our republican institutions remain safe?"

"The Senate is doomed," she said.

"How can they both be doomed? Who will triumph ultimately, then?"

"Caesar will be victorious, and will rule for many, many years."

"I take it back. She does speak gibberish. How can Caesar rule for many years, yet be doomed?"

"Praetor," Iola said, "you have asked three questions and have been answered. Three questions are all that are permitted."

"What? You never said that before we came down here."

"Nonetheless, it is ancient custom. Three questions and no more."

I felt cheated, but I am not certain why. More questions would merely have meant more such nonsense. I backed out of the water and went to rejoin my party. Hermes passed me a flask and I took a swig of good Falernian.

"Reverend Iola," Julia said, "might I approach the goddess?" I suppressed a groan at her piety. She never talked to me like that.

"You may."

Julia stepped into the water and I dreaded what was about to happen. I knew she would ask the goddess about a cure for her infertility, right there in front of all those people. Instead, to my surprise and somewhat to my relief, she screamed loudly.

"Julia," I chided. "The water's not all that hot."

But she was pointing at the water a few feet before her. My thinning hair stood on end as I saw something surfacing there. I dashed forward and jerked Julia back. Now some of the other women were screaming. Some of the men, too, I think.

"What is it?" Iola gasped. Her eyes bugged out.

"Surely nothing can live in this water!" Antonia cried, hustling forward to get a good look.

"Actually," I said, "it's nothing living at all. It's quite dead, in fact." By now I saw that it was a white-robed corpse, floating on its stomach. "Iola, have your slaves take this unfortunate person from the water."

She hissed her orders and a pair of black-robed slaves waded into the water and dragged the corpse ashore. They laid it on its back and I called for torches. A couple were lowered toward the bloodless face and a great collective gasp arose.

"Why," I said, "if it isn't Eugaeon, priest of Apollo!"

"How can this be?" Iola wailed. "How did the priest enter the sacred river?"

"I'm rather more concerned whether he did it willingly or unwillingly," I said.

Sextus Plotius crowded forward and stared at the corpse, his face pale. "Praetor, I do not understand this. There is no access to this river except by way of this tunnel."

"Surely it must surface somewhere near the temple," I said. "And it would have to be upstream from here."

He shook his head. "No, there is no flowing surface water in the vicinity. There are hot springs in abundance in Campania, but none nearer than ten miles from this spot. Even if one of them flows into this chamber, there is no way that he could have gone there, jumped in, and surfaced here in the time since we last saw him, no more than an hour ago."

"Maybe he sneaked down here while we were undergoing the rites above," Hermes suggested.

"Don't speak foolishly!" Iola said. "The sacred black bitches of Hecate would never let a priest of Apollo approach the holy precincts. The very scent drives them wild."

"Be that as it may," I said, "the man is dead and may have been murdered. As praetor, I will investigate this."

"Ah, noble Praetor Metellus," Plotius said diffidently, "you are *praetor peregrinus,* in charge of cases involving foreigners. There seem to be none but natives here."

"Nonsense," I said, gesturing toward the black-clad devotees of Hecate, "these creatures are as foreign as a pack of Britons. I will take charge."

"As you wish," Plotius sighed.

"I want this body carried above into daylight," I ordered. "Now, everyone, back up that tunnel, and I'd better not smell any smoke that doesn't come from a torch or lamp."

"But, Praetor," Iola said, all but wringing her hands, "there are ceremonies we must perform. This holy place has been contaminated by death. There are lustrations and sacrifices . . ."

"Do them later," I told her. "I want none of your people to leave before I have questioned them, either."

She bowed in an almost Oriental fashion. "As you wish, Praetor."

So we made the long trudge back up the strange tunnel, but this time I had no leisure to ponder its oddity. What could this possibly portend? In spite of my matter-of-fact pose, I was almost as unsettled as the rest. First, the whole alien ritual and the descent into the uncanny tunnel, the weird river with its putative goddess, and now a man we had met so recently, dead in an unfathomable fashion. It was enough to unsettle a philosopher.

Then I cheered up. I had been getting bored, and now there was something interesting to do.

Clean air and sunshine quickly restored everyone's spirits, except for Iola's.

The slaves laid the body of the late Eugaeon upon the ground and I took a closer look at him. "Remove his clothing," I instructed the slaves.

"Decius!" my wife cried, shocked. "That is terribly undignified!"

"Oh, he shouldn't mind being naked. He's Greek, isn't he? Was Greek, I should say." She whirled and stalked off, taking the other women of the party with her. Except for Antonia, of course, who came closer to get a better look.

With his clothes off, the man looked shrunken. He was not fat, as so many priests are. His face and body were typical for a man of about forty years, rather spare, but not underfed. The only thing strange about him was that he was completely depilated.

"Not a hair on him," I remarked. "Is this required of priests of Apollo?"

"I wish more Roman men would do that," Antonia said. "I think it's attractive. I have all my slaves depilated." Something else I really didn't need to know about Antonia.

"Has someone gone to fetch the other priests? Maybe they can tell me if they're supposed to be hairless." One of my assistants ran off to fetch them. I could see no mark of violence on the front of the body. "Turn him over," I told the slaves. No mark on the back, either.

"He must have drowned," Hermes said.

"Not necessarily," I said. "There are plenty of ways to kill a man that leave no mark on the body: poison and asphyxiation come immediately to mind."

"Maybe he was frightened to death," somebody suggested.

"He doesn't have a frightened expression on his face," somebody else pointed out.

"I never saw a corpse that wore any sort of expression at all," I told them, "and many of the deceased were plenty frightened immediately prior to expiring."

A moment later the boy sent to fetch the priests came running back. His name was Sextus Lucretius Vespillo, the son of a friend. He was about fourteen, had recently shaved his first beard for his manhood ceremony, and was rather easily excited. "They're all gone!" he shouted. "Not a sign of them."

"Well," I said, "I suppose that tells us who killed the bugger."

"But we don't know he was murdered," Plotius cautioned.

"Then why did they run off like Persians at the sight of a Roman?" I asked. "That looks like guilty behavior to me. I want a thorough search made for those priests. And I want all of you men mounted and out looking for those priests. Also for some way that Eugaeon got into that water. There has to be an access to the underground river somewhere nearby. It's probably hidden, but don't let that stop you."

Julia returned when she saw that the body had been decently covered. "Ah, my dear, you can be of great assistance to me in this matter."

"How so?" she said, suspiciously.

"You seem to be conversant with this Hecate cult."

"I've studied the ancient religions. I wouldn't call myself an expert on them."

"Still, you know more than I do. And it seems that women play a leading role in this cult. I want you to question Iola and the other priests and priestesses or acolytes or whatever they are. Women seem to be more comfortable talking to women than to male officials."

"For good reason," Julia said.

"Exactly. I, in the meantime, will set up a temporary headquarters for investigation here at the temple."

"Do you think the matter is all that important? You are a Roman praetor with imperium. You could assign one of your men to conduct the investigation. You have more important matters demanding your attention."

I looked about at our strange surroundings; the funereal glade with the beautiful temple rising above it. "I am not so sure about that. This is a very odd business and we know how upset people can get when someone of local prestige gets murdered. People are on edge right now anyway. All this tension between Caesar and Pompey and the Senate has people expecting the days of Marius and Sulla to return."

"That is preposterous," she protested.

"Nevertheless, the fear is there. I want a quick end to this business before the whole countryside is up in arms over a common murder."

But I was soon to find that there was nothing at all common about this particular murder.

2

THE TROUBLE WAS NOT LONG IN START-
ing. The first evening ended without either the fleeing priests or the
mysterious access to the underground river found. The temple and its
compound afforded fairly comfortable lodgings for me and the members
of my entourage I chose to assist me. The rest I packed off to the villa
where I was staying. It was an exceedingly luxurious establishment,
built by Quintus Hortensius Hortalus, and one which he had hinted he
might leave to me in his will. He lay even then on his deathbed so I
knew the will would be read soon.

The next morning, people began calling upon me. I sat on the temple portico in my curule chair, which was draped with the customary
leopard pelts, my lictors ranged before me with their fasces. First to arrive were a gaggle of white-robed priests of Apollo from several nearby
temples. They were all Greek, of course. Apollo is a god respected by
Rome, but he is not native to Italy and was imported from Greece. Thus

his principal sacerdotes are Greek and his rituals are performed in the Greek fashion. Personally, I found him quite respectable, unlike some of the truly lunatic deities that had wormed their way into Italy in recent years. For some reason, despite having a perfectly good set of gods to see to their needs, Romans and other Italians were unreasonably enthusiastic about adopting new gods from all over the world, principally from Asia, where they breed gods like livestock. Many of these alien deities were so scabrous and their rites so scandalous that the censors expelled them from Rome with some frequency.

"Noble Praetor," began the leader of this delegation, one Simonides. "We have come to ask of you what has been done about the atrocious murder of our beloved colleague, Eugaeon?"

"The investigation proceeds apace," I assured him. "In fact, I suspect certain others of your colleagues of this murder."

"That is out of the question," he said, scandalized. "No priests of Apollo would ever do violence to one of their own!"

"Say you so? I've never noticed that any sort of person, given a motive, was ever backward about committing murder, priests included. You haven't seen any of these furtive clergy, have you? My men have been searching all over for them."

"None of them has appeared at our temples," Simonides said. "We fear that they have been murdered as well."

"Really? Maybe I should send someone down the tunnel to see if they've come bobbing to the surface. Who do you think would want to murder a whole temple staff?"

"The accursed followers of Hecate, of course!" snarled another of them.

"As a matter of fact," I said, "they are about the only people in the vicinity I do *not* suspect. They were with my party from the time we said good-bye to Eugaeon until the moment he surfaced. I do not see how they could be culpable."

"Do you know that all of them were with you, all of the time?" asked Simonides.

"Well, no. But they are being interrogated by one of my most merciless investigators." The description fitted Julia pretty well.

"They will speak if you use rigorous methods," advised Simonides. "They are no better than slaves, anyway. Use torture on them."

"You speak rather harshly for the priest of the god of enlightenment," I noted.

"They are the enemies of all mankind!" cried yet another devotee of Apollo. "They practice sorcery, necromancy, and all manner of black arts. Many of us have felt their curse."

"Yet you all look healthy enough. I take it this enmity between your temples goes back a long while?"

"For many centuries, Praetor," Simonides affirmed. "Once there were many sanctuaries of Hecate in this vicinity, but the worship of the proper gods prevailed, and one by one they were obliterated. Now all that remains is the oldest of them all, the shrine of the Oracle of the Dead. From that foul tunnel the foreign goddess spews forth her vile lies, to lead the good people of Italy astray."

"I can concur that she speaks in a puzzling fashion, but whether she lies I do not yet know. Rest assured that the malefactor or malefactors shall quickly be brought before me, tried, and judged." After a few formalities they stalked off, not at all reassured or satisfied. I had judged many difficult cases, and never were all parties satisfied; often as not none of them were. That is just how people are.

People of all stations in life began to congregate near the double temple. This usually happens when some remarkable crime has occurred. People come to gawk, though what it is they expect to see is a mystery to me. Nonetheless, they gather, and soon the peddlers show up to sell things to the gawkers, and the mountebanks arrive to entertain the gawkers and the peddlers, and the whores join the throng to service the gawkers, peddlers, and mountebanks. By noon we had a full-blown market in progress.

Despite the holiday atmosphere, I could not help but feel an ugly undercurrent in the crowd. It is a thing common to Italian towns, which are always ridden with factionalism, one district against another, rival supporters of the Blues or the Greens in the Circus, or any other of the justifications for strife the human animal delights in. When Hermes rode in after another futile sweep for the vanished priests, I told him to circulate among the crowd and find what he could sniff out. This was perfect work for Hermes, who would always rather idle his time away at a festival than do serious work for me.

I was eating my lunch from a small table next to my curule chair when Hermes came back, redolent of too much wine but at least not reeling from it. "It's the townspeople against the folk from the country-side," he informed me. "In the towns, Apollo is the favorite god in these parts. They are incensed that Eugaeon was murdered and they think Hecate's devotees did it."

"I saw a delegation of Apollo's priests this morning," I told him. "They told me of their suspicions in no uncertain terms."

"The country people, on the other hand, favor Hecate. She's been in these parts for a long time and they think of her as a native deity, not Thracian. That's the local Campanians and Samnites, of course. They still think of the Greeks as newcomers. They regard Eugaeon's untimely demise in the Styx as a desecration of their holy river."

"Let's not refer to it as the Styx, shall we? It's a powerful word and it makes me uneasy. Besides, except for being underground, it doesn't agree with any of the descriptions of that river. I never heard of heat and foam and turbulence associated with the Styx."

"As you wish. Anyway, we may expect rioting between the factions before long."

"They'd better not riot here," I said. "I have imperium, after all. I can call up troops to suppress insurrection." It was true, but I dreaded taking such a step. I had a feeling that, in the very near future, any Roman official with troops under his command was likely to get thrown into the upcoming struggle between Caesar and the Senate. I hoped to be safely out of office before the break came, and I would use Pompey's law imposing a five-year period between leaving consular or praetorian office and taking up a proconsular or propraetorian governorship in the provinces. Those governors and their armies would also be thrown into the fray.

"So much for the Greeks and Samnites and such," I said. "What about the Romans we've settled here? Are they taking sides, too?"

"So it seems. Most of them have intermarried with the locals by now and they've taken up the local cults."

"Ridiculous," I said. "Have you ever heard of Romans rioting and going at each other's throats over rivalries between Jupiter and Mars, or Venus against Juno?"

"No," Hermes said. "But they certainly fight over everything else."

"That's irrelevant," I said. "There are plenty of worthwhile things to fight about. Fighting over religious differences is absurd."

Sure enough, the next delegation I received consisted of followers of Hecate, an odd mixed group of small merchants and prosperous farmers. They were very irate over the pollution of their sacred river and the damage that this murder might do to the prestige of their Oracle.

"My friends," I said to them, "I am not a pontifex to pronounce upon matters of religion. In any case, our pontifexes are in charge only of the state religion of Rome. Yours is a local cult and I have neither knowledge nor authority to deal with your problems. I am a magistrate, and I will discover who committed this murder. Matters of ritual contamination you must sort out for yourselves." They, too, left looking quite unsatisfied.

Next came a delegation of local merchants of the more prosperous sort, some of them heads of local guilds, like my friend Plotius. Their spokesman was one Petillius, a man who owned a great many properties in Cumae, Pompeii, and other towns in the vicinity.

"Noble Praetor," he began, "we are terribly concerned with the damage this scandal is likely to do to the prosperity of our region. People come here from all over Italy and even from overseas to consult with the Oracle. We fear that this matter may curtail the customary pilgrimage this year."

"I take it that you own a number of inns where these travelers are accustomed to stay?"

"Why, yes, many of us own such properties."

"And taverns, eating establishments, and other businesses catering to the transient trade?" I inquired.

"Yes, Praetor. This matter could be very bad for us."

"I dare say. Well, my friends, I have a feeling that, all too soon, this little matter of a murdered priest may be remembered fondly as a mere diversion in the good times."

"Ah, Praetor," Petillius said, shaking his head ruefully, "there is nothing that such men as we can do about the rivalries of great men. We can only hope that our homes will be treated gently in the strife to come. That is for the future. This, however, is immediate. Something must be done." He was, of course, a practical man, as were they all. The looming catastrophe that seemed so imminent to me, and so potentially fatal for myself and my family, was to these men a remote matter, and no more controllable than storms and earthquakes and other forces of nature, such as that volcano smoking so ominously nearby.

"And something shall be done," I assured him, as I had been assuring everybody lately. "Being done right now, in fact. My men are searching and questioning all over the district. The killer or killers will turn up soon. I expect cooperation from you as well. You locals are the most likely to spot these fleeing priests and I want them reported instantly should they be seen. I will deal very harshly with anyone who seeks to conceal them or hide any evidence from me."

"Of course you shall have our fullest cooperation, Praetor. Nobody wants these murderers found more sincerely than we."

"See that it is so." This another group went off, not truly happy. I wasn't pleasing anyone much that day.

It is in times like this, when some shocking event shatters the customary calm of a district, that the true nature of men's relations with one another come out. The peace between rival groups begins to crack like poor stucco, revealing the rotten timbers beneath. Old grudges, thought to be forgotten, come suddenly to mind. Trivial or even imaginary slights and insults loom large, and thoughts of revenge and retribution prey upon men's minds. Add to that the general tension caused by impending war in Italy, and we had the makings of a full-scale civil brawl on our hands, and all of it set in motion by a death that, however bizarre, had not even been proven to be murder.

I gestured for Hermes to come to me. "Hermes, are you sober enough to do a little more snooping?"

"Are you implying that I am drunk?" he said, swaying slightly.

"Nothing of the sort. Just curtail your intake for a while. We need to know something more. I know that Pompey is powerful here in Campania. He settled many of his veterans here. See what the locals feel about Caesar, and how the lines are drawn hereabouts."

He went off to snoop and doubtless drink some more. The settlement of the Campanian lands had been a thorny one, much disputed in the Senate and fought over for years. Pompey had wanted the land to settle his veterans, who had served for many years and needed farms to retire to. His enemies in the Senate fought this, both because they wanted the land for themselves and because they knew it would give Pompey a strong power base near to Rome. Back then Pompey and Caesar had been friends, Pompey was married to Caesar's daughter, and Caesar had worked hard to get Pompey the land settlement. In time he had succeeded, and now the countryside was full of Pompey's veterans, each man with his arms hung above the hearth, ready to flock to the eagles at Pompey's summons.

Technically, the struggle was between Caesar and the Senate, but here in Campania the Senate counted for little. Here the lines were drawn between the supporters of the great men of the day, and none were greater that year than Caesar and Pompey. In this territory, barely two generations under Roman control, all such loyalties were mutable. Eventually, Hermes returned.

"There aren't very many of Pompey's men in the immediate vicinity.

Most of them settled to the north of here. The few I found to talk to don't seem to care much about Apollo or Hecate."

"That's something of a relief. One more faction in this business would have been one too many."

The presence of all those Pompeians had been a disturbing factor in my otherwise pleasant stay in Campania. Pompey had assured that, should Caesar prove recalcitrant, he could stamp his foot and raise an army. There were those in the Senate, chiefly of the most extreme aristocratic faction, urging him to stamp that foot. The rest of the Senate was more wary, feeling that they could negotiate with Caesar, but the times were bad ones for moderates and fence-sitters. We were drifting into another age of warlords. Sad to say, the Roman soldiers of that day felt their strongest allegiance to their generals, not to Rome. For a general who consistently led them to victory and loot, they would do almost anything.

Pompey's veterans were such men, but I did not fancy their chances against Caesar's troops, who had been fighting hard in Gaul for years. Pompey's veterans were getting old and were long out of practice.

"There are those two legions training up near Capua," I mused.

"What have they to do with this murdered priest and the troubles here in the south?" Hermes wanted to know.

"Eh? Oh, nothing. The thought of Pompey's veterans set me thinking about the disposition of our soldiers and which way they might go if it comes to a break between Caesar and the Senate."

"They're new troops training for a war in Syria," Hermes said. "They have no set loyalties and I suspect they'll follow whoever the Senate sends to take charge of them. I don't think they'll be much threat to Caesar." We had both spent a lot of time with Caesar's army in Gaul, and knew all too well what a savage lot they were. Caesar had been leading them for eight years and they were his, body and soul. He had become their patron and they were his *clientela*.

As the day's business was about to end, Julia came to report her findings. "I've spent all day with Iola and the rest of the Oracle's staff."

"I don't suppose they confessed to complicity?"

"Not likely."

"Pity. It would make things so much easier."

"If only life were as simple as you wish it. No, but I have been learning a great deal about the Hecate cult, about its origins and history. It is quite fascinating."

"I am sure. Anything about murderous enmity between the cultists and the priests of Apollo overhead?"

She sighed. "You are so single-minded when you are on an investigation, Decius. I wish you would give some time to culture and study."

"All in good time, my dear. When I retire, I plan to write many long, boring books, perhaps even look into this philosophy business. Brutus and Cicero and some others of my acquaintance seem to set great store by it."

"By the way, we are invited to dinner at the house of Marcus Duronius."

"Excellent," I said. "I've heard that he sets a splendid table."

She poked my expanding waistline. Rather harder than necessary, in fact. "You should spend less time at the table and more in the gymnasium. This easy life is softening you."

"The demands of office do not permit me much time for the gymnasium," I told her. The derisive snort she made was quite expressive.

"I'm off to confer with some of the other priestesses nearby. I'll meet you at the Villa of Duronius at dinnertime. Do try to show up sober."

Sometimes I didn't think that Julia trusted me. And I knew why she was suddenly concerned with my physical fitness. She expected me to spring to arms at Caesar's call and join his army. Well, I had already been in Caesar's army and wanted nothing to do with it. She thought Pompey was a prize villain and that the Senate was doing Uncle Caius Julius insufficient honor. Personally, I couldn't see a fig's worth of difference between Caesar and Pompey, and the Senate had already voted Caesar more honors than he'd earned. If he'd been denied a few of his demands, that was just the rough-and-tumble of Roman politics as they were in those days.

That evening, with just Hermes accompanying me, I arrived at the Villa of Duronius, quite sober. Well, mostly sober, anyway. Like most villas in that part of Italy, it was sprawling and spacious. Duronius was a wine importer and banker, a formula for riches if ever there was one. The company proved to be an entertainingly mixed lot, chosen to make for good conversation. For dignity, there was my distinguished self. For wealth, we had our host, Duronius. For beauty, there was an intriguing lady of Stabiae named Sabinilla. For wisdom, a philosopher of local repute named Gitiadas. For wit, there was the rising young playwright Pedianus, whose reputation for comedy was growing. For low good humor, we had Porcia, a corpulent freedman's daughter and owner of many commercial properties all over Campania. In Rome it was rare for women to appear unescorted at a dinner party, but it was quite common in Campania. Women could own businesses and had property rights equal to those of men. It wasn't necessary to be a widow to wield control over their own fortunes, and even married women could manage their own finances independently of their husbands. It was all very un-Roman.

There were others, but I have forgotten their names. The banquet was arranged in the Roman fashion, but the Campanians of that time did not always observe the Roman custom of no more than nine diners at any one dinner. For one thing, they thought it unworthy of a rich man to entertain so few guests. In time, Julia arrived and we were conducted to the table. As ranking magistrate, I had the place of honor at the right end of the center couch. Our sandals were removed by servants and our feet sprinkled with perfume. Garlands were distributed and we were ready to get down to business. Before the first course was brought in, our host made an announcement.

"My friends, today we shall observe the ancient custom of the district: before we begin, we must appoint a Master of Ceremonies, to set the order of the banquet, to mix the wine and water, and to determine the direction of dinner conversation. I nominate our most distinguished guest, the Praetor Decius Caecilius Metellus the Younger." There was much applause and cheering. This was another Campanian oddity. Ordinarily, a Master of Ceremonies was appointed for the Greek *symposium*, the after-dinner party when the women had withdrawn and the men got down to the serious business of drinking.

"My host and friends, I thank you for the honor, but I confess I am unsuited for such an office," I said firmly. "The Master of Ceremonies should not be chosen for official dignity, but for taste, elegance, and wit. I propose our renowned playwright, Pedianus." All agreed that this was an excellent choice. Personally, I intended to be far too inebriated by the end of the banquet to direct much of anything. Let the boy try to keep his wits about him while the wine flowed as it does only in Campanian revelries.

A servant placed a wreath of ivy on the young man's head and another draped a purple mantle over his shoulders. A third placed an ivy-wreathed wand in his hand. He stood and declaimed, "My host, great Praetor, honored guests, you do me honor, and I shall in return strive to provide you with an agreeable evening. These rules I decree: One, while guests may be served in order of rank and distinction, there shall be no difference in the quality of the items presented." Everyone agreed that this was an excellent rule. "Two, the wine shall be mixed at one measure of water to two of wine." He caught my look. "Make that one measure of water to three of wine." That was still too much water for my taste, but anything stronger would be considered scandalous. "Three, I forbid all discussion of serious matters. I will hear no debate about Caesar and Pompey. The measures of the Tribune Curio shall not be breathed."

"What about the murder of the priest Eugaeon?" somebody asked.

He grinned. "That's not serious. That is gossip. We must have gossip." Amid much laughter he gestured grandly and the first course was brought in. It was the customary egg course, with the eggs dyed in astonishing colors and painted in fanciful patterns. Some were encased in gold leaf hammered to an incredible thinness. We were supposed to eat these, gold and all. Some were still in their shells, and when cracked open these proved to contain the sort of party favors esteemed by wealthy hosts: perfumes, pearls, gems, golden chains, and so forth. While the ladies made delighted sounds I tried to figure out how they had gotten those items inside the shells, but to no avail. I could see no hole or seam in the complete shells. Maybe, I thought, they just fed the things to the chickens and ducks and this was the result.

More substantial courses followed, each accompanied by the appropriate wines, all of which were uniformly excellent. Between courses we had entertainment, their order directed by Pedianus. There were reciters of poems and dancers, jugglers and tightrope walkers, even an astonishing woman who balanced on her hands while using her feet to shoot a bow and arrow with great accuracy.

In past generations, it had been a custom in Campania to have gladiators fight at banquets. In some houses, this was still done. But I have never felt that blood goes well with food. The *munera* form the proper venue for such carnage. Thankfully, our host seemed to agree.

For a while we spoke of this and that, the upcoming races, events overseas, the latest omens, and so forth. Julia got the fashionably ragged local philosopher Gitiadas to expound upon a theory that the world is round like a ball, which would have been rather interesting had it not been so absurd. He said something about the circular shadow cast upon the moon during a lunar eclipse, which made no sense whatever.

"Praetor," said the abundantly endowed Porcia, "are you making any progress on the murder of the priest?" She popped a honeyed fig into her mouth, making her multiple chins jiggle.

"I confess it is perplexing," I told her. "The priest is dead, the other priests have disappeared, and the devotees of Hecate either cannot or will not help. My biggest headache is figuring out how he got into the river in the first place."

"Praetor," said our host Duronius, "the neighborhood is full of the wildest rumors. Of those here, only you and your wife were actually there when the body appeared. Perhaps you could tell us exactly what happened."

"Of course, but I cannot tell you exactly what happened, only what I observed." At this I saw the philosopher Gitiadas nod approvingly. So I gave them a perhaps overly lurid recitation of my experience, trying to make it as entertaining as possible. Julia then told the tale as she and the other women experienced it. Her account was much more respectful of the holiness of the site and stressed their awe at the surroundings and the uncanniness of the Oracle. Some of the company had visited the Oracle personally, and agreed that their experiences had been much the same, minus the corpse.

"You had an uncommonly straightforward answer from the Oracle, contradictory though it seemed," said the beautiful Sabinilla. She wore a white-blond wig that could only have been made from German hair. Her gown was of transparent Coan cloth and she had a cat's appearance of bonelessness as she lounged on the couch. "I asked her if my husband would recover from his illness and she said, 'Follow the sun to Vulcan's pool.' Later, a physician told me that if we had gone west to Sicily, there is a healing hot spring at the base of Aetna where my husband might have been cured, but by that time he was dead so it wasn't much help." Others agreed that they had been given similarly confusing answers that sometimes proved to make sense in retrospect.

"My men have not yet found an access to the river where the priest's body might have been thrown in. It is most vexing."

"Praetor," said Gitiadas, "I confess I have never visited this Oracle and her mysterious tunnel, so much of this is new to me. You say that the water bubbled violently as if boiling, but it felt no more than warm?"

"Yes, that is how it was."

"Bubbles are merely air moving through liquid. When water boils, air forms somehow and moves upward to the surface, by a process much debated among scholars. Other than by the boiling process, in order to make bubbles, air must somehow mix with the water from this layer of air in which we breathe, which exists above the level of the sea. If the water of the subterranean river has no access save the cave of the Oracle, where are all those bubbles coming from to make it froth so violently? The river must touch the air somewhere very near the spot where it enters the cave."

This was amazingly good sense, and I couldn't imagine why I had not thought of it before. I suppose one must be a philosopher to deduce things so logically. It gave me much to think about, and I fear I was rather withdrawn company for a while. Eventually the best wine came out—a Cretan vintage I had never heard of—and I got back to my duties as a guest.

"Does anyone know," I asked, "why the cult of Hecate has lasted so long in these parts while it has died out almost everywhere else in Italy?"

"Hecate has the Oracle," Porcia said, "but the Oracle was there before Hecate."

"That's just an old tale," Sabinilla protested.

"Oh, tell us about it," Julia urged.

"Well," Porcia began, "we Campanians hold ourselves to be the original people of these parts, and we regard the Greeks and Romans as newcomers, but truth is there were people here even before we came here from somewhere else. I've heard them called Aborigines, but that's just a name the Greeks gave them. They called themselves something else. It's said they were great magicians, and they used to have all of Italy and the islands to themselves. They built their temples of huge stones and you can still see some of those here and there. It's said they carved that tunnel down to the river, and they had the Oracle, or some sort of god, in that place. The temple above was built by their descendants on top of an even older one, before the Greeks changed it to their liking."

I remembered the sense I'd had that the decorations of the temple covered older, cruder figures, and the carvings around the tunnel entrance had struck me the same way. About the Aborigines I was more Skeptical. Certainly, some sort of people inhabited Italy before the first

Latins arrived, and I had seen some of those temples and monuments of ponderous stones as large as any the Egyptians had utilized that Porcia spoke of. But it seems to me that all the defeated and subjugated people in history somehow acquire the reputation of having been great sorcerers. I find myself wondering how, if they had such potent magic at their command, they always got themselves conquered by unmagical but soldierly people. To carve and move big stones all you need is a lot of time, a lot of manpower, and an odd idea of what it is the gods want.

"Personally, I don't believe any of that," Stabinilla said.

"Oh," I asked. "Why is that?" I wondered if she shared my own doubts.

"The Aborigines were nothing but savages, like Gauls or Germans. There are none of those giant stone monuments here in Campania, or anywhere else in Italy that I ever heard. Whoever cut that tunnel had skill and good tools. I don't think it could be older than the earliest Greek settlers. They had the skills and tools necessary. They knew how to survey and how to mine. No pack of primitives drove that tunnel straight down to an underground river."

"I don't care what you say," Porcia put in. "Even a mathematician from Alexandria couldn't find that river so far down. It was sorcery." Then she went on in a lower voice, "But there's some even stranger tales about that place."

"Such as?" Julia asked.

"Well, there are some old tales that say the tunnel wasn't driven down from the surface. Some think it was carved *upward*, from below." There were gasps and mutters from around the table. People made gestures to avert evil. Talk of the underworld always makes people uneasy.

"Well," I said, "I suppose it is relatively easy to find the surface from the river, compared to going the other way."

"And the precise alignment on the solstice?" Julia asked.

"Well, underworld demons would know how to do something like that, wouldn't they?" Porcia said. I couldn't argue with that.

"What do you think, Gitiadas?" Julia asked.

"Here we only speculate," the philosopher said. "We are presented with certain remarkable facts: a tunnel carved with great precision in alignment with a celestial event, an underground river with no known source or effluent, and the appearance of a corpse therein. From these things we can spin theories both natural and supernatural, but our speculations have little value, because we are not in possession of enough facts from which to draw informed conclusions."

"You make uncommonly good sense, for a philosopher," I commended, while Julia rolled her eyes, as she often did when I spoke with learned persons. "What we need is more basic facts. We need to know where that river comes from. We need to know who had it in for the priest and perhaps all the priests."

"We also must dismiss those things that are facts but are nonetheless irrelevant to the case at hand. Too many facts can be as inimical to clear thought as too few."

"Exactly!" I said. "Personally, I don't care if that tunnel lines up with moonrise on the anniversary of Cannae. Nor does it matter if it was carved out by the Aborigines, the Greeks, or our host's grandfather. The circumstances of this murder are both immediate and local, and we need to concentrate on these matters, not upon ancient tales."

"Most astute," Gitiadas commended. "And, one must ponder certain other matters concerning this killing."

"Such as?" I queried.

"Well, there must be a motive for the slaying."

"Mmmm. Here we are confronted with an embarrassment of riches. People are killed for a great many reasons. Speeding up an inheritance is a classic motive. Revenge is another and forms a whole subcategory in itself. An insult may be a call for vengeance, or a tit-for-tat killing as is common in blood feuds. I've known many killings to result from jealousy and more from political rivalry. Killing during a robbery is common, and manslaughter can be the result of an accident, as when a blow meant merely to chastise results in a broken neck or crushed skull. I could go on all evening on the subject of motive alone."

"Then," said Gitiadas, "you must eliminate all save those that may apply in this case. Another factor must be the means of murder, be it a weapon or an opportune circumstance."

"People are killed with everything from swords to chamberpots," I observed. "Daggers, garottes, spears, bricks, clubs—I even knew a woman who strangled her victims with her own hair. This is, I believe, the only case where the weapon was a sacred river."

"If he was drowned," Julia said. "That hasn't been proven yet, nor whether it was murder at all, rather than an accident."

"As a matter of fact," I said, "I would be inclined to believe the death the result of an accident, if a rather bizarre one, save for one fact: the disappearance of the other priests. That makes it smell of foul play."

"Has it occurred to anyone," said the playwright, "to wonder why, of all times to carry out a murder, the perpetrator or perpetrators chose a day upon which the shrine was visited by a Roman praetor?"

"And one famed for his successful criminal investigations," Duronius put in.

"Ah! Most excellent points," said Gitiadas. "What says the praetor to this?"

"Socratic method, eh?" I said, letting him know that I was not entirely ignorant of philosophical matters. I pondered the question, which was indeed a good one. "First off, they did not know we were coming. The visit was suggested in idle conversation and we set off forthwith. The killing must have been plotted well in advance and had to be carried out at a specified moment. It seems that they could not alter their plan."

"Quite logical. And the sudden appearance of the body in the river—do you think that it was intended or an accident?"

"I can hardly think that someone who wished to carry out what must have been a rather difficult murder should have intended that the victim appear before our very noses," I said.

"The goddess took a hand in it," Porcia said with great conviction. "She was offended that someone would pollute her sacred river with a dead body, so she threw it up before the praetor's party. She wishes justice from you, sir."

I was about to rebuke her for dragging the gods back into the matter, but I saw Julia nodding agreement and held my tongue.

"Oh, rubbish," said Stabinilla, coming to my rescue. "The gods don't interfere in human affairs as petty as a mere murder, unless it's patricide, and even then I rather doubt it. I have half a dozen neighbors I'm pretty sure helped their fathers along into the afterworld, and they are doing just fine. As the praetor said, people get tired of waiting to inherit." For the first time I noted the understated elegance of her jewelry. Unlike most Campanian women, she did not favor ostentatious amounts of gold and precious stones and pearls. Instead, her bracelets, earrings, and necklace were of bronze—but it was not plain metal. It was the old Etruscan work, in which the surface was covered with minute beads of bronze so close set that they give the piece an exquisite texture. It is said that only children had a touch delicate enough to set the bronze beads in place for soldering, and that it could not be done past the age of twelve. The art of making this jewelry has been lost; it was only in recent years that Romans had begun to appreciate it, and the old pieces were eagerly sought after.

"You're one of those Skeptics, I take it," said Porcia.

"Are you a follower of Aenesidemus?" Gitiadas asked, apparently referring to some philosopher of that school.

"Never heard of him," Sabinilla said. "But I believe in good sense. I like to see evidence. If you buy a horse, do you just listen to the seller blather on about the perfection of this beast he wants you to buy? No. You go look at the horse. You check its teeth and punch it for wind. You examine its legs and hoofs for evidence of illness or injury or poor breeding."

"You can't know everything by empirical observation," Julia said.

"Who wants to know everything?" Stabinilla countered. "I just want to be clear about the things that affect me personally."

"I merely meant," Julia said, "that there are such things as instinct, and inspiration, and divine revelation."

"Difficult concepts to use in court," I said. "Evidence works better there, although imaginative vituperation and character assassination can be more persuasive."

"Not to mention showing off your scars," Julia commented drily. In those days any man in public life was expected to be a soldier and it never hurt to remind a jury of one's honorable service. In these recent, decadent times many men practice law who never lifted a sword.

"Also excellent legal technique. Look at this," I said, hiking up my tunic to show the huge furrow that slanted from my left hip diagonally down almost to the knee. "Got that when I was run over by a British chariot. That one's won me many a favorable verdict. Not a lawyer in Rome can match it, not even Marcus Antonius, and he's been cut and stabbed and speared more times than all the heroes in the *Iliad* combined." The other guests murmured admiration at the spectacular scar, but Julia just rolled her eyes again and turned away. It wasn't as if she'd never seen it before.

This little entertaining moment was interrupted when Hermes appeared at the entrance to the triclinium. He made his way around the couches and stood by my side. As highest-ranking guest and a serving magistrate, I was of course given the "consul's place," the right end of the center couch, where it was convenient for a man on public service to receive and dispatch messengers, for a Roman official was never off duty.

"Praetor," Hermes said in a low voice, "we've found the other priests."

3

OF COURSE THE WHOLE BUGGERING lot of party guests, including half of the slaves, had to come along. You don't get to see a spectacle like this every day, and all my protests and fulminations did no good. So much for the dignity and majesty of Roman office. Like some great traveling festival, we all descended upon the precincts of the Temple of Apollo and the Oracle of the Dead.

The evening was well advanced, and thus the uncanniness of the venue all the more pronounced. A mild wind blew, causing a sinister rustling among the funereal trees and shrubs, like small deities of the underworld conversing just below the level of human hearing. I was just as happy to bypass the gloomy grove and go to the temple instead.

"So close," Julia said, stepping down from her litter. "Just a few steps from where it all started."

"I felt it must be so," I told her. "There was just no time for them to have gotten far, or that no one would have seen them."

My lictors arrived from our quarters and I directed them to stand guard on the steps of the temple and let no one enter save myself and the members of my party.

Hermes came to join us, accompanied by a few of my other young men. They had that smug look of men who know something important that nobody else knows yet. I suppose I've worn that expression myself from time to time.

"It was easy to miss," Hermes said. "The Oracle isn't the only place around here with odd passageways."

We followed him into the temple. The lamps glowed warmly and the god smiled down upon us benignly, above all human foolishness.

"Well, let's get to it before the word spreads and the sightseers start to gather," I said.

Hermes nodded to young Sextus Vespillo, and the boy, trying not to swell with importance, went to a decorated paving stone just before the plinth supporting the statue of Apollo. He bent and fiddled a moment with a bit of carved ornamentation. Then he worked free what looked like a loop of stone vinework. He twisted the loop and tugged and up came the stone, and not just that one but about eight adjacent blocks. The whole must have weighed the better part of a ton, but the boy raised it as easily as a wooden trapdoor in a house. Another piece of that mysterious engineering we had come to so admire.

Julia and the other women gasped. The men muttered. I merely asked, "It's well hidden. How did you discover it?"

"I am a brilliant investigator like you and—" he caught my look. "Actually, Sextus Lucretius here got on rather well with one of the temple slave girls. She told him she'd spied on the priests opening this trap one night."

"If only all my assistants exercised their gifts to such beneficial effect," I said. The boy blushed furiously. "Where is the girl?"

Hermes signaled and the girl stepped from the shadow of a column. "Her name is Hypatia."

"Come here, child." The girl was about sixteen, and quite beautiful.

This was to be expected. Apollo is associated with all that is beautiful, so his temples never employ ugly slaves. Any physical imperfection bars one not only from Apollo's service but from his priesthood as well. This girl had hair as yellow as that of a German princess and huge blue eyes. Her simple white shift was modest enough, but it left no doubt as to the perfection of her body. She stepped near me and lowered her beautiful eyes.

"Hypatia, how did you come to be spying on your master?"

"I did not spy, Praetor," she said softly. "I was new here, and did not know the rules. One of my duties is to extinguish the lamps just before we slaves retire to our quarters for the night. I did not know that upon certain nights, no one was to enter the temple except for the priests. That night I came in and went to the first lamp niche." She pointed to one of a pair that flanked the doorway. "But I heard a noise. I looked up here toward the god's statue and I saw all the priests gathered before it with lamps and torches. The high priest, Eugaeon, stooped and twisted the stone loop that I revealed to your assistant. I saw him raise the doorway and I was amazed. I thought he must be very strong to lift such a weight. They went down and never even glanced in my direction. I left the lamps alight and hurried to my quarters."

"I see. Did they close the doorway behind them?"

She thought for a moment. "No, they lowered it but it seemed to me that they left it slightly ajar. I didn't go close to look. I was afraid."

"And why did you not come forward when the priests disappeared?"

"Again, I was afraid. I feared that just speaking of it might violate some ritual law. This place has many such rules. And I feared being called to testify." That I could understand. A slave can testify in court only after being tortured. It's nothing severe, but certainly not an experience to be anticipated with pleasure.

The irrepressible Porcia stepped over to young Sextus Lucretius Vespillo and tickled him under the chin. "And this lad had just the thing to get you talking, eh? Praetor, may I borrow him when you're done with him?" Everyone laughed, but a little nervously. Vespillo's face flushed scarlet.

"How long have you been here at the temple?" I asked the girl.

"About two months."

"And who was your former master?"

"Aulus Plantius, sir."

Duronius spoke up. "Plantius is an itinerant slave trader who comes through here two or three times a year. I remember he was here about two months ago. He deals in high-quality stock. I bought a cook from him."

"I see. Girl, I may want to question you further, so don't go anywhere."

"Where would I go, Praetor? I belong to the temple."

"So you do. Just don't let yourself get sold anywhere else. Now," I said, turning to my audience, "let's have a look at this new tunnel."

I stepped cautiously to the lip of the opening. The light from the lamps revealed a steep stairway descending into obscurity. "Bring a torch. I want only Hermes with me for now." There were sounds of disappointment behind me. I was used to such sounds. Luckily I was not wearing my ponderous official toga. The *synthesis* had recently come into fashion for dinner party wear and the lightweight garment is much easier for negotiating steep stairways. I thought of simply removing it, but dignity of office forbade going about in only a tunic.

Hermes preceded me down the stairs. In the smoky, uncertain light of the torch I examined the walls and ceiling. I was no expert on the subject of stonework, but the workmanship appeared identical to that of the tunnel leading to the chamber of the Oracle. I did notice one difference: there were no niches for lamps. This was never intended for regular ritual use, I thought. So what was its purpose?

Without the ceremony, the chanting, the smoke, and all the other appurtenances of my earlier journey underground, this one was not as frightening. It was, however, uncomfortable, cramping and confining. Though there was no real reason for it, I found it hard to breathe. The weight of the stone above seemed to bear down upon me. Clearly, I was never meant to be a miner.

I became aware of a faint breeze in the tunnel. It made the torch flicker and it was coming from below. Above the smell of the torch it carried a disagreeable but all too familiar scent: blood and death. But below these there was yet another scent: water. I had expected something like this and the philosopher's remarks that very evening had suggested it.

As we descended, I tried to keep the layout of the whole double temple compound in my head: how far and to what extent this tunnel paralleled the Oracle's. It seemed to be far steeper and thus required a stairway. As near as I could judge, its direction was almost parallel to the lower one, but I had no idea of its depth.

After what seemed an interminable descent, we came to a large chamber, and now I could hear the sound of water. There was a thin fog, not as dense as that in the chamber of the Oracle. The blackness all but swallowed the light of Hermes' torch. "They're over here," he said.

He stood beside a round hole in the floor about five feet in diameter. It was a fine piece of masonry, with a slightly raised lip all around. It was from this hole that the fog and the sound of water issued. Lined up just before the hole, in a neat row, were five white-clad bodies.

"Did anyone touch them?" I asked.

"We found them exactly like this. Laid out for a funeral. Has a ritual look, don't you think?"

"This place is about nothing but ritual," I groused. "Oracles, temples, ancient, forgotten gods, and Aborigines . . ."

"Aborigines?" Hermes asked.

"Oh, yes, you weren't at the dinner party."

"No, I was out doing your work, and very productive, if I may say so."

"Yes, well done. I want to examine them in better light, but first I want a look around this chamber before anyone else comes down here. Let's start by walking the periphery."

Hermes leading with the torch, we went to the wall and began to pace it. The chamber proved to be circular, with the hole in its exact middle. The wall sloped gently inward, so that it was shaped like the rustic beehives farmers weave from wicker. Like the tunnel and chamber of the Oracle, it had been hewn from solid rock, resembling certain tombs I had seen in Egypt. The hole in the center reminded me horribly of the trap in the Tullianum prison, where the bodies of strangled enemy kings are thrown after taking part in the victor's triumph. Some have been thrown in while still alive. Nobody has ever come out, living or dead.

We began to pace back and forth across the floor, searching it for any sort of evidence. Long before, I had learned that people are careless and often leave behind evidence of their deeds. I had tried to teach my methods to other investigators, but they could never quite understand what I was getting at. Only my old friend the physician Asklepiodes understood, because he used a similar technique in his medical diagnostics and prognostics..

We went over the floor, but found nothing. Except for the bodies the place was incredibly neat, as if it had been thoroughly swept, perhaps even scrubbed. Why go to such trouble to tidy a place but leave dead bodies behind? I told Hermes to leave the torch and go summon the rest.

"It looks like this floor has been swept recently. There's some dust in the angle where the wall meets the floor, but the rest is clean."

"You're right. Even a place like this should collect a little dust over the ages."

Hermes went back up the stairway and left me brooding in the chamber. Several things about the place disturbed me. Here we had a second tunnel driven down through solid stone to water, yet there were numerous differences between them. For one thing, there was the shape of the chamber. The chamber of the Oracle was an elongated, irregular rectangle. This one was circular. It reminded me of a very ancient tomb

I had been shown in Greece, one rumored to date to the time of Agamemnon. That one had the same beehive shape, though it had been built of massive stone blocks. The chamber of the Oracle had been cut down to the surface of the river. This one ended above it, with a well in its center. It was approached by a stair, not a ramped tunnel. And somehow—I cannot quite describe this—it did not have precisely the feel of antiquity that the other oozed like dampness from its walls. It was certainly not recent, but it did not feel so ancient.

Minutes later, the rest of the party arrived. I had decided to let a number of people see this rather than allow rumors to run rampant through the district.

"Well, this settles it," Duronius said. "It wasn't accident or suicide. It was murder."

"But why kill a whole temple staff?" said Pedianus, still wearing his purple mantle and ivy wreath.

"More to the point," Julia said, "why kill five and lay them out like this but throw Eugaeon down this well into the river?" She walked around the corpses, stepped to the lip of the hole, and peered down. Roman ladies of those days weren't upset by dead bodies, what with all the disorder and combat in the City. These days they are more delicate. With all the peace and quiet enforced by the First Citizen, everyone has gotten disgracefully soft. I've seen patrician ladies turn pale at the sight of a gladiator being killed.

"Perhaps he wasn't thrown down there," said Gitiadas. "Perhaps he jumped in, hoping to escape the fate meted out to these five."

"A valid speculation," I approved.

"I'm not so sure," Julia said. "Sextus Vespillo, bring that torch." At her direction, the boy knelt at the lip of the well and lowered his torch inside. "The river is only a few feet down," she reported. "The current seems fairly swift. I don't think the chamber of the Oracle can be more than a few paces from here. Yet he was thoroughly dead when he arrived in our midst."

"Another valid point," I mused, "but Gitiadas was right about one thing: he said there had to be another access to the river near the chamber to account for all those bubbles. Now, has anybody here ever heard of a second tunnel? Even an old tale or rumor? I find it hard to believe that the Oracle's tunnel to the Styx is so famous while this one is unknown." The locals looked at one another and shrugged. No help there. Our host had thoughtfully brought along some burly slaves who carried sizable jugs of wine and others with cups; girls passed around cups to us all, and soon we were standing around the bodies sipping at the excellent vintage like guests at an embassy reception.

"Praetor," Hermes said, "do you want to examine the bodies here or shall I have them carried above so you can see them when the sun is up?"

"Take them up," I told him. "Torchlight is never adequate for a thorough examination." That, and my aging eyes, I thought glumly. I was nearing my fortieth year.

Hermes went up to fetch some slaves. A while later he returned with them and the chamber grew very crowded. Already, the torches and lamps were making the air very close and we were all glad to vacate the premises. Once outside, everyone breathed deeply and with relief.

"Hermes," I said, "first thing tomorrow, I want you to find the master of the local stoneworkers' guild and summon him here."

"Why?" Hermes asked.

"To answer some questions, of course. I also want to speak with Iola as well." Then I addressed the others. "This is likely to get very ugly. As long as it seemed likely the other priests did Eugaeon in, things were under control. It might have been some personal vendetta. But now we know they were all murdered. The different factions will be accusing each other and we may have the countryside up in arms."

"There is still a possibility that they were not murdered, Praetor," said Gitiadas.

"Eh? If you can tell me how that may be, I will be grateful."

"We all saw how close and confined that room is, how quickly the torches and our own exhalations staled the air. Perhaps they were engaged in some ceremony that involved burning some noxious substance. In fact, an ordinary charcoal brazier has been known to suffocate people in a confined space. Eugaeon may have fallen down the well when he was overcome, ending up in the Oracle's chamber."

"But there was no sign of such a thing," I said. "And how would it account for the bodies being laid out as they were?"

"It does not, but it may be the best story to put about, to keep things quiet until you can fathom what really happened."

"Sly as well as philosophical, I see. Not a bad idea. It would account for the lack of any marks on the bodies, not that I've examined these others thoroughly as yet. All right, everybody. For official purposes, we shall maintain the pose that these men met their fate through misadventure. I don't believe it for a minute, but it's in all our interests to maintain the fiction. I want no wild speculations or rumormongering. As far as the public is concerned, the staff of the Temple of Apollo died through some frightful accident. Maybe we can keep things from getting riotous for a few days while I sort all of this out." They all nodded and promised to heed my warning. Fat chance of that happening. Futhermore, I knew the slaves would talk to other slaves. The district would hum with rumors before the sun was up. No help for that.

I just hoped I would not have to call any soldiers in.

AT FIRST LIGHT WE EXAMINED THE bodies. As with Eugaeon, there were no wounds to account for the fatalities, but the hands of two of them were somewhat battered. Hermes pointed this out. "Looks like there was some fighting down there."

"So they resisted," I noted. "But how did the killers overcome and kill them without leaving more marks on the bodies? They haven't been strangled. Their necks aren't bruised. Even smothering with pillows should have left their faces darkened and their eyes red."

"Poisoned?" Hermes hazarded.

"Possibly, though how it was administered remains perplexing."

"We had to drink that stuff before we were allowed to go down the tunnel. Maybe they had a similar rite and someone poisoned the drink."

"Not impossible, though most poisons have rather violent effects. You would expect them to have thrashed about a bit, perhaps foam at the mouth. There also was their neat, side-by-side arrangement."

Hermes shrugged. "Whoever did it had plenty of time to clean up before we found the bodies."

"Exactly." I sighed. "There are just too many explanations for everything. We need to narrow them down somewhat."

"That's what you are supposed to be good at," he pointed out.

The master stoneworker was named Ansidius Perna. He was a big man with scarred hands and eyes permanently reddened by rockdust. Hermes had needed to do some searching to find the right man. It turned out that there were all sorts of stoneworkers: quarrymen, drillers, cutters, smoothers, polishers, fine carvers, and decorators, men who did nothing except cut the precise holes for placing the drumlike stones of pillars, and, of course, the masons who stacked the prepared stones into buildings and temples. Perna was head of the guild that represented quarrymen, drillers, and cutters. He stood before me as I lounged in my curule chair, draped in my purple-bordered toga, attended by my lictors.

We were in the temporary headquarters I had set up next to the double temple. The minor festival of a few days before had turned into a veritable regional bazaar and more people were arriving every day. The place buzzed with word of the new killings, but so far no riot had broken out. The news was too fresh. Everyone was agog to hear more about the matter that had them all enthralled. Probably, I thought, they are hoping for even more killings.

"Perna," I said, "have you been in the tunnel that leads down to the chamber of the Oracle and the St—that river?"

"I have, Praetor." He was well dressed, barbered and bathed, as befitted the master of an important guild, but the dust was embedded in the creases of his skin as permanently as any tattoo. Plainly, he had been a common hammer-and-chisel man in his younger days.

"And what is your impression of the stonework?"

"Well, it was cut by men who knew their business. Every stroke is straight and true, the marks are still there to see. Strange how they did it, one or maybe two men working at the rockface. Must have taken them twenty years to drive that tunnel in such a fashion. With a good team of a dozen cutters I could drive a tunnel that long in a year. It would have to be wider, of course. But then, how can we judge the way ancient people did things? They must've thought the gods wanted it done that way, and who's going to argue with the gods?"

"Quite so," I mused. I had been inside one of the great pyramids outside Thebes, and none of it made any sense at all, with shafts leading nowhere and chambers containing nothing and slots no wider than your hand that led a hundred feet or more through solid stone to the outside, and nothing to be seen through them but a star or two. They were different people with different gods and how are we to understand them?

"Perna," I said, "I heard a rumor that the tunnel was cut *upward,* from below. Any way that could have happened?"

"How is that possible?"

"I didn't say it was possible," I said testily. "I just wondered if it could be true."

He chuckled. "No, sir. I know how to read chisel cuts, and that tunnel was driven downward like any other, and it was done with normal mallet-and-chisel work. Hard to even swing a sledge in such a narrow space."

"Have you any idea how it was driven straight to the river?"

He shrugged. "That I couldn't tell you. I suspect the gods were involved."

"I was afraid you'd say that." I rose from my seat. "Come with me. I want you to tell me what you think of this new tunnel we've found beneath the temple." My lictors followed us.

"I've never heard of this tunnel," Perna said, "and I've lived in this district all my life."

"That's what everyone says. Somebody has been very good at keeping a secret."

Inside the temple, I had one of my lictors raise the trap. Perna grunted and examined the door, then peered into the hinging arrangements. "The counterweight is hidden in the foundation," he pronounced. "This is Greek work, but not local. I've heard of this sort of device being used in Alexandrian temples. They're fond of spectacular effects like raising the god up through the floor during ceremonies."

"Yes, I've been in Alexandria and have seen that sort of thing. Now for the tunnel." We went down the ramp and Perna examined the walls, floor, and ceiling.

"Greek work again," he said. "The pattern of cuts is the same that's been taught by Greek stonecutters for generations. Very different from the cutting done in the Oracle's tunnel."

"That's as I suspected. Is there any way to judge how old this work is?"

"That's harder to say. Under the surface like this, there's no natural wearing to age the stones."

I nodded, remembering the pyramid. It was more than two thousand years old, the priests said, yet the stonework in the interior looked as if it had been finished the day before.

"It's much newer than the Oracle's tunnel," said Perna. "And this temple is far older as well. It's a Greek temple now, but a lot of the stonework is pre-Greek. The foundation here is made of huge blocks, nothing like native work, more like something Egyptians would use. The temple dates from later than that. It's pure Campanian work. Then the Greeks came along and altered it to their own taste."

It was not an uncommon thing in a place like this, which had been overrun so many times by various conquerors as well as peaceful immigrants. I had seen more complicated structures in Sicily. Why waste a good, solid foundation or sound walls when you can just build on top and redecorate?

"How long has your family been in the district?" I asked him.

"You mean how was this tunnel built without anyone outside knowing about it?" He was not without a certain native intelligence. He rubbed his chin. "I'd say it could be done without great difficulty. If someone were to give me a contract to accomplish such a task, I'd bring in foreign workmen and keep them here in barracks under guard. They could work at night, since night and day are the same thing underground. The rubble could be carried out in baskets and scattered in fields or in the nearby rivers." He thought for a while. "But I can think of an even better way."

"What might that be?"

"Do it when the temple is being restored. That way, nobody at all would wonder about the work going on. You wouldn't have to disguise the rubble. Just keep sightseers away. Priests can always do that by threatening curses, or promising ritual contamination or talking about omens."

"You possess a certain sophistication in these matters," I told him.

Perna grinned. "One of the plagues of the building trades is that, for some reason, idlers always want to hang about construction sites, gawk, and get in the way."

"I've noticed the phenomenon."

"Well, I've hired more than one priest or soothsayer to keep them away. Usually, it works."

"Thank you, my friend," I said, with a hearty politician's clap on the shoulder. "You have given me much to think about."

"I am happy to be of help," he said. "But, if you don't mind my asking, what has the stonework to do with what happened here?"

"I have no idea," I admitted, "and ultimately this may be of no assistance. But I long ago discovered that learning everything there is to know about a place or a scene or a family can have great bearing upon the solution of a crime."

"If you say so, Praetor," he said doubtfully. Another one who didn't understand.

Next I summoned Hermes. "Find me the local historian," I ordered him, and this time he knew better than to question me. I knew that there would be one. There always is. Usually it is some tiresome old pedant, one with nothing better to do, who busies his normally worthless time with compiling the trivia of local history: its mythical antecedents, the wars fought and social movements, local genealogies. Rome was full of them, having so much history. Having created so much history, for that matter. The virtue of such people was that they needed little provocation to talk about their favorite subject. The problem was to narrow their recitations to the topic you were interested in.

About lunchtime, Julia appeared with Iola. The priestess looked considerably less haughty than before. Her eyes were haunted rather than illuminated with a self-induced religious fire. "Praetor, how may I help you in this terrible matter?"

"First of all, please, both of you, be seated." Julia conducted her to a chair, then took one herself. Julia was usually not slow to assert herself, but when I was seated in the curule chair she had to comport herself humbly. Cato at his most patriotic never had greater respect for Republican traditions than Julia.

"Now, first," I said, "Iola, I want you to swear to me, before all the gods, that you and your people had nothing to do with the killing of the entire staff of the Temple of Apollo. I will summon whatever priests or other sacerdotes you require to make your oath binding. But you must know that to make such an oath before a Roman magistrate, you already swear before Jupiter, Juno, and Mars."

She closed her eyes and breathed deeply through her nose. "I am quite aware of this, Praetor. Your gods are not mine, but I acknowledge their sovereignty. I swear by Hecate that I will tell you nothing but the truth—and I swear by the Styx." Julia jerked a look at her. By tradition, only the gods of Greece swore by the Styx, but her cult was a peculiar one, with a special relationship to that dread river.

"That will do. Now, has your cult any knowledge of the tunnel leading from the Temple of Apollo to the subterranean river?"

"We have—long suspected such a thing," she said uncertainly.

49

"How so?"

"The adepts of our religion can detect disturbances in our communications with our goddess. We felt that someone was conducting ceremonies concurrent with our own, to destroy our communion with Hecate."

This was exactly the sort of supernatural drivel I was hoping to keep out of my investigation, but it seemed to be unavoidable. "Had the staff of Apollo's temple threatened you?"

"Never directly. There has always been a policy of strict silence between us."

"Indirectly?"

She was silent for a while. "While the priests themselves would never speak to us, the people of the district who follow their god made no secret of their hostility."

"Yes, I've heard a bit about the local religious rivalries. But that's been going on forever. Were there any threats, serious threats, quite recently?"

"No, Praetor, there were not."

I had to take her word for it, but I held my reservations. It was not in her best interests to admit that she had a good reason to kill the priests. I dismissed her and sat brooding for a while.

"What are you thinking?" Julia asked at length. It was a question I heard often from her. Usually, I kept a store of innocuous answers in readiness for it. This time, though, I saw no particular reason to prevaricate.

"The girl saw the priests go down into their tunnel carrying torches and lamps. We found none down there. Not only the bodies but the whole chamber had been tidied up. It suggests that a number of people conspired in the murders. Yet so far as we have been able to ascertain, no parties of visitors arrived while we were consulting with the Oracle. It suggests that the murderers were already in the temple."

"Then you should put the whole temple staff to the question," she advised.

"I am not ready to go to such an extreme yet. Perhaps only one person was required to administer the poison or whatever method was used. Accomplices could have come in later, while we were scouring the countryside."

"You are too softhearted to be a praetor," she said, not without affection.

The local historian arrived just in time for lunch. Scholars have a way of doing that. His name was Lucius Cordus, and he was a small man with ink on his fingers and eyes permanently asquint from constant reading, even by lamplight. After exchanging the customary amenities, we sat at a table set up beneath my canopy. It was laid with a plentiful lunch, to which Cordus applied himself as if he intended to do it full justice. I waited until he was replete and well lubricated with wine before broaching the matter of the day.

"How may I be of service to the noble praetor?" he said, when the edge was off his appetite.

"I am told that you are the foremost authority on the history of this district."

"I would not style myself so," he said modestly. "I have some small knowledge of the subject, and what I know is of course at your service."

"You are familiar with the events of recent days here at the temple?"

"Several versions of them, in fact. I could not say which if any are correct. As a historian, I am all too aware of the mutability of information."

"Facts can be slippery indeed," I agreed. "What I need to know is something of the history of these two oddly juxtaposed holy sites."

"Ah, this is a fascinating subject," he said, taking a quick bite of cheese and bread, and washing it down with an even quicker swig of his wine.

"I take it the tunnel of the Oracle is far older than the temple?"

"By a great margin. As you may have discerned, there have been at least three temples on the site, possibly more."

"I've noted that the foundation blocks are quite different from Campanian stonework, and that the Greek temple was adapted from an earlier one of Campanian style."

"Exactly," Cordus agreed." It is my theory that the tunnel was dug at the same time that the Cyclopean stones of the foundation were put in place. The method of stonecutting seems to be the same. Whether these great stones supported an earlier temple, or were just a platform for the image of a god, or were for some other purpose entirely, we cannot know. It dates from long before the art of writing came to Italy. The earliest writings I have found, inscribed in a very archaic Campanian dialect, speak of the tunnel as being ancient even then. There is one curiosity, though."

"What might that be?" I asked him.

"There is no mention of an Oracle, nor of an association with Hecate. The subterranean river is mentioned, but is not called the Styx."

"Interesting, indeed," I said. "Have you any idea when these ideas became associated with the location?"

"The Greeks came to southern Italy about seven hundred years ago. Some were Dorians, others Achaeans and Corinthians. First they settled in the east, founding Brundisium, Then up and down the eastern coast, then into the Bay of Tarentum, finally through the strait of Messina to found the towns of this district. Those were wild and dangerous times, and the sea swarmed with pirates, so they built inland roads to connect their settlements. Soon all of southern Italy was known as Magna Graecia. I do not think that Hecate moved in down there before this time, because her devotees are Greek, as are her ceremonies and all of the terminology used in her worship." He shook his head. "No, I think that tunnel was there for many centuries before the Greeks came. And there is another discrepancy."

"And that would be?" I asked, fascinated. At least this fellow did not drone on endlessly like so many scholars of my acquaintance.

"Hecate is not an oracular goddess. Oracles are usually associated with snakes and there is no snake cult here. She is one of the true

Greek *autochthonoi*, but she doesn't speak to petitioners. Only here. In fact, I have found no mention of her Oracle here earlier than about three hundred years ago, and that was only in the form of a reference to the sacrifice of black dogs, her traditional tutelary animals."

"Do you believe the Oracle could be fraudulent?"

"I hesitate to make pronouncements concerning the doings of the immortals. If it is fraudulent, it has succeeded longer than most. The human will to believe is a powerful thing."

I sat back in my chair and mused. "So, we have a tunnel of great antiquity, of unknown purpose, which may have lain unused until the cult of Hecate moved in."

"Needless to say, the writings are very fragmentary, but I can hardly believe that something so remarkable would escape more frequent mention. As for local traditions, I would grant them no credence whatever. Anywhere peasants live, they create mythologies around their district and their ancestors, often mutually contradictory. Few people are trained in the art of rigorous thinking."

"So it would seem," I agreed. "What of the Campanian temple erected atop the foundation?"

"The Campanians pushed their territory southward and reached this area about the same time as the Greeks. Before, there had been only the primitive settlements of the Aborigines."

"You believe the Aborigines really existed?"

"They must have. There are many burials that predate the people we have been discussing. Whether they were the people of legend I cannot say, but the burials I have examined indicate a very low level of culture. They built nothing in stone that has survived."

"So, things got lively here between Greeks and Campanians around the time Romulus and Remus founded Rome." The official date of that event was some 704 years before this time.

"Very lively, I would say. They were two aggressive, warlike people who wanted the same land. Plus, the Greek cities, being Greek, fought endlessly among themselves. That temple may have been erected and demolished a number of times. It was dedicated to the god Mamers, who can be identified with Mars. But a far grander Temple of Mamers was erected at Cumae, and eventually this one was abandoned. In time, the Greeks turned it into the Temple of Apollo. That was about two hundred years ago."

"Did the rivalry between the followers of Apollo and those of Hecate date from the time that the Campanians and Greeks were fighting over this territory?"

"Something like that. I think that it came to serve as a substitute for open hostilities, especially after Rome imposed peace on the region."

"Well, sometimes you can keep people from fighting, but you can't stop them from hating one another. The Greeks and the Trojans would probably still hate each other, if there were any Trojans left."

"Such seems to be the nature of men," Cordus said.

"So it's always good to be the strongest. That is what Rome determined to do. Always be the strongest. That way it doesn't matter if people hate you, because you can always whip them and they know it and don't dare say anything aloud."

"Ah, that is very true, Praetor. We are the terror of the world." This to remind me that he was a citizen, too. "A terror in a good way, of course. Where Rome has conquered, Rome establishes peace."

"Yes, well, we seem to be straying from the subject. In all your studies, have you seen any mention of this tunnel beneath the temple, where we found the dead priests?"

"In fact, I have."

"What? The thing seems to have been a mystery to everybody else!"

He smiled. "How many people bother to read records of construction work from two hundred years ago? In the city archive of Baiae I ran across a contract between the founders of the temple and one Skopas of Alexandria for 'the construction of a crypt beneath the Temple of Apollo by the Bay of Baiae.' It does not specify a tunnel, but as far as I know, there is no rule limiting how far down a crypt can be."

"Wonderful!" I said. "This is the virtue of paying attention to paperwork. One document is worth any number of legends."

"And this knowledge will be of use in your investigation?"

"I have no idea. But it is wonderful to actually *know* something in this maze of myths. Earlier today the master stoneworker said that the workmanship on the trapdoor looked Alexandrian. He also said that the easiest way to do it without the locals noticing would have been when it was remodeled to Greek taste."

"Very sagacious," he said, nodding. "The question remains: Why did they do it?"

"I don't know, and I certainly hope that it has no bearing on the investigation."

We spoke a while longer but he had nothing further to offer, though he promised to pitch into his studies with great zeal to find me more information. I thanked him profusely, for he had proven to be of real assistance. I gave him a small sack of gold and silver "in case he had to travel," and he went away beaming, happy to have the money, a full stomach, and, above all, to have his wisdom praised and appreciated by one in authority. The path of scholarship can be thankless and unrewarding.

That evening, my kinsman Marcus Caecilius Metellus came down from Rome for a visit. He was a young man just setting out on his political career, and he had been in my traveling entourage since I entered the praetorship. A month before, I had sent him to Rome to gather the latest gossip for me. For true Romans, being separated from the City is an almost physical affliction. One can stand being separated from the center of the world for only so long. This is why we consider exile such a terrible punishment. Many exiles go insane or commit suicide in despair. At dinner, we were all ears to hear the latest.

"First, the best news, Decius," he began. Here at dinner, among close friends and relatives, he was free to address me by my praenomen instead of my title. "You know that Appius Claudius has been going through the senatorial roll like a great scythe, expelling senators for corruption, bribery, debt, and immorality?"

"Everybody knows that," I said. This Appius Claudius was the brother of my old enemy Clodius, but was a man of the highest rectitude for whom I always had the greatest respect.

"Well, among others, he expelled Sallustius for immorality!"

I laughed so hard that wine shot out of my nose and it was a few minutes before I regained possession of myself. "Wonderful! Too bad it was only immorality, though. He's guilty of every one of the practices Claudius is so determined to stamp out."

"One was enough," said Marcus. "He doesn't dare show his face in the Forum."

This Sallustius was a wretched climber I had known for far too long. He was as corrupt as any senator who had ever disgraced the curia, and in those years that was very corrupt indeed. He was always trying to ingratiate himself with me and I could not stand his insinuating manner. In later years, with no further political or criminal activity to distract him, he styled himself a historian.

"On a less happy note," Marcus went on, "Caesar and the Senate seem to be on a collision course."

"Well," I said resignedly, "it's been coming." Caesar wanted to retain his extraordinary command in Gaul and Illyria. He also wanted to stand for consul in the elections for the coming year. The problem was, the Senate demanded that he return to Rome to stand for office in the traditional manner, but a Roman propraetor or proconsul lost his imperium the moment he stepped across the *pomerium*. The Senate already had Caesar's successor picked out.

"The Senate has decreed that Caesar, if he wants to keep his proconsulship, is to stay north of the Rubicon." This river was the border between Italy and Caesar's province.

"He won't," I said. "He'll cross, and he'll bring all his legions with him. I know him and I know his soldiers. After what he's accomplished the last ten years, all the victory and loot he's brought them, those men will lay siege to Rome if he asks them. And he will."

"Rubbish!" Julia said heatedly. "Caesar will never oppose the

Senate with armed force. He has too great a respect for Roman traditions. There are senators who foolishly wish to dishonor him, but he respects that august body like any good Roman. What has Lepidus to say?" Lucius Aemilius Lepidus Paullus, one of that year's consuls, tried to support Caesar, who had, among other favors, given him the money to restore the ancestral Basilica Aemilia. Unfortunately his colleague, Claudius Marcellus, was Caesar's deadly enemy and a much more forceful man. Julia's affection for her uncle led her into the dangerous paths of wishful thinking.

"Lepidus tries, as always, to support Caesar. But that is getting to be a minority position in the Senate. The Assemblies, as always, favor Caesar."

"Cicero," Marcus went on, trying to lighten the mood, "has already run from Cilicia. He made huge efforts to prevent having his proconsulship prorogued. He's already petitioned the Senate for a triumph."

"A triumph?" I said. "For that trifling victory?" Cicero, that most reluctant of soldiers, had gone to govern Cilicia and had eventually scored a win over what amounted to a pack of bandits.

"His troops hailed him as imperator." Marcus said.

"The standards of Roman legionaries have fallen if that lot declared Cicero imperator." Ordinarily I did not speak disparagingly of Cicero, whom I admired above most Romans and counted as a friend. Although in his later career he became foolishly grandiose and self-important. The very thought of the spindly, unmilitary Cicero riding in triumph through Rome for so trifling a victory was deeply embarrassing.

"Curio continues to be controversial," Marcus went on. "He's gone over to Caesar wholeheartedly now, after months of vacillating." Scribonius Curio was the most remarkable Tribune of the People in a long time. His rise to power had been phenomenal, and he was uncommonly effective, proposing and ramming through the Assemblies a program of legislation unprecedented in its scope and volume. Rumor had it that Caesar had suborned him with a bribe of unprecedented extravagance and now it appeared that the bribe had been successful. If so,

Curio was a man of character, for in the years to come he hewed faithfully to Caesar, right until his death in Africa. I had always liked him, even when we ran afoul of one another.

"Oh, enough of this dreary political blather!" Antonia cried. "Let's have the real gossip! What's Fulvia been up to?" This Fulvia was one of those scandalous women who livened Roman discourse of the day. She had been briefly involved with some ill-fated political rogues and had been a center of attention ever since.

"Well," Marcus began, "she has been linked with the aedile Caelius Rufus, who has been prosecuting those who illegally divert water from the aqueducts. And, since her own family are notorious for just that crime—" and so on. I was eager for the political news, but petty gossip about who was sleeping with whom, who was bribing whom for financial gain, who had murdered whom for banal motives, left me utterly unconcerned.

Still, I was grateful for the way Marcus had turned the conversation to lighter subjects. It was well that we ended the evening on a cheerful note, because the next morning brought us yet another murder at the temple.

4

"WHAT?" I SHOUTED. "WHO'S LEFT TO kill? The whole staff of priests are gamboling happily amid the Elysian Fields already!"

"Calm down, dear," Julia admonished. "With all you ate and drank last night you're liable to bring on a seizure."

It was early morning, never the best hour for me. Hermes had come in to wake me more than an hour before my accustomed time. It was still dark enough to need lamps. I threw on a toga, ignoring Julia's demands to wait for her. I knew she would take far too long to get dressed and made up. Preceded by torchbearers, we made our way up to the temple. In what had become the market area, I could see the embers of some campfires still burning, though most of the visitors were fast asleep. A steward met us at the entrance to the temple grounds. He looked distressed, and understandably so. Temples of Apollo were supposed to be serene places and this one was anything but.

He led us to the stable area, where horses and asses shifted quietly in the cool morning. There on the straw lay the body, and the torchbearers lowered their flames so that we could see, but it was scarcely necessary in the growing dawn light.

It was the slave girl, Hypatia. I closed my eyes for a moment. Such a beautiful child.

"Well," Hermes said, "at least this time there's no mystery about how she died."

Indeed, she had been stabbed just beneath the sternum. It was an expert's blow, sure to kill quickly with one thrust slanting upward into the heart. Hermes parted her gown to view the wound.

"It was done with a broad-bladed dagger or a short sword, maybe a soldier's *pugio*."

"I wish Asklepiodes were here," I said, not for the first time.

"He probably couldn't tell you much. This looks pretty straightforward."

I spoke to the steward. "When was she found?"

"Less than an hour ago, Praetor. The boy who cares for the animals is always here before first light. I am afraid he tripped over her. He came running to me and I sent word to you at once."

"Commendable. Besides the boy, how many people have been trampling around here since she was found?"

"Just ourselves, sir."

"Hermes, go get my lictors and have them guard this area. We'll make a thorough search at full light."

He was back in a few minutes, and Julia arrived as well, looking grim when she saw the body. "That poor girl," she said. "She was afraid to speak out and she had reason to be, it seems."

"I blame myself for this," I told her. "I should have taken her into custody. I said right in front of everybody that I might be questioning her further. Clearly somebody did not want her to talk."

"Do you think she saw more than she told you?"

"Probably not, but sometimes it is best not to take chances. Whoever is behind this decided to eliminate a possible problem. They didn't see fit to employ arcane murder methods this time."

"Why at the stables?" Julia mused. "What was she doing out here in the middle of the night?"

"I've been pondering that myself. Perhaps she was frightened enough to try to escape and she came down here to steal a mount. But it can be no coincidence that the murderer was here waiting for her."

"She must have been summoned here by someone she thought she had reason to trust."

"If so, she was mistaken in that belief. In fact, it causes me to wonder about her depth of involvement in this matter."

"You think she might have been an accomplice?" Julia said.

"It wouldn't be the first time someone suborned a slave to spy on a master. Nor would it be the first time an accomplice was eliminated in just this fashion."

With full light we went over the scene. As is common with stables, the ground in front, where the body lay, was a mash of trampled mud and straw. Footprints, both human and animal, were so plentiful that they told us nothing. I examined the ground closely for any foreign matter, but there was nothing. Just the beautiful girl, whose eyes stared up at nothing, expressing nothing, not even the reproach I deserved.

"Well, my dear," I said, "I don't think we're going to learn anything here."

"Don't be so sure, my love," Julia said. To my horror, she further opened the unfortunate girl's gown and felt her breasts, then her belly. Apparently satisfied, she straightened. "This girl is—was, I should say, pregnant. About three months along."

Her words did not shock me at all, but her actions did. Romans do not at all mind turning live bodies into dead ones. We do it all the time. However, we have a ritual revulsion for touching dead bodies before the proper rites have been performed. Death contaminates, and the purificatory lustrum must be performed before the body can be handled. And here was Julia, the very personification of patrician rectitude, touching the body of a murdered slave.

Mind you, I did not doubt for a second that her judgment was correct. Few women knew more about pregnancy than Julia, since the subject was her passion. She suffered from the Julians' famous infertility and she had been to every midwife, medium, and quack physician in Rome to find a cure. Still, as many years as we tried, she had achieved pregnancy rarely, carried a child to term only twice, and these infants had not survived their first four months. I accepted this as the gods' will where it came to the Julians, as opposed to my own family, whose fertility was little less than pestilential. In our circles, where you cannot produce heirs, you adopt. But Julia resisted this expedient, still hoping to produce an heir of good Julian-Caecilian stock.

"What of it?" I asked, when I got over my shock. "Girl slaves get pregnant all the time, and a beauty like this one must have had more opportunity than most. Julia, you've contaminated yourself! We'll have to summon a priest and perform a lustrum."

"Don't be an idiot!" she snapped. "Touching the dead can't contaminate anyone. The gods aren't that petty."

I was astonished. This was the first time I had ever heard Julia speak against ritual law. Of course, I never truly credited all that primitive mumbo-jumbo myself, but I had never seen any point in taking chances. Moreover, I had always thought that old, patrician families like the Julians were even more tradition-bound than mine. But Julia had become something of a freethinker. She had been consulting with Alexandrian philosophers.

"All right, I grant your point. What difference does it make that this poor child was pregnant?"

"We can't know, but it's something we didn't know before. As you've so often intoned to me in such portentous tones, my love, 'every fact, however innocuous it may seem at the moment, may have a crucial bearing upon the case.'"

"Yes, I did say that, didn't I? I think it was that lecture I delivered in the Basilica Julia just after that business with the flood and Scaurus's death."

"Maybe you just practiced on me," she said, with that tired patience she sometimes showed when she judged me an especial idiot. "But we have here a temple whose staff are expected to be renowned for chastity. This girl's condition coincides with the mass murder of its priesthood. Might there not be some connection?"

"Well, I suppose so," I said, still having trouble dealing with the fact that Julia had just handled a corpse with her bare hands. "But what might that connection be?"

"That's your field, dear," she said, turning away. "As for me, I will concentrate upon the staff of the Oracle, and the women of the district." She left a warning unspoken: I had better be circumspect about the women of the district. I had learned to heed Julia's warnings in such matters.

So I summoned young Sextus Vespillo. He appeared with commendable dispatch, and turned pale when he saw the girl's corpse. He was old enough not to be dismayed by the occasional corpse, but he clearly had been fond of the girl. I gave him a moment to regain his composure.

"I heard there had been another killing," he said, when his color returned. "I didn't know who it was."

"It's time you told me how you encountered this girl and how she came to reveal the hidden tunnel to you." We walked from the stables and turned our steps toward the temple. I had no urgent business there but it was more pleasant than the crime scene.

"We'd been combing the district for the priests and using the temple as our base of operations, as you instructed. Hermes often left me behind here because he says I'm a wretched horseman and would just slow the rest down. Actually, I'm quite good at—"

I raised a hand to silence him. "That is of no account. Let it suffice that you remained behind here at the temple instead of riding off with the rest. What then?" We had come to the space before the temple where I had set up my headquarters.

"I, ah, that is, I was—sitting over there—" he gestured idly toward the low dais, hoping that I would not grasp the implication. Not much chance of that.

"Were you sitting in my curule chair?" I shouted, drawing many curious stares from the idlers all about. I have not mentioned that the impromptu market had by now swollen to the size of a modest town, so we were well supplied with such persons.

"Forgive me, Praetor, but it seemed harmless enough, with you and your lictors absent—"

"And just the thing to impress pretty serving girls with your importance as the close associate of a Roman magistrate, eh? I will remind you that that chair is a part of the regalia of imperium, and no one who has not had imperium bestowed by the Senate is permitted to use it."

"Yes, sir," he said, gaze downcast. "I am sorry, sir. It won't happen again."

"If it does, I'll have you before me on charges of sacrilege or *maiestas* or some other charge that carries gruesome penalties, which I will proceed to inflict."

"But you only try cases that involve foreigners!" he protested.

"A petty legal quibble. I can have you executed and when I step down from office your relatives can try to prosecute me. They won't be successful because my family is more important than yours. It won't do you any good anyway, because you'll be dead."

"But—"

"All right, so there you were, lounging feloniously in my curule chair. What happened next? Did you order wine from my private stock?"

"Nothing of the sort. A few people approached me, mostly with questions about your investigation—"

"What sort of questions?" I kept interrupting him because it is an excellent trial lawyer's tactic. It keeps people off-balance and in such a state they frequently say things they would not if given time to think and frame their statements.

"What you would expect. Had you made any progress, were the

missing priests found, and so forth. Some wanted to accuse their neighbors or enemies."

"Were any of those credible?"

He shook his head. "Clearly deranged or just petty troublemakers."

"Did anyone have political questions, questions not concerning the case?" This concerned me because, with the countryside so full of Pompey's adherents, some of them surely would be sounding me out. My family had not yet picked a side in the upcoming showdown between Pompey and Caesar. I was of two minds myself. No, I was of three or four minds, and none of them had a satisfactory answer for me.

"That lady from Stabiae, Sabinilla, she came by. Asked the usual questions and then wanted to know if you were in the confidence of your wife's uncle, Caesar. She acted as if that made you fascinating."

"It would, to some people. Anyone else?"

"A man called Drusianus badgered me, acting rather drunk. He hinted that he's the spokesman for Pompey's veterans in the area. He said you'd better settle this matter quickly or there will be trouble."

"He said that, eh? I had the impression that Pompey's men aren't very numerous in the region, but there may be more than I thought."

"Or he may be some local bully trying to pretend he's a power in the district."

"Most likely," I concurred. Still, the prospect of trouble from that quarter made me uneasy. "Now, at what point did you go after the girl?"

"I didn't go after her!" he said indignantly.

"Yes, far beneath your dignity, I'm sure. How, then, did the two of you happen to occupy the same space at the same time?"

"It was just past noon. The girl came from the temple and asked if I would like some refreshment—"

"Refreshment," I said tonelessly.

"Well, I thought she meant some lunch or wine, something like that. I followed her into the temple."

"A temple being, of course, the sort of place where an impromptu luncheon is always likely to be laid out."

"All right, I wasn't really all that eager to ask questions."

"That's more like it. So you followed that shapely backside into the interior of a dark and deserted temple. A very promising prospect, I admit. After all, the word 'refreshment' is subject to generous interpretation. What next, if I may make so indelicate an inquiry?"

"Nothing that's very indelicate to tell about, I'm afraid." He looked downcast like any other unsuccessful would-be swain. "She got—ah—very friendly and pulled me behind a pillar and while I was preparing to—"

"Do something indelicate?" I prodded.

"Very indelicate," he said, perking up at the thought of his intention. "But then she pulled back and stared at the statue of the god, as if she feared his disapproval."

"I don't see why," I said. "Old Apollo was as randy as the rest of the male gods, always chasing mortal women and getting them turned into plants, like Daphne."

"My very thought. In fact, I was making exactly that objection, only using the example of Castalia, the girl of Delphi, who got turned into a fountain."

"Yes, and some yielded to his advances," I said. "Back in the days when a mortal woman had a chance to bed a truly exalted lover, he sowed the world with little bastard demigods. So, how did the girl respond to this eloquent line of reasoning?"

"She said that it was not my ardency that upset her, but the memory of the last time she had stood upon that spot, when she had witnessed something that disturbed her."

"And that was the incident of which she informed us."

"Exactly."

"Well, at least you have hope for the effectiveness of your masculine charms. Take me to the spot where you stood during your abortive tryst."

He indicated the pillar and we stepped behind it. "It was just about this time of day, wasn't it?" He concurred that it was.

The interior of the temple was dim, as is always the case with temples, which have doorways but no windows. I could just barely make out the statue of the god. The pedestal below his feet was even more obscure. What, I thought, must it have looked like at night, when the only illumination was the flickering light of the torches?

"She claimed that she went no closer than this spot, did she not?"

"That's what she said."

"Yet somehow she saw clearly the bit of carving, among such a profusion of floral stonework, that is the concealed latch to the trapdoor."

"This is the sort of thing you're so famous for, isn't it?" Vespillo said. "Examining scenes and circumstances and picking away at the—the inconsistencies?"

"It's a simple and logical process," I said. "People lie and sometimes they trip themselves up. Unfortunately, I am not now able to interrogate the girl about this improbability. I suspect that this is the reason for her murder."

We left the temple and I saw a woman on the dais, her ample bottom perched on the arm of my curule chair, which seemed to have become a public convenience on these days when court was not in session. Catching sight of us, she smiled and waved. It was Porcia, the wealthy freedman's daughter.

"Praetor!" she yelled, turning heads for acres around. "And if it isn't the handsome young Vespillo! Do you have any plans for lunch?"

I drew closer so I wouldn't have to shout. "As a matter of fact, we are entirely at loose ends."

"Then you must come to my house and have a bite. It's quite nearby."

"Vespillo here yielded to just such an invitation, and bad things can come of it."

"If I hadn't, you'd still be looking for those dead priests," he objected.

"You are right, so we must accept this invitation. Lead on."

She led us to a huge litter that stood near a fountain, the bearers squatting by the poles, taking advantage of the cool spray. We climbed in and were hoisted. The bearers set off through the motley, alternately festive and sullen crowd.

Her house lay only a mile from the temple complex, a great, sprawling villa surrounded by orchards and lovingly sculpted formal gardens. We were carried up the steps of the main house and through its extra high and wide doorway and set down in a huge atrium graced with a number of family portrait busts. They all had the look of Italian peasants and no attempt had been made to ape aristocratic practices like a formal chest full of spurious ancestral death masks. I had known social climbers to haunt estate auctions and snap up a whole family tree of spurious ancestors to dignify the atrium.

"Welcome to the Villa of the *Mundus*. It's what my father named the place."

"You have a *mundus* here?" I said. "Is there anyplace in Campania that isn't in direct contact with the underworld?"

She laughed raucously. "It's just a hole in the ground! An old peasant who used to own a piece of this land claimed that people could get in touch with their dead by leaving offerings in his *mundus*. As you've figured out by now, people in this area will believe just about anything. He salted away a lot of denarii before he croaked. He usually charged a denarius per offering, but he was a shrewd judge of what people could afford and he had a sliding scale. He'd accept a copper *as* if he thought that was all he could get out of you."

"A man of enterprise," I said. "An example of the drive and initiative that have made Italy great among the nations of the world. He should be an inspiration to us all."

Again, the great, hooting laugh. "Praetor, you are priceless! Come, you must be famished. I've had something laid out by the pool."

"Nothing too lavish, I hope," I said, hoping just the opposite. "After all, you might not have found me in time for lunch."

"Oh, I always have a bit laid out just in case I bring someone home from town. I usually do." We entered a wide, colonnaded court-yard with a central pool.

"I can see why you have many takers," I said, eyeing the long tables stacked with every imaginable delicacy and endless pitchers of wine. Half-naked Egyptian girls wafted huge ostrich-feather fans to keep the flies away. We took couches, and Asian slaves not only took our sandals but washed our feet in the Eastern fashion, finishing by rubbing them with aromatic oils.

We were handed tall beakers of solid gold filled with a wonderful vintage I recognized as Coan. Vespillo, no veteran, sipped his and made a face. I tried mine and raised my eyebrows, glancing at Porcia.

She grinned. "I noticed at Duronius's dinner that you don't favor too much water in your wine. My own idea of the proper proportion is no water at all."

"I can see that we are going to get along famously," I commended, downing half of it in a gulp.

Since this was an informal lunch, not a dinner or formal banquet, there was nothing resembling the customary progression of courses starting with eggs and finishing with fruit. Instead, the slaves brought us a succession of small, bite-sized snacks, each very different from the others and all delicious: small skewers of venison wrapped in bacon and broiled over coals; whole squab, each about two bites; ground duck mixed with pine nuts and rolled in grape leaves; squares of melon wrapped in parchment-thin slices of ham cured in the northern fashion; little squid deep-fried in a thin crust; bits of bread toasted with cheese on top and sprinkled with capers; and other things I no longer remember. It was all delicious and, lavish though it was, it was without the vulgarity we commonly associate with rich freedmen. There were no ridiculously rare tidbits or ostentatious servings or grotesque ingredients or preparations. It was all rather simple food, superbly prepared and presented.

In time I lay back, replete. "Campania is famed for its cuisine," I said, "but I do not think I have eaten better since coming here, and I've been entertained in some of the finest houses."

Porcia beamed. "I thought I'd read you right. People who want things like sow's udders stuffed with Libyan mice and German bear stuffed with oysters just want you to think they're sophisticated. I like to serve the things I enjoy eating myself and forget about impressing people."

"Consider me impressed," I said.

"It's all pretty silly," she said, "lowborn people like me trying to use their money to gain acceptance by aristocrats. It's just not going to happen. I'll always be a freedman's daughter and I don't pretend to be anything else."

"A wise philosophy," I said. "Speaking as an aristocrat myself, I can tell you that the advantages of high birth are greatly overrated. You get to hold high office, which can get you killed or prosecuted; you are qualified for the highest priesthoods, and I cannot imagine anything more boring than that. Worst of all, you have to spend a lot of time with your fellow aristocrats, most of whom are bores, insane, or congenital criminals. Be content with wealth and luxury. Those will get you all the respect and deference you could ask for, without all the other headaches." Vespillo looked scandalized at my disloyalty toward my own class. Perhaps I exaggerated, but throughout my adult years I had been growing more and more embittered toward my class, the senatorial aristocracy, who in their self-seeking folly were dragging the Republic down to ruin and destroying much of Italy and the Roman world in the process.

Her eyebrows went up. "Well, that's blunt enough! It's what I always suspected, though. My father wasn't born a slave. His parents sold him when there was a famine here. He never held it against them. They had a lot of children, and by selling a couple of them, they could save the rest from starving. He never thought it made him better than the other slaves, either. Being a slave is a matter of luck, not breeding or the favor of the gods. Some are born slaves, some get made slaves, some stay free all their lives. He worked hard for his master, learned how to handle money, and made a fortune for him in property."

"Commercial properties, were they not?" I asked.

She nodded. "That's right. His master was interested in farmland, because that's what the highborn consider respectable. My father pointed out that squeezing rents from peasants was a lot of trouble and there'd be years when you couldn't get any money out of them at all, because the crops would fail. Buy shops and factories, my father said. Merchants always have money, and if they go broke, you can evict them and rent the place to another merchant. They're always clamoring for properties they can use. It made the old boy a fortune, and he freed my father and staked him to a good bit of investment money. As you can see"—she made a wide gesture, taking in our surroundings—"he did well out of it."

"So he did." I belched politely. "Now, if it is convenient to you, I would like to see your *mundus*."

"That old place?" she said, astonished. "Whatever for? Like I said, it's just a hole in the ground."

"Nonetheless, I am a collector of odd places, and Campania seems to be full of them. Please indulge me."

"Your wish is my dearest pleasure," she said cheerfully, clapping her hands. Moments later the litter reappeared in the atrium and we tottered, full of food and wine, toward it, with slaves at each elbow just in case we should need assistance. Poor Vespillo had said almost nothing throughout the minor banquet. This was partly because he was young and unsophisticated but mostly because he could make nothing of either Porcia or me. He thought I showed a very unpraetorlike lack of gravitas in consorting with the hospitable but lowly Porcia, and a freedman's daughter who was richer than his own family was an unsettling prospect for a naive boy brought up on his mother's tales of the nobility of his ancestors and their natural right to rule. Age and experience would disillusion him, but that was in the future.

The slaves packed us into the litter, along with a great basin of crushed ice in which a large pitcher of wine cooled. This would have been a wonder in Rome, but I had seen the artificial caves where Campanians kept ice and snow, carted down from the mountains in winter, to cool their drinks all summer long.

"You think of everything," I said, holding out my cup to be filled by a rather beautiful Arab girl, who happened to be some sort of dwarf. Her tiny size made her an ideal attendant for a litter, taking up little space and burdening the bearers much less than a normal-sized human.

"Wouldn't want you to go thirsty," Porcia said, accepting another golden beaker herself. She offered it to Vespillo, but he shook his head, already nodding. The boy had little capacity. He needed training. I resolved to undertake this myself. My attendants had to be able to keep up with me if they were to be of any use.

Our progress took us through the abundant orchards and past a broad vineyard that would soon be ready for harvest. Slaves were readying the great trampling vats where the workers would caper like satyrs and nymphs to the music of flutes, stained purple to their thighs as they extracted the gift of Bacchus. That was always my favorite time of year on an estate, where I could watch other people working from a place of comfort and ease.

The bearers took us along a road paved with smooth-cut white stone, lined with watchful herms that were draped with fresh garlands, their phalli standing at attention as if in salute. The fields were cultivated, but the many small prominences had been allowed to grow wild and were topped by small forests.

"You allow plenty of wildland," I said to Porcia. "I like that. So many slave-worked plantations are overcultivated to increase profits. It ruins the land, in time."

"I'm not a farmer, I'm a businesswoman. This place pays for itself, and it supports me and my chattel. I don't ask more than that and I'd rather watch the deer and foxes than see people sweating all day long. I also like to hunt from time to time. Learned it from my father. He was a keen hunter."

"Would that all people were so sensible."

Eventually we came to a little swale, deep-shaded by trees and shrubs, where stood the circular ruins of what had once been a peasant's hut.

"This is as far as we can get by litter," Porcia announced, as we were set down. "From here, we march like legionaries." I prodded Vespillo to wakefulness and we alighted. Swaying only slightly, Porcia led us past the ruins and into the little valley. It was pleasantly cool in the shade and from time to time I sipped from my chilled wine. Slaves followed behind with the pitcher and its basin of ice.

We came upon a small altar in the form of a stubby pillar with a carved serpent spiraling around it; the usual shrine to the *genius loci*. Someone had placed on it cakes, a wooden cup of wine, and, oddly, a few small arrows.

"Did you leave those?" I asked, pointing to the altar.

"No, I hardly ever come here. The local folk keep up their traditions, though. These are probably offerings to someone nobody five miles away ever heard of."

"What do the arrows signify?" Vespillo wanted to know.

"I've no idea. Maybe some hunter wanting to find game here."

We ventured farther into the valley, which I now saw was actually a cleft in almost solid stone, perhaps left over from some upheaval of the earth such as might be wrought by the nearby volcano. Over the ages, the stone had acquired a covering of soil and from this soil sprang the dense growth and twining vines that shaded us. Everywhere, though, crags of solid stone thrust upward through the growth like the snaggled teeth of some long-dead dragon.

"It's over here somewhere," Porcia said, poking about in the undergrowth. "Ah, here it is."

We went to stand beside her. She stood on the brink of a broad, circular well, perhaps three yards in diameter. It merited better than her description of it as a hole in the ground. The rim was of finely cut stone, unornamented but bearing the remains of what was once a fine polish. Careful of my clothes, I knelt on the rim stone and leaned over. A few feet down, the cut stone ended and the well was carved into solid rock. The walls were smooth and the bottom was lost in obscurity.

"I think it's just an old well," Porcia said. "It must've gone dry and was abandoned."

"Awfully wide for a well," Vespillo said.

"A sacred well gets more attention than the ordinary sort," I pointed out. "We have more than one in Rome as elaborate as this one." I looked about and found a black stone streaked with green the size of my fist. I dropped it in and a few moments later was rewarded with a solid *thunk*.

"See?" Porcia said. "It's dry."

"So it would seem. Did the old peasant's callers claim any extraordinary results arising from their visits here?"

"Not that I ever heard of. It's a *mundus*, not an oracle. I think they just left offerings and prayers and good wishes for their dead."

I was vaguely disappointed and unsatisfied, and I wondered, as we passed the little altar on the way back to our litter, why people had left arrows there.

5

For BREAKFAST WE HAD CHERRIES IN cream to go along with the fresh, hot bread I insisted on every morning. Cherries had been introduced into Italy only about seventeen years before this time, and they were still something exotic and a bit of a luxury. Lucullus had brought cherry trees from Asia as part of his triumphal loot after his victories over Mithridates and Tigranes. He had planted a lavish orchard, and had made seedlings and cuttings available at nominal cost.

Julia finished a dish of them and called for more. "Long after people have forgotten who Mithridates was," she said wistfully, "they will praise Lucullus for the gift of cherries." She was passionately fond of the little fruit, and had a cook whose only employment was dreaming up new ways to prepare and present them.

"An estimable accomplishment," I admitted. "It's been my misfortune to campaign in places already well picked over, or else that have nothing of culinary interest to offer. Britannia is just more of Gaul, only colder, and the Germans eat little except meat." These two being the only places I had visited ahead of most Romans. Egypt and Cyprus and the rest were well-worn territory where we'd already looted whatever was useful.

Along with her second helping, Julia received a letter. She opened it and read while popping cherries into her mouth. As usual she took her time. From Uncle Julius she had learned the useful skill of reading silently, something I had never fully mastered. I dipped hot bread in a pot of honey and waited, knowing that it was no use trying to hurry her. From the intensity of her attention, I knew that it was something significant. Making me wait was annoying to me, something she enjoyed.

"Well, who's it from?" I demanded at last.

"It's from my aunt Atia." This woman was actually a niece of Julius Caesar, married to Caius Octavius, who had been proconsul in Macedonia and had died about eight years previously. Octavius had been what we called *novus homo,* a "new man," meaning that he was the first of his family to achieve curule rank at Rome. After his death she had married the very distinguished Lucius Marcius Philippus.

"Well, what does she say?"

"She tells me that young Octavius is the darling of the public. You'll recall that he delivered the eulogy at his grandmother's funeral last year. Everyone was astonished that so young a boy could speak with such dignity and eloquence."

"I remember the event." I had attended the funeral, since there was a family connection, but I was busy politicking for the office of praetor and paid little attention to the speakers.

"Atia hints that Caesar may wish to adopt young Octavius."

This almost made me choke on a cherry. It wasn't so surprising that Caesar might want to adopt. He was famously infertile, despite his multiple marriages and innumerable affairs. The death of his single, beloved daughter had devastated him and severed the last connection between him and her husband, Pompey. But little Octavius?

"Why would Caesar want to adopt that wretched little brat?" I exclaimed.

"He is of the noblest lineage, at least on his mother's side," Julia said. "Caesar has spent a great deal of time with him and is clearly impressed with his intelligence and potential."

"Then he's losing his grip. There are plenty of others with family connections that are better candidates for adoption. Even Brutus, dull as he is."

"You only think he's dull because he's a serious student of philosophy. Do you know what I think? I think you secretly imagined that Caesar might favor you."

"Me!" I sputtered.

"Admit it! You've been close to him, you married his niece, you were his closest confidant in Gaul, you practically wrote his account of the Gallic War yourself."

"I was a glorified secretary, transcribing his wretched scrawl into something readable. At best I amused him, which is a poor recommendation for adoption. Besides, he's barely ten years older than I am."

"That is a nonsensical objection. Men adopt sons older than themselves, for sound political reasons. Clodius, for instance, was a patrician. He wanted to stand for the office of Tribune of the People, which is barred to patricians. So he had himself adopted into a plebeian family, his adoptive father a man his own age."

"That particular adoption was met with a good deal of senatorial opposition."

"It was an extreme example, I admit. But it was done, and the adoption of young Octavius by Julius Caesar makes far more political sense."

"I suppose," I sighed, no longer very interested. "After all, what is there to inherit? It's not as if he's passing on his offices, which must be won politically. He's built a substantial fortune where he used to have a mountain of debt, that's something. Otherwise, there's the prestige of a very ancient patrician name. He'll get nominated for some of the priesthoods, at least."

"Decius, envy ill becomes you."

"Envy? Where did that come from?" However, she would say no more, for which I was thankful.

That morning, I held court. Ordinarily, I would have sat in one of the nearby towns, but it seemed that the countryside had come to me instead, so I employed my temporary tribunal on the temple site. Since it had become as noisy as a Greek funeral, I had my lictors call for silence. When the noise abated a little, I addressed the mob.

"This is not a festival day, no matter what people around here seem to think. It is a day appointed for official business. I won't put a stop to your activities, but I insist upon decorum and quiet. Anything boisterous will be heavily fined." A threat to a man's purse is usually more effective than a threat to his body. Things quieted down and I proceeded with what was almost a routine court day: a Syrian merchant accused of selling an inferior dye as the pure murex (I dismissed the case for lack of evidence); a Cretan slave dealer who accused his citizen colleague of embezzlement (I sentenced the citizen to be sold into slavery, and would have liked to give the Cretan the same treatment).

I was about to adjourn for the afternoon when I saw an odd group of men making their way toward my podium. There were about a dozen of them, all wearing togas, some with senator's stripes on their tunics, a few wearing red sandals with the ivory crescent of the patrician fastened at the ankle. In the forefront was a man who walked barefoot. He wasn't even wearing a tunic, just an old-fashioned toga wrapped around his stocky, muscular body.

I covered my eyes and groaned. "The gods have deserted me. Cato is here."

"Did you forget to sacrifice?" Hermes asked.

"It must have been a greater offense than that." Marcus Porcius Cato was my least favorite senator and almost my least favorite Roman, now that Clodius was dead. The men who constantly accompanied him were what we had come to call "Catonians"; men who admired or professed to admire Cato's harsh, abrasive style. Most of them were just looking for an excuse to be rude.

"Hail, Praetor!" Cato yelled, saluting. He was always a stickler for the honors due public office.

"And a fine afternoon to you, Marcus Porcius. I think it's time to break for lunch. Will you join me?" My lunch was already laid out beneath an awning nearby. A praetor usually has guests, so there was always at least enough for twenty people on the tables. As soon as I left the podium, the fair went back to full roar.

"I didn't expect to see you here," I said, as we took our seats. No couches for an informal luncheon like this.

"I didn't expect to find you presiding over a country fair."

"Sometimes these things happen. Are you on your way to Sicily?" He had served as praetor a few years before, during the consulship of Domitius and Claudius.

"Not until after the elections. I've been sent down to sort out the matter of the Campanian lands."

"Good luck with it," I said. "Nobody has been able to sort out that mess as long as I can remember. Too many conflicting interests."

"The only conflicts are those of greed," he said, taking a cup from a servant, draining it at a gulp, and holding it out for more. "And it may not be a problem much longer. Pompey wants that land to settle his veterans and the Senate is looking to Pompey to save their necks from Caesar. He'll probably get what he wants."

"What has them panicked this time?" I asked.

"Caesar wants to stand for consul in absentia."

"I know all about that. Why not let him?"

"It flouts all traditional law!" Cato barked. "Since the days of Romulus, any man on foreign service who wished to stand for consul has had to return to Rome to stand for office." His pseudo-Catos growled agreement. They were good at growling.

"Would it hurt to bend the law just a little, just this one time?" I said, knowing how it would enrage him.

"The law isn't something you can bend and trim to suit the occasion. Who knows where it could end!"

"This course could end in civil war," I pointed out.

"What of it?" said one of his sycophants. "Pompey is the greatest general in the world, and his soldiers are the most numerous and the most loyal. He will crush Caesar like a gnat."

"Pompey's been away from the wars for a long time," I said. "His soldiers have been living at ease while Caesar's have been fighting almost constantly for eight years. I agree it won't be much of a match."

"Time enough to worry about war if it comes," Cato said. "I have another message for you. Pompey wants this business that's upsetting the district settled quickly."

"Oh?" I said. "And has the proconsul of the Spanish provinces some sort of authority over the *praetor peregrinus*?" I realized that Pompey had spies in this area and they had fast horses if he was keeping up with events here almost as they were happening. During the time he was proconsul of the Spanish provinces, the Senate had allowed him to govern those provinces through his legates while he remained in Italy to oversee the grain supply. His proconsular status forbade him to enter Rome, so he lived in a villa south of the City.

"He has a vested interest in southern Campania," Cato said. "His *clientela* is vast in this region and he wants nothing upsetting the peace here."

"Is that so?" I said, feeling my face growing red. Or maybe that was just the wine. "A pack of dead priests should be of no concern to him."

"Oh, but he finds it of great concern. That temple is one personally endowed by Pompey. That makes those priests his clients."

I found myself gaping foolishly and quickly stuffed a fig into my mouth to give it some occupation. Then I washed it down with some undiluted wine and said, in the quietest voice I could manage, "Why have I not heard of this? The priests never mentioned such a thing. I do not see Pompey's name engraved on the pediment."

"Gnaeus Pompeius *Magnus*," Cato said, giving that honorific a sarcastic twist, "has no need to aggrandize his name through so trifling an act. He's built whole cities and temples the size of sports stadiums." He held out his cup for a refill. Cato was another believer in undiluted wine, probably the only taste we shared. "This temple has for generations been under the patronage of the Pedarii, a very ancient patrician family."

"The Pedarii?" I said. "I'm no genealogist, but I thought that family died out before Hannibal learned to use an elephant goad." I remembered the name only vaguely, from some poems about the early days of the Republic.

"They are very distinguished," Cato said, "but fallen into poverty long ago, and unable to support senatorial pretensions."

"So Pompey has a stake in this business?" I suppressed a groan. "Next you'll be telling me Caesar's family donated the land or paid for the statue."

"Eh? Why should I say such a thing?"

"Never mind. You've made my life sufficiently complicated, thank you."

"Sometimes you make no sense, Metellus."

That evening, Cato and his coterie went on to Cumae, which he had chosen as the headquarters for his mission. Capua was a much larger city, and closer to Rome, but he reasoned that it was too faction-ridden and too dominated by great Roman landlords. Whatever he lacked, and it was much, Cato had sound political instincts.

That evening I invited the historian, Lucius Cordus, to dinner. Since I didn't want a lot of political and social blather to dominate the conversation, the only other diners were Julia, Hermes, and the philosopher Gitiadas. I had come to appreciate his incisive intelligence. Five was an almost scandalously small number of participants at an important man's dinner, but I considered this simply an extension of my workday.

After the first courses and a bit of small talk, I got down to business.

"Lucius Cordus, what can you tell us about the Pedarii? They were once prominent in Rome, but I thought they had long since died out. Today I learned that a remnant still live here and are patrons of the Temple of Apollo." I had already told Julia of what Cato had told me.

"Ah, the Pedarii," Cordus said. "In fact, that name has turned up in my recent researches on your behalf, Praetor. It seems that one Sergius Pedarius, a half-legendary figure, was a comrade-in-arms of the Brutus who was the first consul, after the Etruscan kings were expelled from Rome. The family was prominent during the early years of the Republic, but never consular."

"Was Sergius a praenomen or a nomen?" I asked him. By our generation, the name Segius was used only as a nomen, but far back in history, it had been a praenomen.

"It was a praenomen. The Pedarii were never connected with the gens Sergia," Cordus informed us. "At some point in history, about the time of the First Punic War, the Pedarii were afflicted by a series of catastrophes. Their lands were flooded, many of their livestock died. Then, in a pestilence that afflicted most of Italy, their district was especially hard-hit, and many of the family members perished, along with their slaves and peasant tenants. In those days, senatorial families were nowhere near as wealthy as they are now. The survivors sold their lands and moved south, to the land of some distant relatives. Here they prospered modestly and were esteemed for their status as patricians, but they never returned to Rome, where once they had been great."

"As Romans among Greeks and Campanians," I said, "their situation must have been precarious."

"Although as Romans they weren't part of the local conflicts," Cordus said, "and by endowing the temple as soon as they had a bit of surplus wealth, they acquired the status of local patrons, though there are many families far wealthier."

"I shall have to meet with the heads of the family," I said. "I wonder why they have not presented themselves before this? Usually all the most prominent people present themselves to the Roman praetor upon his arrival."

"Perhaps," Julia opined, "they are embarrassed to show themselves, having become so humble since their family's heroic origins."

"Maybe," I said. "But they shall hide no longer. I want to see them." Something else occurred to me. "Cordus, yesterday young Vespillo and I visited the putative *mundus* on the property of Porcia. Do you know anything of it?"

"It is one of several such in the vicinity. I believe that it is the largest and the oldest. According to the local legend, Baios, the steersman of Odysseus, descended into it to visit the underworld and ask the shade of King Agamemnon whether he should found his city nearby—but you know already what I think of such legends."

"Not to mention that the underworld is not very far down. I tossed in a stone and heard it strike just moments later. There was an altar nearby and someone had left the usual offerings of bread and wine, but also some small arrows. Does this mean anything to you?"

"Arrows?" He considered for a while. "This is very odd, and I had been thinking upon this very subject."

"You had?" I said, surprised.

"Yes. You see, in our Temple of Apollo, he is depicted with a bow and arrows."

"'Apollo the Far-Shooter,'" I said, "as he's described in the *Iliad* and elsewhere, as in the story in which he and his sister slaughtered the children of Niobe."

"Exactly. Well, every year at the Festival of Apollo, small arrows are among the offerings brought to the god, although the petitioners usually bring them after dark."

"Why is that?" I asked. "Apollo is a solar deity, and his sacrifices always take place in the daytime."

"Because Apollo of the Bow is the god in his aspect as avenger. The arrows mean the petitioner is asking his aid in taking vengeance upon his enemies."

"Quite interesting," I said. It seemed there was no way I could keep the gods out of my investigation.

"Cordus," Julia said. "You said you had been thinking about this very subject. Why is this?"

"Because I was struck by an odd coincidence in names. Do you recall the Greek name for Apollo Far-Shooter?"

I thought about it. "Why, it's—" Then the light dawned. "It's Apollo *Hecatebylos*."

"Exactly. I am sure that it is a mere coincidence in sounds, but the first three syllables of the cognomen form the name of the goddess of the temple below."

"Could this have some bearing upon the rivalry between the temples?" I asked.

"It is possible, though I am at a loss to explain why. Confusion among the names of gods is not unknown, sometimes causing an alteration in their forms of worship."

"That's interesting," Julia said. "Can you give us an example?"

"Well, there is the case of the god Plutus, from very ancient times honored as the god of wealth. People confused his name with that of Pluto, Roman god of the underworld, whom we identify with the Greek Hades. As a result, most people think of Pluto as a god of wealth, which was not his original role at all."

"I am intrigued," I said, "by something you brought up at our earlier meeting, that Hecate is not an oracular deity. Yet Apollo is. In fact, the most prominent of the oracles—those of Delphi and Cumae and Dodona and such—are priestesses of Apollo. Might this have been a source of this strife? Do the devotees of Apollo see those of Hecate as usurpers of their god's functions?"

"Perhaps taking advantage of the local peoples' confounding of the two names?" Julia put in.

Cordus nodded. "Quite possible."

"But," said Gitiadas, "this conflict has been going on for centuries. Why have these multiple murders occurred now?"

"That is the question," I agreed, "and it causes me to think that these murders have little or nothing to do with the ancient strife between the strangely superposed rival temples. I think it is something local, immediate, and most likely based on something mundane, such as money."

"That would be disappointing," Julia said.

"We have seen a great many murders in our time," I told her. "Were any of them motivated by anything elevated? It's always politics, power, jealousy, insult to personal honor, or money. Usually, money. Men seldom prize their own honor or their wives' chastity above their purses."

"My husband is a Cynic, to the extent that he can be said to have a philosophy at all," Julia commented.

"The doubt of human motives is one of the bases of Cynical philosophy," Gitiadas said. "Or, should I say, the doubt of human motives *as stated*. Diogénes said that when a man claimed to be doing something for honor, or for patriotism, or for love of his fellow man, or any other such high-flown reason, you could be certain that the real motive was something base and shabby. This is a perfectly respectable philosophical premise, and the older I get, the more I am persuaded that it is true."

"Alas, it is so," Cordus agreed.

"That is because you are all men," Julia informed us. "Men gain wisdom with age but continue to behave like boys their whole lives."

"My wife is not an admirer of the male gender," I told them. "Her uncle Caius Julius always being the exception, of course."

"One must always make an exception for such men," Gitiadas said, smiling.

"My husband has an unreasoning distrust of Caesar. He suspects a Sulla-like dictatorial ambition. This is quite foolish. His Diogenean example is an underhanded way to question a great man's integrity."

We were straying onto dangerous ground. "But, returning to the question of the temple and its annihilated clergy, there is the matter of the girl, Hypatia. It is clear to me that she was killed because she had some part in the murder of the priests. She was primed to tell me what she did, but someone thought she was going to tell me more and she was silenced."

"What might she have known?" Julia wondered.

"For one thing," I said, "the identity of the person who killed her, who is probably also the one who suborned her into her part in the murder. It seems to have been someone she trusted."

"A lover, perhaps?" Julia said. "After all, she was pregnant." This was news to our guests, and Julia explained.

"This adds another dimension," Gitiadas said. "Now there is scope for jealousy, love, treachery, betrayal, and a host of other motives. You should have invited the playwright. I'm sure he is far better regarding matters of the heart than dusty philosophers and historians."

"Just more complication," I groused. "As if this matter didn't have enough of that already."

6

THE NEXT DAY I TOOK MY PERAMBU-
lating court to Stabiae. It is another of those charming towns on the
bay, blessed with a wonderful climate and views fit for the enjoyment
of the gods. For part of the way the road took us along the top of a pre-
cipitous cliff, causing the ladies of the party (yes, the ladies were along
again) to cry out with fright and pretend to faint. We men just looked
Stoic.

The town was founded by Oscans, but about forty years before
this time they had chosen the wrong side in the Social War and had
risen in rebellion against Rome, a famously bad decision for any town
to make but especially foolhardy for a tiny resort like Stabiae. As a result, it was destroyed by Sulla and the site was given to the Nocerians,
who had remained loyal. They had resettled and rebuilt the city, and
now it was once again a favorite resort, with the town plan centered on
its medicinal springs instead of the usual forum or temple complex.

As we neared the city, our party was joined by an ornate litter carried by a set of Gauls who wore the twisted neck rings common to that race, their blond hair and mustaches dressed identically. As it drew alongside my saddle, a hand with gilded nails pushed its curtain aside. "Praetor! You should have told me you would be visiting my city." It was Sabinilla. This time she wore a red wig, to complement her green gown.

"I knew you would insist that I stay at your home, and I have no wish to impose a party this size upon you when there is a perfectly good official residence available in the town."

"Nonsense! I *do* insist you stay with me! I'm sure I am not so poor that I can't afford to entertain a praetor's entourage properly. I shall be insulted if you refuse."

"In that case, how can I say no? Give my freedman directions to your home and I will join you there as soon as I conclude my business for the day." She was overjoyed, or put on a good show of it. I had indeed not let her know I was going to Stabiae for precisely this reason. I knew that she would try to outdo everyone else who had entertained me in the lavishness of her hospitality. At another time this would have suited me perfectly, but now my pleasant stay in Campania had turned serious, and I wanted no more distraction. I told Hermes to get the party settled at Sabinilla's villa while I went to confer with the city officials.

"Cheer up," he advised me. "There are worse fates than being entertained to death."

With a few of my helpers and preceded by my six lictors I rode on into the beautiful city, where I was greeted with the usual choruses of children and girls in white gowns who strewed flower petals in my path and local poets who read panegyrics composed in my honor. At least, I think they were panegyrics. I've never been too clear on the distinction between a panegyric and an ode. Oh well, as long as it's not a eulogy, I've no cause to complain.

The city offices were in the Temple of Poseidon, which was Stabiae's finest. The town is located on the sea, so the sea god is naturally held in great reverence there. Also, the region is very prone to earthquakes and Poseidon is the god of earthquakes. Furthermore the locals revere Poseidon as the patron of their hot springs, so he is held in triple reverence.

Of course I was taken in to see the statue of the god, a stunning bronze by the sculptor Eteocles, only a bit larger than life-size, and in an unusual pose: standing, his left arm thrust forward in the fashion of a javelin thrower, right extended rearward, balancing the trident as if for a cast. His hair and beard were enameled blue, a treatment I had never seen before on a statue, paint being more commonly used. His eyes and teeth were likewise enameled, rather than the more common ivory and silver treatment. Everything about the image was exquisite, and I was not sparing in my praise. The trip would have been worth it just to see the statue.

We retired to an office and took care of the modalities: the location for the morning's court, the officials to be present, and the order of hearing the cases to be presented.

"Will there be any special complications in any of these cases?" I asked. "Right now, I am in no mood for unpleasant surprises."

"All very straightforward, Praetor," said the town's own praetor, an official lacking the imperium and broad powers of a praetor from Rome. Since the locals had full citizenship, his judgments could be appealed to a Roman court. This was usually an unwise move, since Roman magistrates hated to have their dockets cluttered with the petty complaints of provincials. Only someone able to pay a hefty bribe dared try it.

With these petty matters settled, I decided to wander about and see the town. I dismissed my lictors, telling them I would meet them at Sabinilla's villa. They protested, saying it was unworthy of a praetor to walk abroad without an escort. I told them I had imperium and could do anything I wanted to. I exchanged my *toga praetexta* with its purple border for a plain white one and bid them be off.

I was utterly tired of having an entourage dog my steps every waking minute. I pined for the days when I was an anonymous citizen recognized by few people and could prowl about and get into trouble as I wished. It was the sort of juvenile thinking for which Julia was forever scolding me. But she was right. We men only learn to fake maturity and wisdom. Inside, we are perpetual adolescents, heedless and foolhardy. Well, what of it? That was the way I liked it.

Not that I was totally unwary, of course. I had my dagger and *caestus* tucked away in their usual place inside my tunic. To tell the truth, I was half-hoping to get into a brawl. I hadn't been in a good fight for several months, and felt that I was losing my edge. Not a serious brawl, of course, just a little fist-swinging and bench-throwing to get the blood stirring.

Unfortunately, Stabiae turned out to be a quiet, peaceful town, full of wealthy visitors come to take the cure in the hot springs and vendors to see to their wants and relieve them of excess money. I went into some low sailors' dives, but there was nothing to be had except bad wine. The sailors drank and rolled dice and exchanged the names of especially skilled whores, but that was all. After a while I left the dockside area and went back into the city proper.

I was about to give up and go to Sabinilla's place when I heard someone hissing at me, and saw a hand beckoning me toward a doorway. I was passing through a street not much wider than a typical alley, one which I hoped would lead to the forum, where I could get my bearings and find the landward gate. The hand was white and fairly shapely, adorned with a number of rings, though none of them looked terribly expensive. I assumed that it was a whore in search of a customer, but as I drew near the door, the woman thrust her head outside. She wore a shawl over hair that fell straight to her shoulders, a fashion not much in favor with prostitutes, nor was her dress, which was typical of any matron's.

She looked quickly up and down the alley, then she said, "Aren't you the Roman praetor? The one who's investigating those killings at the temple?" She spoke barely above a whisper and seemed agitated, clearly in a state of fear.

"I am."

She reached out and took me by the arm. "Come inside, quick!"

My hand went inside my tunic as I stepped across the threshold. I'd scarcely been in town long enough for anyone to set up an ambush, but you never know. As soon as I was inside, she scanned the alley again and shut the door. The room was illuminated dimly by some clay lamps, but I was all but blind coming in from the bright daylight outside. Slowly my eyes adjusted and I saw that this was the dwelling of an ordinary citizen, neither wealthy nor especially poor; a typical shopkeeper's house.

"Your business had better be urgent," I told her, "and it had better not be about any of the cases to come before me. I take it ill when people believe that I may be suborned."

"Oh no!" she said. "Nothing like that. It's about the killings."

"What is your name?" Her face twitched as I jerked her from whatever terror held her to something mundane. I have found it a useful interrogation technique many times: If you destroy a person's concentration on what they are trying to tell you, sometimes they reveal things they'd rather not.

"My name? Why, it's, it's Floria, Praetor."

I knew instantly that the name was false. She'd taken too long to make one up, but informants often don't want their names known. It didn't mean that her information was bad, just that I would have to be suspicious. As if I wasn't already. People lie more often than they tell the truth, even if they have nothing to gain by it. They lie to officials even more often.

"Well, Floria, you should know that I have taken a very personal interest in the doings at that temple—those temples, I should say—and I wish very much to have some reliable information. On the other hand, I will punish very severely anyone who tries to give me false information. Is that understood?"

"Certainly, Praetor!" she said, looking even more scared. "I would never—" My raised hand silenced her.

"Yes you would. I just want you to know that it would be a terribly bad idea. Now, tell me what you have for me." My eyes had adjusted to the dim light and now I could see that she was a handsome woman of perhaps thirty years, with broad cheekbones and huge eyes, a look common to southern Italy.

"I know things about the priests of that temple, Praetor."

"You mean the Temple of Apollo?"

"No, the Oracle of Hecate."

I thought this odd, because she had said "priests" when it seemed the staff of the Oracle was dominated by women. But I let it pass. "Go on."

"Well, sir, ten years ago I was in service to the house of Lucius Terentius. He was an oil importer of this city. He died childless and freed me, along with the other household slaves, in his will. This was the year that he died. I blame those priests for that." She paused, seeming intimidated by the seriousness of her accusation.

"You believe the devotees of Hecate killed your former master?"

"Not directly, no, but they—"

"Just go on. Tell your story, and don't worry about reprisal. I will put you under my own protection, if you wish." I was remembering the girl, Hypatia.

"Oh no. I wouldn't want that. I don't want anybody but you to know what I'm telling you. Anyway, my master was preparing to make a voyage to visit his oil suppliers in Greece and in the islands: Crete, Cyprus, and one or two others. He imported the highest quality oils, the kind used for bathing and for perfumery. Every year he would make a voyage in the spring, to go over his factors' accounts and bid on new contracts. He said the competition for the best pressings was pretty fierce, and you had to be there at the right time with the money. He wouldn't leave that sort of thing to a factor.

"Every year, he would go to the Oracle of Hecate to ask if he would have a safe and profitable voyage. It seems every year he got a favorable prophecy, and since he'd always done well, he set great store by the Oracle. This year was a little different. I went with him, along with some of the other slaves. I'd accompanied him twice before. He was an important man and wouldn't go unaccompanied on an occasion like that. The priests put him through the usual ceremony, with the drinks and the sprinkling and so forth. We slaves stood off to one side, along with the servants of the other people visiting the Oracle. We waited in a little grove of trees while our masters visited the underworld. It was a hot day, and this time some of the temple slaves brought us cool drinks while we waited. This seemed very thoughtful. One of them was a girl, perhaps a year or two older than me. She was very lively and talkative, and she went on about this and that, and she asked me about myself, and about my master, and what he did. I told her pretty much what I've told you about him, only at greater length. In time my master came out of the cave looking very thoughtful. Seems the Oracle priests had told him to come back the next day, that the will of the gods was unclear."

"Just him?" I asked. "Did none of the other petitioners get the same message?"

She frowned. "That I could not tell you. Anyway, we did not come all the way back here. We stayed overnight at the home of one of his friends near the temples. Next morning we went back and he went through the same ceremony. We waited in the grove as before, only this time there were no cool drinks. I didn't see any of the temple slaves except for the ones who assisted at the ceremony. In time my master returned and this time he was elated. It seems he got a really favorable prophecy from the Oracle. He was practically singing all the way home, and as soon as we got there, he sent for his banker.

"I heard later from the steward that our master went into the shrine of Hecate and was told there that his luck would be tremendous on this voyage, and that great opportunities awaited, and he should be prepared. He figured that meant that some prize contracts were going to be up for bidding, so he took along far more cash than he usually carried. The steward said it was five times as much."

"I see. And what was the outcome of this voyage?"

"The first leg took him to Piraeus. That was where he usually took ship for the islands. When there was no word from him in over a month, his business manager here started an investigation. He sent a couple of the freedmen to Piraeus to ask questions and follow the master's trail. They were back in no time. He'd stayed just one night at the inn where he usually stayed. He went down to the harbor to find a ship headed for Delos. The harbormaster said he saw him get onto a small ship that had just arrived from Italy. It cast off right away, like he was the only thing they were waiting for, though they hadn't discharged or taken on any cargo since docking. Nothing has been heard of him since. After a year passed, the will was read and I was a free woman."

"And you suspect the Oracle staff was behind the disappearance of your master?"

"Sir, he was set up! They as much as told him to take along plenty of extra cash this trip. And I never heard of an oracle saying anything outright like that. Worst thing is, I helped them do it." Apparently she had been fond of her master. We always want to believe that our slaves love us, but this is seldom the case.

"You are blameless. How could you suspect that an idle conversation would lead to your master being waylaid by robbers? You divulged no secrets. No court would hold you accountable."

"I still feel terrible about it."

"You needn't. Now, Floria, you must tell me something else."

"I've already told you what I know."

"For that I am quite grateful. You have been a great help to my investigation. But when you called me in here, you were very apprehensive. Frightened, in fact. Why?"

She was quiet for a moment, her arms crossed before her as if she were cold on this warm afternoon. "Word has been going around, Praetor. Nothing open, but when I go to the market or down to the corner fountain for water and some gossip, I keep hearing the same thing: It's going to be bad for anyone who helps this Roman praetor in the matter of the temples and the killings. It's something everybody just seems to know: This is a local matter, no need to get Rome involved. Keep quiet if you know anything, or it'll be the worse for you."

"I wish you would let me place you under my protection."

"In a few days, this matter will be over one way or another and you'll be gone, Praetor. But I'll have to live here the rest of my life. I don't know any other place and I don't want to start over somewhere like Rome."

"Very well, but if you feel in any way threatened, come to me instantly."

"I will, Praetor, and now I think you should go." She went to the door and opened it just enough to stick her head out. She scanned the alley both ways, then motioned for me to go. I stepped outside, hand on dagger again, but the alley was deserted.

As I made my interrupted way toward the city gate and my waiting horse, I thought about what I had just heard. Of course, my first thoughts were of how I might have been tricked and gulled. Was she a plant? It was known that I would be in Stabiae that day, but nobody could have known that I would on a whim choose to wander about the city alone. I had chosen that particular alley because I did not know the town and it seemed as good a way as any to find the forum and thence the gate. Try as I might, I couldn't see how she could have been planted in my path.

As for the rest, it sounded plausible enough. It hardly seemed shocking that a foreign cult was acting as a cover for a robbery ring, though ten years at the minimum seemed a long time for it to stay under wraps. Of course, the late Lucius Terentius had been neatly disposed of in a manner that would not have cast suspicion on the Oracle. People are lost at sea every year, hundreds of them even in a year of good sailing weather. Also, they need not fleece all of their customers, just the ones who present a prospect of high profit and safe disposal somewhere far away.

Still, this said nothing about the murder of the priests of Apollo. I could not tie them to a ten-year-old murder, and the circumstances of their deaths had no apparent connection with the fraud, larceny, and murder perpetrated by the Oracle below them. There was always the possibility that the woman had some other motive entirely. Perhaps she had some personal grudge against the cult of Hecate and merely wished to blacken them in my eyes, not that I required much in that direction.

At the public stable by the gate, I retrieved my horse and mounted. The guard at the gate gave me directions to the villa where Sabinilla lived. The ride was pleasant and nothing occurred to disturb my fruitless cogitations. A fine, paved road turned off the main road, leading to the villa. It was situated on a cliff-lined spit of land jutting into the sea, with breathtaking views in all directions. I could hardly have imagined a more dramatic setting. The main house occupied the very tip of the spit, so that a suicidally inclined occupant could simply dive off a back terrace to end all his problems. There were times when that extreme act seemed attractive to me. As I had feared, Julia was waiting for me at the top of the steps leading to the house.

Of course she didn't shout. She was too proper a patrician wife for that.

"Decius!" she hissed. "Have you lost your mind?" Her hiss could probably be heard in Rome. Maybe in Gaul. "What are you doing wandering off alone?"

"I'm grown, my dear. I don't require a *pedagogues*."

"You require bodyguards! In fact, you require a keeper, like those idiot children of the richest families! Have you any idea of the danger you are in? Quite aside from the local feuds you're meddling in, there are probably idiots around here who think your head would make a fine gift to Pompey or Caesar or any of the other rivals for power. In any case, it is beneath the dignity of a Roman praetor to gad about like a carefree bachelor, without a following or even his lictors."

"Yet," I told her with a broad smile for anyone who might be watching us, "one may learn things in this fashion that would be impossible otherwise. Let me tell you all about it."

"You'd better!" she hissed again. She led me to our quarters, a cluster of rooms with balconies overlooking one of the cliffs. The geography of the spit of land made the standard domestic design unfeasible, so the house was long and rather narrow in conformity with the plot, though it lacked nothing in luxury and splendor.

"So," she said, when we were alone, "what did you learn?" So I told her what the woman Floria had told me.

"It seems too fortuitous," I said, when I had finished my recitation. "What are the chances that I should just happen by the doorway of this woman who had information vital to my investigation? Yet I can't imagine how she might have been planted in my path."

Julia nodded, her natural curiosity and prying instincts at last overcoming her righteous rage. "It does seem improbable. Still, there might be an explanation."

"What might it be?"

"It is possible that this town and all the others around here are full of people with similar stories to relate, only they are afraid to approach you. Most of them are probably slaves, as this woman was when this vicious deed occurred. At least she was manumitted, and this may have given her the courage to approach you, even if in a fearful manner. At least, as a free woman, she can't be made to testify under torture."

"I hadn't thought of that," I admitted. "I may have passed the doorways of many people victimized by the Oracle. This one saw me alone and took a chance. But I am certain she gave me a false name."

"Nothing strange about that. She hopes not to be drawn into it at all, but you can find her house again." She looked at me sharply. "Don't tell me you didn't memorize its location." It was an order, not a question.

"Have no fear, my dear. I could lead you there blindfolded on a moonless night." This was a bit of an exaggeration, but I was pretty sure that I could find my way back. Stabiae was not as chaotic as Rome, but it wasn't designed as a rigid grid like Alexandria.

"And we now know something: The voice of the Oracle is false." She seemed bitterly disappointed at this, whereas I was not at all surprised. Julia dearly loved her oracles, prophets, augurs, and haruspexes.

"At least," I said, "we know that it was ten years ago, assuming that this woman's tale is true. I was surprised at her use of the word 'priests.' I should have questioned her more closely about it. Perhaps the Oracle had a different staff then. We shall have to make inquiries."

"Cordus may know, or at least he may know how to find out."

"I'll send a letter to him at once," I said, gratified to see that Julia's anger had cooled, distracted now by a question to solve. She had philosophical leanings and considered these investigations to be philosophical conundrums. I approached them in a different way, knowing that they were shaped by human passions and weaknesses rather than by mathematics or natural forces at work, and I relied as much on instinct and inspiration as on rigid logic. Between us, we usually got to the bottom of whatever was going on. Unless, of course, it involved her uncle.

That evening, we were entertained by Sabinilla. For the evening she had chosen a startling silver wig, and in the odd fashion of such things, this set me to pondering almost obsessively what her real hair might look like. This is one of my many failings, though I hope a minor one. She took us on a tour of the strange villa, which was built on several levels to accommodate to the slope of the stony spit. We climbed many stairs and saw odd-shaped dining rooms and reception areas, colonnades and courtyards. All of the walls were decorated with beautiful frescoes, none of them the then-popular black walls decorated sparsely with fantastic vegetation and spindly pillars, a style I found intensely depressing. These were colorful paintings of the doings of gods and goddesses, heroes, demigods, nymphs and satyrs, fauns and other sylvan deities. Campanians like color, as do I. The floors were uniformly covered with vivid picture-mosaics, mostly displaying marine subjects. To my astonishment, even the ceilings were painted, this time with Olympian gods disporting themselves among the clouds, and one astonishing room had its floor decorated with night-blooming plants while on the ceiling above Diana and her retinue hunted constellations in the night sky. Julia immediately wanted our ceilings painted.

Most unusually, Sabinilla showed us her personal gladiator troupe. Many wealthy Campanians invest in gladiators, but seldom keep them in their own houses. The schools are usually located in the countryside, well away from the towns. She had a barracks for twenty of them, and an oval exercise yard surrounded by a low stone wall lined with seats. For our amusement she had them come out and go through their paces, mock-fighting with wooden practice swords. They fought almost naked, wearing only the bronze belt and brief *subligaculum* traditional to Campanian gladiators, their skins oiled to catch the torchlight prettily. They were all Gauls, which was no surprise. Caesar's wars had flooded the market with cheap Gallic slaves, many of them warriors too dangerous for domestic service. They were armed in their native fashion, with a long, narrow, oval shield and a long sword. They wore no protective armor at all save for a simple pot-shaped helmet.

"How can you sleep," Julia asked, enthralled, "with such men so nearby?"

"Oh, these fellows seem quite content with their lot," Sabinilla assured her. "You should have seen them when I bought them: filthy and verminous and wearing enough chains to anchor a ship. Once I had them washed, barbered, and fed decently, and I assured them all they had to do was fight, they couldn't have been more grateful."

"I could name you their tribes," I said. "These are warriors, Julia. Gallic warriors do no work, unless it involves horses. All their lives they do nothing but fight and train to fight. They are aristocrats, by their own reckoning. Their lands are worked for them by slaves. To them, fighting to the death is nothing. Being set to work would be an unthinkable degradation. They'd commit suicide before they'd pick up a shovel. No, these men wouldn't want to be doing anything else, since they can no longer be warriors in Gaul. Sabinilla, who is your trainer?"

"Astyanax. He's the best trainer in Campania. In his fighting days he contended as a Thracian, but he's expert at all the styles. He had fifty-one victories. He comes here three days in ten to work with my men. He trains several of the small private troupes in the district." This evening her nails were silver-gilt, and she wore all silver jewelry in place of the bronze she had worn earlier. Her gown was a shimmery white, about as close to silver as you can get with cloth.

Dinner was the usual lavish affair, with a huge number of guests. Sabinilla couldn't resist showing all her neighbors that she had the Roman praetor under her roof. There were local officials, some of whom I'd already met, priests from various temples, the most prominent *equites,* even a few senators who had villas in the area. As it Romanized, the district was becoming more and more popular with the Roman elite, with its resorts, its beautiful landscape, and its wonderful climate. After all the meeting and a lengthy dinner, at which I was uncharacteristically moderate, I found myself huddled with the senators. This was inevitable. No matter the location, Roman politicians have to get together to talk politics and intrigue.

"Praetor," began a man named Lucullus, who was a distant relation to the great Lucullus, "what do you think Caesar will do next?" As ranking man, they all deferred to me. Plus, through Julia, they expected me to know all about Caesar's doings.

"He'll cross the Rubicon and he'll bring his army with him and there will be civil war." I was heartily sick of the subject and wanted to keep my answer short.

"Surely not!" all of them chorused.

"Surely so," I said.

"It will be the days of Marius and Sulla come again," said one, his face pale. "All Italy will be devastated. The carnage will be terrible."

"That I rather doubt," I said, enjoying the offshore evening breeze. We stood on a beautiful terrace behind the main house. It stood at the very tip of the spit of rocky land, high above the sea, and was rimmed by a marble balustrade topped with beautiful Greek statues of heroes, also of marble. The surf crashed musically below, foaming over jagged rocks.

"How can that be?" said the pale-faced one. "The minute Caesar crosses that river, the Senate will declare a state of civil war and Pompey will raise his legions to meet him."

"Pompey has not seen Caesar move and I have. He'll come down on Italy faster than the Gauls or the Carthaginians or the Teutones or Cimbri ever did. Pompey won't have time to get his troops together, much less drilled and provisioned for war. He'll have to run for it and have his men join him elsewhere, maybe Greece, maybe Illyria. There will be plenty of fighting and it will be bloody, but I doubt there will be much of it in Italy."

I am not trying to appear prescient in hindsight. It is exactly what I said that evening, and events bore me out. This is because I did indeed know Caesar well, insofar as anyone really knew that man. He was perfectly happy to exterminate whole nations of barbarians on Rome's behalf, but he had a strange reluctance to kill citizens and applied the death penalty more sparingly than most ordinary judges. It was, incidentally, this magnanimity that eventually got him killed. He was assassinated by a conspiracy of men most of whom he had spared or called back from exile when he had every reason and every right to kill them. Let that be a lesson to anyone who seizes absolute power: Always kill all your enemies as soon as you have the power to. You're just making trouble for yourself if you don't. It was a lesson our First Citizen certainly took to heart.

Sabinilla appeared like a silver vision and suddenly I understood why she had chosen her fantastic color scheme. It was so that she would be dazzlingly visible after the sun was down and everyone was gathered outside, on the terraces or in the formal gardens and courtyards. It was a clever bit of planning. She outshone every other woman there.

"You men shouldn't be huddled here plotting," she said. "Come and enjoy the evening's entertainments."

"You mean there's more?" I said.

"Of course there is! And you gentlemen must let me borrow the praetor for a while. Come along, now." She took my arm in an elegant but viselike grip and dragged me away from the clump of white togas.

"I had to rescue you," she said. "I heard them bringing up Caesar and I knew you've had your fill of that."

"I can only express my gratitude," I said, sure that she had some other motive. I was getting suspicious of everyone lately.

Abruptly, a crowd of dancers and mountebanks stormed the terrace. Like every other bit of the evening's festivities this was contrived to be spectacular at night, for all of the acts involved fire. The outdoor lamps and torches were extinguished and fire-eaters rushed among the guests, breathing flame like mythical beasts, making the ladies scream delightedly. Then dancers performed an act I had never seen before. They were all women, naked and sparkling with oil in which flecks of mica glittered like stars all over their lithe bodies. They twirled short torches with flames at both ends, so swiftly that they formed great, glowing circles, and they did this without ever missing a step of their elaborate, acrobatic dances. After that, tightrope walkers traversed and did handsprings high above the terrace on ropes that flamed furiously, yet their hands and feet seemed to be unburned, and the ropes never burned through.

"How do they do that?" I said, like a yokel who had never seen such mountebanks before.

"It's the secret of their art," Sabinilla answered. "My master of ceremonies devised this entertainment some time ago and scoured Italy and Greece and Sicily for entertainers with the requisite skills."

Something occurred to me. "You only learned this morning that I would be coming to Stabiae. Surely you didn't throw this evening's entertainment together just since we met by chance on the road?"

She laughed at my cloddish lack of subtlety. "Of course not! As soon as I heard that you would be visiting Campania and staying at the Hortalus Villa, I started planning this. I knew you'd eventually make your way to Stabiae for the assizes, so I had all in readiness for that day."

"You mean you've been housing all these people here for months?"

"Actually, the dancers only arrived about ten days ago. They're from Spain, where all the greatest dance troupes are trained. I'm so glad they arrived in time for this. The evening wouldn't have been complete without them. Oh, look!" She pointed to a sidespit of rock that jutted out from the main formation about a hundred paces away. A tongue of flame had sprung up and now it spread with incredible speed until a huge bonfire was burning at furnace heat. It lit up the terrace like a rising sun and was almost as unbearable to look at directly. A blast of heat reached us even across that distance and the flames leapt into the sky as high, it seemed, as the Pharos lighthouse at Alexandria. I knew that only oil-soaked pine could blaze so high, so fast.

"Surely," I said, "this is the climax of your evening. I must say it's awe-inspiring. It's like watching an enemy city burn."

"Not quite the end," she said, "but soon."

I looked around. "Where is Hermes? I haven't seen him since dinner. He's supposed to attend me at functions like these. If I know the scamp, he's sparring with your gladiators. He's never been happy about his proficiency with the Gallic longsword. If you will excuse me for a moment, I must look for him."

"Oh, don't bother, Praetor! I'll send a slave to fetch him."

"No, I want to catch him red-handed so I can punish him savagely."

She laughed happily, giddy with the success of her evening's entertainment, which would make her the envy of the local aristocrats and parvenus for months. "Oh, go on, then. But be back soon. You don't want to miss the real climax."

In truth, I wanted to be away from the press on the terrace, as I had wanted to be away from my entourage that morning. The rest of the villa, all but deserted, seemed dreamlike as I passed through its strung-out, meandering rooms and courtyards, so different from the usual square or rectangular villa plan.

Sure enough, when I came to the training pen, there was Hermes, stripped to a loincloth, his body covered with glowing welts that would soon be bruises from strikes by the long sticks they used for swords. A goodly knot of fight fans were gathered, cheering on the combatants. Campania is the home of what might be called the gladiatorial cult. The *bustuarii,* to use the old term, were fighting here for centuries before the first *munera* was displayed at Rome. There were people here from all walks of life, from slaves to senators, who were happy to miss the spectacular entertainment on the terrace in order to watch a good fight.

For a while I stood in the dimness of a colonnade, content to watch Hermes as he contended with a tall, long-armed Gaul who grinned happily as he fought, the way Gauls usually do, even after they've been mortally wounded. The boy was a joy to watch, strong and graceful as a panther. He was a match for anyone save these professionals. The Gauls had been fighting all evening for the entertainment of the guests, and they were unwinded, scarcely even sweating. That is what training all day, every day, at nothing but swordplay will do for a man, especially one who is a born athlete and swordsman in the first place, which pretty much describes Gauls of the noble class. Finally, I decided I had indulged him enough. I stepped from the colonnade into the light.

"Hermes!" I barked in my best parade-ground voice.

He paused and turned his head, a mistake a professional never would have made. The long-armed Gaul landed a blow on his helmet that rang like Vulcan's hammer on an anvil and must have had him seeing stars.

"Let that be a lesson to you!" I shouted. "Never take your eyes off your opponent, even when the patron calls. Now stop making a spectacle of yourself and come attend me as is your duty."

Amid raucous laughter from the spectators and the Gauls, Hermes put on his best falsely sheepish, repentant manner and went to the bench where he'd left his clothing. Once he was decently dressed, he joined me in the little courtyard above the fighting pen where I was sitting on the rim of a little fountain.

"You should have seen me earlier, Patron," he said, unable to keep up his humble facade, bubbling with enthusiasm. "I almost beat one of them! And the Brigante named Isinorix or something taught me the most amazing maneuver with the longsword. You don't even need a shield to pull it off—"

"Do be quiet," I said. "And go find me some wine. I've been politicking all evening and Julia has been keeping her eagle eyes on me the whole time. I could feel her gaze all over me from clear across that terrace."

"At once," he said, grinning. He knew his work well and was back a few breaths later with a silver pitcher and two silver cups. Sabinilla had even matched the tableware to the night's theme. He poured for both of us and sat by me. He took a deep gulp and I grabbed his wrist.

"Drink slowly. The way you're sweating, that wine will hit you like a German's club. Drink some water to take the edge off your thirst."

"Now who's the spoilsport?" Then said, "Sorry, I forgot." He tossed the lees from his cup and dipped it in the fountain, which ran with perfectly sweet, clear water, piped to that rocky crag from only the gods knew where.

"I'm troubled," I said.

"You usually are. What is it this time?"

First I told him about my strange interview with Floria and about my own thoughts on the matter, and Julia's. He listened attentively, keeping his mouth shut and his thoughts to himself, as I had taught him.

"Nothing quite makes sense," I told him. "Nothing adds up. Either we don't have enough information, or we're looking at it the wrong way. I've been examining it all from my own peculiar viewpoint and experience and Julia from her philosopher-trained stance. What are your thoughts?" He took a while before answering. Hermes had been a slave for most of his life and had a view of things that Julia and I, aristocrats that we were, could never share.

"This rivalry between the temples," he said at last. "That's been going on a long, long time. This profit-making scheme may be much more recent. Ten years isn't so much time in the scheme of things. The priests of Apollo just may have been in on it. We've been thinking that they were uninvolved with the doings of the Oracle except for some sort of long-term effort to thwart or destroy the Hecate cult. What if they were killed to silence them before they could betray their own complicity?"

"I hadn't thought of that." I admitted. "I don't know why, since it's my custom to suspect everybody of everything."

He grinned. "You're getting slow, being so preoccupied with politics, and you've been talking with the wrong people. I think that now we should concentrate on finding out what the local slaves know. Leave that to me, I know how to talk to them. I'd especially like to find that temple slave this woman Floria spoke of."

"If she exists at all," I cautioned. "The story could be a total fabrication."

He took a cautious drink. "I think it's true, most of it, anyway. It has a feel to it. In the morning, I'll start working with the slaves. I'll just get rid of my toga and hang around the fountains and the bars that cater to the slave trade."

"You'll seize any excuse to get out of court duty."

"Wouldn't you?"

At this moment a little slave girl padded up to us on bare feet. "Praetor, my mistress and your lady say you must come to the terrace for the most wonderful spectacle."

"How could I resist either the temptation or the command?" I said, standing. Hermes got up as well and started to walk a bit stiffly as he began to feel his stripes. The little girl led us by the shortest way to the terrace, where the company were gathered at the railing that faced the fire-topped crag.

"Way for the praetor!" Hermes shouted, as if he were one of my lictors. Amid much inebriated jocularity, we made our way to the railing, where Julia and Sabinilla stood with the guests of greatest prestige.

"Ah, there you are, Praetor." Sabinilla said. "Just in time."

"And very rude of you to abandon our hostess and her guests at the height of the evening's entertainment," Julia said, glaring daggers at me and Hermes indiscriminately.

"Duty called, my dear. A Roman in service to Senate and People must never neglect duty." This raised a drunken laugh from the guests nearby. Julia had had a few too many herself, or she never would have berated her ultradignified praetor husband in front of all and sundry. Sabinilla clapped her hands for attention, and perhaps to prevent an unseemly scene.

"Watch, everybody!" She signaled to a musician, who blew a series of shrill notes on his double pipes. It is a peculiarity of pipes that they can be heard at greater distances than a trumpet, and are clear even above a loud clamor such as that of a battle.

All eyes turned to the bonfire atop the cliff opposite us. It had burned down, for pine burns very hot but very swiftly. What was there now was a huge heap of glowing coals with tongues of flame spurting up from it at intervals. At the signal from the pipes we heard a groaning, grinding, scraping sound. I could not guess at its origin until the heap of coals began to rise and hulk up in its center, as if it had come alive. The crowd gasped as if they were seeing some supernatural apparition. I was just a bit startled myself, though I am completely free of superstition.

Then we could see two teams of oxen to either side of the coals and I understood. They were dragging a huge scraper like the sort that is used for leveling roads and grounds for building projects. I think it is called a grader or something of the sort. In any case, this time one was being used to drag that gigantic heap of coals toward the cliff. The coals continued to tower ever higher until, abruptly, the forward edge reached the rim of the cliff, which was all but invisible by this hour, just a blackness with a faintly visible mass of seething whiteness at its base, where the waves broke upon the rocks.

Everyone gasped, all but stunned, as the coals poured over the cliff. They formed a huge cascade of glowing light, like a waterfall of fire. Flames burst anew from the coals, and in an instant there was a solid, broad stripe of living fire from cliff to surf, and when the coals hit the water below there was a hissing noise like a thousand dragons waking up and angry about it. Steam billowed upward in a cloud Jupiter could have hidden himself in. It flowed over us in a strange, warm wetness, lit from within so that the cloud glowed orange.

Then the last of the coals dropped, the light and the hissing faded, the cloud dispersed, and we were all standing there, stunned, and there was no trace left of what had just happened. A long-pent sigh escaped from every throat, including mine, and I turned to our hostess. She looked at me with an almost demented eagerness.

"That was the most spectacular thing I've ever seen in my life," I told her.

She smiled with maniacal relief and signaled the musicians. They began to play as if the evening were just beginning, but clearly it was at an end. Absolutely nothing could have topped what we had just witnessed. Everyone prepared to go home, but I was the ranking man and all would await my departure, then the rest would go, in order of rank.

Julia and I took our most effusive leave of our hostess and told her we simply must retire to our quarters because I had a full day in court on the morrow. It truly had been an extraordinary evening. Amid loud ritual farewells from the other guests, we retired.

In our luxurious chambers, Julia said, "Sabinilla is the happiest woman in Campania tonight. This must have cost her a fortune, but her position is assured. It's given me some ideas about entertaining when you are consul and we are back in Rome."

"I was afraid of that. Sadly, there are no good cliffs in Rome."

She thought about that for a while, as her girl dressed her hair for bed. "Do you think we could build one? A tower about four hundred feet high would do it. You could build it in the Valley of Murcia and people could gather on top of the Aventine to watch."

"Good night, dear," I said, going out to the sitting room that adjoined our bedroom. Doubtless she was joking, but with Julia I could never be sure. I summoned Hermes and he came in, walking like a man of eighty. His bruises were in full flower now, and he winced with every step.

"Tomorrow afternoon after court is over," I told him, "we'll go to the town palaestra. I want you to teach me that move with the longsword."

7

TWO DAYS LATER WE WERE BACK AT MY temple headquarters. This time the crowd seemed no larger, but it didn't seem any smaller, either. I also learned something else. They weren't all here for the festive atmosphere. The times were unsettled, with everyone on edge over the possible outbreak of civil war, and all the oracles, both traditional and impromptu, were doing a booming business, with nervous people asking them about what was to come and would they survive it. Or else, how to make a profit from everyone else's upcoming misery, always a popular concern.

I was just getting comfortable in my curule chair, about to start the day's proceedings, when something utterly unexpected happened. The crowd fell silent. This unprecedented quiet piqued my interest. Some sort of commotion was coming down the road to the north. It looked like a lot of men, some walking, some riding. I didn't see any glitter of polished armor or standards, but it had a definite military look to it.

"What is all that?" I asked no one in particular. "Am I never to have a peaceful court day?"

Just moments later, the procession began marching into what had become my little town. First to arrive, to my unutterable dismay, were twelve lictors in a double file. Only a consul is entitled to twelve lictors. Or a proconsul. The consuls were in Rome and wouldn't leave in times as uncertain as these. And there was only one serving proconsul in Italy.

Sure enough, a bit later there rode in none other than Gnaeus Pompeius Magnus himself. My lictors lowered their fasces in salute to a higher magistrate. I had, perforce, to stand and descend the steps of my dais to greet him.

"Hail, Proconsul," I said, as the throng gaped. "What brings the distinguished Pompey to my court? Surely the demands of office should require you in the north."

He looked down at me from his lofty horseback perch. Looking down at people was something he did well, having had so much practice. "Indeed they should, but it seems a matter here puts greater demands upon my attention. Why has this business of the murdered priests not been cleared up?"

I held on to my temper. He was, after all, the great Pompey. "Perhaps you could dismount and we can discuss this in a more quiet environment."

"Very well." He heaved himself from his saddle—and "heaved" was the word for it. The once hard, soldierly Pompey had gone soft and corpulent in his long years of peace. Even this effort left him winded and his aides had to catch him to steady him lest he fall. It removed the last vestige of uncertainty I nursed for the outcome of a showdown between Pompey and Caesar. It would be no contest.

We climbed the temple steps and sat in the shade of the portico while slaves quickly brought a table, pitchers of wine and water, and platters of food, all with great and silent efficiency.

Pompey took a great gulp of watered wine and I did the same, only with less water. "Now, Metellus, why is this business not re-solved?"

"By what authority do you ask?"

"By the authority of a proconsul, by Hercules!" he all but shouted.

I remained admirably calm. "You are proconsul in *Spain*. Here in Italy you are overseer of the grain supply. It is an important and respon-sible position, but its duties are administrative, not military and not ju-dicial. I, on the other hand, am *praetor peregrinus*, with imperium and the authority to judge cases involving foreigners all over Italy."

He dropped the bluster and grinned slyly. "Then why are you em-broiled in this case that, as far as I can tell, involves no foreigners? Why not leave it to the local authorities?"

He had me there. "Because I want to, just as you do whatever you want, no matter what rules the Senate and law tables have laid down."

He barked out a short laugh. "Spoken like a true Metellus. You're an arrogant lot, no doubt of that." He leaned close. "Look here, Decius Caecilius. I need this matter settled quickly. I'll be knee-deep in a war with Caesar soon and I can't have any distractions plaguing me here in the south."

"Why do you think whatever happens here can amount to a dis-traction for the likes of Gnaeus Pompeius Magnus? This is a piddling, local affair. It's nothing on the big game board of world power. There are only two players on that board now, you and Caesar." The game board image was one Clodia had thrown at me years before, along with her withering contempt for my not being one of the big players. Clodia was the sister of my old enemy Clodius, and the most notorious woman of that time.

"Never mind that," he said, suddenly cagey. "I have my reasons for wanting this matter over and forgotten, and they're none of your business."

"None of my business?" I said, feeling my face begin to flame. "You come in here with no authority and tell me to hurry up and solve this mess and you say your reasons are none of my business?"

He jumped up and his chair went over backwards. "My authority is the authority of a man who can whistle up twenty legions, all loyal to him alone. Nothing else counts these days. Remember that, Metellus."

I stood too, wanting to tell him how useless his twenty legions would be against Caesar's veteran killers. But I didn't and I felt it was incumbent on me to keep the peace. "Oh, sit down. We can discuss this in a civilized fashion. No sense drawing swords before the war has even started."

He sat without looking back to see if a slave had put his chair under him. Of course, the chair was right where he wanted it. That was always the way with Pompey. "Actually," he said, "it's about those legions that I'm here, not your case. I want my men to be prepared to mobilize at a minute's notice. If Caesar dares to cross the Rubicon, which I doubt he will, he won't leave me much time."

He wasn't a total dunce. He just didn't understand how little time he would really have. "Will you be here long?"

"Longer than you'd like, but that's just too bad. Before I leave, I want the crime solved and the killers executed."

"This is a criminal investigation, not a military campaign. You can't rush it along with a few floggings and summary executions."

"I don't see why not. Who are the most likely suspects?"

"At the moment, the devotees of Hecate."

He spread his hands. "Well, then, there you are. Try them and execute them. Problem solved."

"Somehow I knew you would suggest the simplest possible solution. I take it then that you are more interested in having things done with than finding the actual killer or killers."

"As you've said, I have far more important matters to concern me. Personally, I don't care who killed the priests, and what matter if some half-crazed priests of a foreign goddess are done away with? As long as the countryside is quiet, I will be satisfied."

"The countryside will not be quiet if I execute the priestesses—most of Hecate's clergy here are women, by the way—without glaring proof of their guilt. The cult is very ancient and deeply rooted in these parts. It has many more adherents than the Temple of Apollo. Plus, the local merchants have come to depend on the business that the Oracle brings to the district."

He fumed for a while. "Just find someone to execute and do it soon." He stood. "I'll be off. I'll be raising at least one legion from this district. I will need to requisition supplies from all the local towns. The men have their own arms and equipment, but I'll want animals, tents, wagons, and a hundred other things."

"See the city officials of the towns about that," I advised him. "I'm just visiting."

When Pompey rode out, amid much pomp and fanfare, the crowd cheered him lustily. As I've said, Pompey was a popular man in the south. Of course, they would have cheered Caesar just as happily. They were both popular men, but few of the men present planned to enlist in their legions. Whoever won, they would be content.

I heard my cases and there were few of them. In fact, I could have left at any time. I was only prolonging my stay because of the murders. That, and because I just liked the place. I had a pile of cases to hear in the north and in Sicily. That was a thought. Go to Sicily and dawdle there, wait out my year, and when I returned to Rome perhaps everything would be settled and I could keep out of it. At lunch that day I broached the subject to Julia and wished I hadn't.

"What?" She looked at me as at some vile reptile. "You want to be clear out of Italy when great events are happening here?"

"It's not so far," I protested. "You can see across the Strait of Misenum to the Italian mainland."

"It ill becomes you to behave in such a cowardly fashion. I think you should write to Caesar right now and offer him your services."

"I still have the rest of the year of my praetorship to conclude," I said.

"You have imperium," she said pitilessly. "You do know what that means, don't you? In case you've forgotten, I'll tell you. It means you have the power to raise and command armies. What are you going to do when the Senate orders you to raise an army and march against Caesar? Have you thought of that?"

"Believe me, Julia, I've thought of very little else for months."

"Then it's time to make up your mind and decide which way you are going to go."

"I have decided," I told her. "I've decided that Sicily is a very fine place to be. I will go there as soon as this murder business is settled."

She was furious but, for once, she held her tongue. This may have been for any of a number of reasons. She might have decided to comport herself as a good, patrician Roman wife and bow to her husband's will. What a laugh. Or she may have decided to hammer at me late at night when I should be tired, a favorite tactic of hers and, I suspect, of all wives. She may have actually given the matter some sober thought and realized what a terribly dangerous predicament this put me in. Moreover and most likely, I suspected she was already writing her uncle and plotting with him, wangling a high position for me on his staff. Between Julia and the Senate and Pompey and Caesar it was like having my limbs tied to four elephants, each of them with orders to seek the home of one of the principal winds.

That afternoon, there being no nearby public baths, I walked into the virtual tent city that had sprung up near the Temple of Apollo. The place had become nearly self-sufficient, as food vendors and farmers and shepherds from the countryside had established a little forum where the transient population could purchase necessities. No more than a hundred paces from the encampment a stream furnished abundant water of excellent quality. As for what they were using for sanitary facilities, I did not inquire.

Some tents, sheds, and lean-tos housed nothing but individuals and families. These were the ones who had come with questions for the Oracle. I was tempted to tell them to watch out for oracular advice concerning money, but forebore. I was certain that my trial, when I should hold one, would expose the fraud sufficiently. The larger and more colorful shelters belonged to traveling merchants and mounte-banks who lived on the roads all the year round, stealing when they could and selling when they had to. Italy had veritable tribes of these peripatetic folk, whom no one trusted but who seemed to serve a nec-essary function and were therefore tolerated, albeit with suspicion.

An itinerant cutler displayed his wares from an ingenious upright chest that opened out into three large panels on which hung everything from sickles to cleavers to daggers. Leaning against the chest were a dozen or so fine swords, some with jeweled sheath mounts suitable for officers and centurions. These piqued my interest and I spoke with the man, a bald-headed Bruttian.

"Do you always travel with so many swords?" I asked him. "I would think agricultural implements would be your stock in trade in this area."

"You think that's a lot of swords, Praetor?" he said, inclining his shiny head toward the display. "That's just the fancy pieces for officers and the rich men's sons who'll be joining the cavalry. In my wagon I have six chests of plain legionary's swords and now Pompey's here I imagine I won't have a single one in ten days. I wish now I'd brought more."

"Men of your trade have been preparing for trouble, eh?" I said.

"If you deal in arms, you keep your ear to the ground. War's been in the air this last year and every cutler and arms maker in Italy's been laying in swords, daggers, spearpoints, and arrowheads for a long time. Go to a port and you'll see pig lead coming in from everywhere it's mined. Do you think it's all for plumbing pipes and roofs?"

"Slingstones?" I said.

"There you are. Men who make it their business to know such things say war is coming and a wise man had better be ready to meet the demand for arms."

"Civil war, you mean," I said.

"Well, that means you can sell to both sides, doesn't it? Most wars, you only get to sell to one." This simple commercial philosophy was fairly typical of the times. Deplorable as the situation might be, it presented wonderful possibilities to a man of enterprise.

Of course, it presented noncommercial possibilities as well, especially for men of my own class. My family had been prominent in Roman political life for centuries, but we had become the greatest of the plebeian families when we backed Sulla against Marius. There is much to be said for picking the right side. Now my family had thrown in their lot with Pompey, which I thought an unwise move. Yet, should I choose to join Caesar, the great men of the family would not object. Why? Because it is always a good idea to have a family member or two on the other side, just in case. That way, should the majority have chosen wrongly, at least the family would survive and would not lose all its lands. Such were the realities of politics and family in those days.

At other vendors' booths I saw a similar enterprise at work: soldiers' tunics and belts, hobnailed boots, canteens, oil flasks suitable for hard campaigning, all the gear a man needed for war. The legion would have stores from which to draw such gear, but it was often ill-fitting and overpriced, so a wise soldier showed up at muster with all his own equipment.

Not all the itinerant business people were so sanguinary in their wares. There were the usual souvenirs of the site, statuettes of Apollo and Hecate, lamps decorated with those deities or their symbols. One such vendor had no stall but sat on the ground with her wares displayed on a cloth before her. Among them were a number of the little arrows I had seen near the *mundus* on Porcia's estate. Alongside them were bundles of fresh and dried herbs and small amulets made of bone, intended to ward off the evil eye or protect health. The woman was some sort of *saga*: a low-level witch.

"How is business here?" I asked her. "People seem to be on edge, so I suspect it has been brisk."

"Oh yes, sir," she agreed, smiling to show a small number of yellow teeth. "Just since you've been here I've had to go home three times to replenish my stock. Between the murders here at the temple and all this talk of war, people can't have enough protection."

I nudged the arrows with my toe. "And these?"

"Why, they're offerings to Apollo, Praetor. He's Apollo the Archer at this temple."

"Doesn't this offering have a specific meaning?" I asked her.

She lowered her eyes. "None I know of, sir. Just an offering, like. To ask the favor of the god."

I didn't blame her for prevaricating. Selling baleful charms might get her charged as an accomplice in murder, for which the penalties were severe. They were not as bad as those for selling poison, but bad enough. People fear supernatural evil more than a dagger in the back. Important persons fear poison most of all. Poisoners are regarded as witches of the worst sort.

So somebody wanted revenge. People always want revenge, for some reason, good or bad, but usually bad and not only bad but petty and unworthy. It told me nothing. Fortune-tellers were doing a thriving business as well. Fortune-tellers were the poor man's oracle. Oracles are not paid, of course. That would be sacrilegious. They do, however, accept gifts, and if you aren't able to offer a generous gift, you might as well not even ask the priests for access to the Oracle. Fortune-tellers, on the other hand, will oblige you for a few copper coins. There were diviners who threw bones, those who gazed into bowls of clear water, even some who used the behavior of small animals or snakes to foretell the future.

Fortune-tellers were frequently banned and driven from Rome by the aediles for fomenting popular discontent and influencing politics. After all, if the fortune-tellers get the populace to believing that some calamitous event will happen, it just might. Naturally, they always came back. Somehow, when there is a demand for services, the services always appear.

It was as if all Italy was sick with anticipation.

That afternoon I called Hermes to my side. "We're missing something," I said.

"You've been saying that for some time," he said. "What do we do about it now?"

"You know what I've taught you. We can't expect new evidence to come to us. The woman Floria was a stroke of luck unless she was something more sinister. We have to find it ourselves. So how do we do that?"

He thought a bit. "We go back and reexamine what we've already seen and look for what we missed."

"Right. We'll start where this all started, in the tunnel of the Oracle. This time with no mumbo-jumbo to distract us. No drinks, we bring our own torches and make our own smoke, and it had better be clean smoke with no funny colors in it. Come to think of it, get new torches with linen-wrapped heads and soaked in the best olive oil. I don't care about the expense, I want as little smoke as possible. Same oil for the lamps. No chanting, no prayers, no uncanny voices. It will be just like when I was an aedile and we went down to inspect the sewers or the basements of buildings."

He grinned. "I always loved sewer-crawling."

"Bring three or four of our best men to carry torches and lamps; I want plenty of light. All armed. We know that there are people who don't want us finding out things. They've committed a number of murders already and won't scruple at a few more."

An hour later we were in the valley of funerary growth and standing before the tunnel. Our purposeful little band, clinking with swords and daggers on bronze-studded military belts, had attracted some attention and a number of idlers, bored with the ongoing festival, had followed in hopes of seeing some action.

Iola rushed up to us with some of her acolytes or whatever they were, robes disheveled and dignity lost in their haste. "Praetor! What is going on?"

"Iola, I am going down into your tunnel to find out whatever is to be learned there. Everyone here has been lying to me or at least withholding the truth. I intend to get to the bottom of this and I propose to begin at the literal bottom, in the chamber of the Oracle."

"You cannot do this!" she shouted, eyes and hair wild. "It is sacrilege!"

"Iola, Roman law recognizes sacrilege only as an offense against the gods of the state. Hecate is not a god of the state, but a foreign deity. My good friend Appius Claudius is censor this year and he is purging Rome and Italy of evil influences. He is a very upright and energetic man and he hates foreign cults. If you don't want to be driven from Italy and your tunnel filled with rubble, you had better not hinder my investigation in any way. Do I make myself clear?"

She looked fit to have a stroke, but abruptly she caved in. "Very well, Praetor."

"Now tell me something, Iola. Who was the chief sacerdote here ten years ago? Was it you?"

"No, Praetor. I came here from Thrace, homeland of the goddess, seven years ago. The priest ten years ago was Agathon, but he died right about that time. Then Cronion succeeded to the high priesthood. He was quite old and perished about the time I arrived. Hecabe became high priestess then and made me her acolyte. She died three years ago from the bite of a serpent and I succeeded her."

"Yours is a hazardous priesthood." I observed.

She shrugged. "People die. It happens all the time."

"You stay up here. I want none of your people in the tunnel while we are there."

She closed her eyes and let out a deep sigh. "As you will, Praetor. But this is a terrible violation of our shrine. I shall make protest to the Senate."

"Feel free to do so. But you have no idea how busy they are going to be soon. They will have very little attention to spare for the likes of you."

I got my men together at the entrance of the tunnel. "I want two of you to precede us with torches. We will descend very slowly. I want to examine everything very closely—the walls, the ceiling, the floor, everything."

"What are we looking for, Praetor?" asked one of the men.

"Anything that doesn't have an obvious reason for being there. If you see any sort of opening, anything that looks like a door or access to some other place, I want you to draw it to my attention. Now, let's go."

The two torchbearers went ahead, one before the other due to the narrowness of the tunnel. The uncommonly fine torches I had specified indeed made almost no smoke as we crept slowly down the passageway. I examined every niche, lifting its lamp and feeling the level spot and its back. Hermes and my other men ran their fingers over the walls and felt the ceiling, trying to find any irregularity. The work was so exacting that we felt none of the supernatural trepidation of my previous visit, and little even of the natural discomfort that comes with being in cramped quarters underground.

"Here, Praetor," said one of the men. He had found a narrow slot in the ceiling. It was as long as a finger and no wider. I held a torch to it and the flame fluttered slightly away from it.

"Probably a ventilation shaft," I said. "But I can't imagine how they cut so fine a hole. Whoever did this did things with stone I can't comprehend." We found more such slots, evenly spaced about every five paces along the shaft. The walls, however, yielded no secrets, nor did the floor. In this laborious fashion did we make our way to the chambers at the bottom. First, we searched of Hecate's shrine. The men were apprehensive at first, working under the gaze of the uncanny statue of Hecate.

"It's just stone," I said. "And not very well carved stone at that."

"Maybe you should perform a little propitiatory rite," Hermes whispered. "It might make them feel better."

So I asked the goddess's indulgence for thus profaning her shrine, pleading the necessity of one bound by duty and on the service of the Senate and People of Rome. Then I cut off a small lock of my hair and burned it on her altar among all the other rubbish. Then my men set about their work with lightened spirits. I resented losing the lock. My hair had been getting thinner of late and I could ill afford to lose more.

This work was even more tedious than searching the tunnel, though far less cramped. The roughness and irregularity of the stone walls made it difficult to detect cracks or protuberances that did not belong there. Polished or at least smooth stone would have been far more accommodating.

"There's something odd about this," Hermes said, as the other men worked over walls, ceiling, and floor.

"You mean there's something about this that *isn't* odd?" I said.

"It's just that the tunnel is so straight and relatively smooth-sided—a bit rough, but flat and true all the way down, while this chamber and the Styx chamber below are no more regular than a cow's stomach. They're more like natural caves."

"It's another oddity to go along with all the others," I commented. "I suppose it should be no surprise. If the tunnelers could drive their shaft through solid stone straight to the river, why shouldn't there already be some natural caves already down here to make their task a bit easier?"

I personally searched Hecate's altar and her statue. First I had one of the men clear away all the accumulated rubbish from the altar, a task he performed efficiently but with no small repugnance. I could hardly blame him. Along with everything else, I inspected the altar litter and it was as strange an assortment of items as I had ever run across. Predominating were bones, some of them quite familiar, including the aforementioned skeletons of infants. These gave us pause.

"Could we prosecute them for human sacrifice?" Hermes asked. "It's strictly forbidden."

"Do you see any traces of blood?" I asked him. "As near as I can see, nothing living has been sacrificed here. These could be the skeletons of stillborns for all we know. It's bizarre, but in violation of no law familiar to me."

There were other bones, the skeletons of birds, of small animals, nothing bigger than a fox, a great many dogs, and some of creatures never native to Italy, at least not in many generations. One appeared to be the skeleton of a tiny man, but I recognized it as a monkey. I had seen the skeletons of monkeys and apes on display in the Museum at Alexandria. There were reptiles of conformations I had never seen anywhere.

"Remind me to ask Iola about this," I told Hermes.

"I will. Speaking of that woman, she says she's from Thrace, but she doesn't have a trace of Thracian accent."

"She has a rather odd accent," I said, "but I agree it doesn't sound Thracian."

"I think it's fake," he said. He would know. As a slave, he had socialized with other slaves from the far parts of the world. We masters tend not to notice these things.

The altar itself, cleared of its exotic detritus, was a natural block of stone, hewn from the same rock as the floor. At first it seemed awfully convenient that an altar-shaped stone should be here, but then I saw that the statue of Hecate, too, was in one piece with the floor. I saw how they lined up, and that the wall behind Hecate was planed smooth, unlike the rest of the chamber wall.

"There used to be a rock outcropping coming out from that wall," I said. "The tunnelers, or at least whoever converted this place into Hecate's shrine, carved the altar and the statue from that outcropping."

"You don't think it was the same people?" Hermes said.

"Unlikely. The tunnel is unthinkably ancient. You can feel it. This statue is old, but nowhere near that old. If the Aborigines carved the tunnel, it was for some Aboriginal purpose, incomprehensible to us. This must have been carved within recent generations, maybe a few centuries ago."

"Do you think there's anyone who could tell us when it was made?" Hermes said. "I don't know much about sculpture, but it looks pretty crude to me."

"Probably not," I said. "I know a lot of art connoisseurs, but they always think that there was no sculpture worth noticing before the great age of Athens and don't pay much attention to the older stuff. I doubt it's very important to our investigation in any case. It just tells us what I expected: that this unbelievable place has served a number of peoples in a number of functions over the centuries. That means there's nothing terribly sacred about the relationship of the Hecate cult with this place. They're just another pack of immigrants who moved in and adapted it to their own purposes." In addition I was beginning to suspect that the Hecate cult itself, or at least some of its adherents, had been using this convenient facility for a number of differing purposes, among them murder and robbery.

We found a few more of the vent holes, but nothing more. "All right," I said. "To the river chamber." So we made our way lower into the chamber where this had all begun, when the priest Eugaeon had surfaced in the bubbling water. Here I had extra torches ignited and lamps lit. Soon we had a very tolerable light, dimmed and diffused somewhat by the ever present mist from the water. While I set the other men to searching walls, floor, and ceiling, Hermes and I stripped and went into the water. In the excellent light, this was quite pleasant, making up for the lack of a decent bathing facility near the temples.

I went first to the place where the water, as we now knew, emerged from the other place, an unknown distance away, where it was accessed from the other tunnel. The current was quite strong, making it difficult to hold my place. The water was chest-deep to me, the bottom perfectly smooth beneath my feet. There seemed to be no growth of lichen or any of the usual slimy stuff that grows where water and stone meet. The heat of the water may have accounted for that, or possibly its sulfur content. The channel where the water entered seemed to be almost as wide as my outspread arms, and the same distance from the surface of the water to the floor. I felt that, had I been able to make my way against the current, I might have walked to the access from the other temple.

From there I went to the opposite wall of the chamber, where the water ran out. Hermes was examining the bottom, feeling every inch of it carefully, with his feet. "Absolutely smooth," he reported. "No rocks, no sand, nothing—wait." He stooped, ducked under the water, and came up a moment later with something. "Felt it with my foot," he said, handing the thing to me. It was a bone pin about as long as my hand, the sort women use to dress their hair.

"Let's keep searching the bottom," I said, and commenced to feeling with my soles. In a short time we came up with a bronze stylus for writing on wax tablets, a necklace of blue Egyptian beads with the clasp broken, and a woman's sandal, but nothing more.

"What do we make of this?" Hermes said. "Offerings?"

"It's an impoverished god who'd accept such trash as sacrifices," I said. "Petitioners have to wade into the water to get their prophecy. Maybe this stuff just got dropped and lost in the water over the years."

I waded on, still feeling with my feet, until I was almost at the far wall and the current around my feet and calves began to quicken. I turned to the men who were searching the chamber. "Anything yet?"

"Nothing, Praetor," said one man who stood on another's shoulders to search the ceiling. "Not even one of those vent holes in this room. It's probably why the mist stays here."

"Well," I said, feeling my way closer to the outlet, "you just keep on . . . Awwk!" Something that felt like a giant hand grabbed my ankles and jerked me beneath the water. I was almost to the wall and I grabbed at it, my hands scrabbling at the rough rock, nails scraping and splintering against it as I was dragged into the outlet fissure, feeling my legs scrape against the side. I was drowning and I knew that this was definitely not the way I wanted to die, unable to breathe in the utter darkness of a subterranean tunnel.

I was losing what little purchase I had on the rough stone, knowing I was lost forever, when strong hands seized my wrists and pulled hard, almost disjointing my shoulders, so powerful was the current that was trying to drag me the other way. Then other hands grasped me and tugged and I was free of the fearful current. My head broke water and I coughed and sputtered and they carried me from the water and sat me on the stone floor.

After a few minutes I got my breathing under control and my

lungs cleared of water and, best of all, my heart stopped hammering like a mad blacksmith pounding hot iron which, incidentally, is what my chest felt like.

"What happened?" Hermes wanted to know. He'd just saved my life, but then, that was his job. His expression was decidedly odd and I took that to mean he was relieved that I was alive, but there was something more to it. He looked *amused*. I looked around at the other men and they were all trying to hide smiles, unsuccessfully. One began to chuckle, then they all chuckled, then roared with laughter.

"Let me in on the joke," I said in my deadliest voice.

"P-Praetor," said one when he could talk. "If you could have heard the sound you made just before you went under!"

"And the look on your face!" said another. Then they were all off laughing again.

"I can only regret," I said, "that I didn't drown and make your mirth complete." This set them rolling on the floor. Hermes, too. True, they had saved my life, but there is such a thing as carrying gratitude too far. I waited until they returned to sanity. I needed the time anyway, to get my breath under control.

"What *did* happen?" Hermes asked at length.

"Something I should have anticipated. I'm no aqueduct engineer, but I know a little about how water moves. The tunnel where the water comes in is almost man-height and just as wide. Where it goes out is a tunnel not one-fourth as large. Yet the level of the water here in the cave stays the same. How can that be?"

"The same amount flows out as flows in?" Hermes hazarded.

"Precisely. And how does it do that?"

He thought for a moment. "It has to flow out a lot faster than it flows in."

"That is right. Just as when a river flows through a narrow canyon. At the spot it enters, the water speeds up and foams and rapids form. Same here. The current is strong coming in, and it has terrible force going out. I should have been more cautious. So you found nothing else?"

"Nothing, Praetor," reported one of the men.

"Very well. Let's get out of this place."

Hermes and I resumed our clothes and we began the trudge back to the surface. "Do you think we've learned anything?" he asked. "Other than to watch out for fast water?"

"I think we have. It may not be apparent just yet, but we know more of that cave than we knew before, and when we know a little more, these things may fall into place."

"I hope so," he said. "At least we're through wandering underground."

"No, we are not," I told him. "Now we're going to do the same thing with the other tunnel." Hermes groaned. So did the others. Now it was my turn to smile. Laugh at me, would they? We'd see about that.

At least the priests of the Temple of Apollo were all dead and didn't try to hinder us. I got a good close look at the trapdoor first. There were what appeared to be bloodstains on its underside. I thought about this for a while, then I realized what I was looking at.

"Hermes, you remember when we found the bodies of the priests and their hands and forearms were battered?"

"Yes, we figured they'd been defending themselves from their attackers."

"We were wrong. They were bashing their fists against this stone, trying to get out after it had been shut behind them."

He thought about the implications of this. "Then we're back to the possibility that there was just a single killer. Let them suffocate down there, then dispose of the bodies afterward at your leisure."

"That is how I see it. I suspect there was more than one, but it was certainly an easier task than it appeared at first."

Next we examined the tunnel, and I left a man to guard the trap with drawn sword to make sure that it stayed open. I had no desire to emulate the example of the late priests. The tunnel told us nothing at all. The smooth-dressed stone would have revealed any irregularities immediately and there were none.

The chamber below was no better. It looked no different than it had before, except for the absence of corpses. As before, the air quickly grew close from our profusion of torches and lamps and our own exhalations.

"Greeks are supposed to know everything," Hermes said. "Why didn't they think to provide ventilation, when those Aborigines thousands of years ago did?"

It was a good question. "Maybe," I said, "they didn't think it would be needed. A small number of men don't require a lot of air if they're only going to be down here a short time, and with the trap above open, it isn't too bad."

"I was wondering about that," Hermes said. "There's enough air coming up from the hole there to keep us breathing here. Why did the priests suffocate so easily?"

"I can't say I know much about the properties of air," I admitted, "any more than I do about those of water. But it seems to me that the air rises from the water tunnel and is sucked up the passageway. Maybe when the trap is shut, the flow of air stops." Something struck me.

"That's how Eugaeon ended up in the water! He was leaning down into the hole to get what air was left, lost consciousness, and fell in to resurface so fortuitously in front of us!"

"Why not the others?" Hermes asked.

"He was the ranking man and the others let him have the water hole. Or maybe they were all up the shaft, pounding their fists against the stone. They probably suffocated even faster up there."

I had the men lower torches into the well and stuck my head down there, like the late Eugaeon. What I could see looked like natural tunnel. I was tempted to have the men lower me into it, but somehow I had had enough adventuring in water for that day. I came back up.

"I wonder how we can measure the distance to the other chamber?" I mused. I sat down and tried to think like an engineer.

"We could tie something that floats to a piece of rope," Hermes suggested. "Tie a knot every cubit. Toss it in, and when it comes out the other side, count the cubits."

I nodded. "That makes sense. How would you know when it came out the other side?"

He thought a while longer, as did I. "Have a man in the other chamber. As soon as it comes out, he grabs it and gives a tug. Then you know not to pay out any more line."

I clapped him on the shoulder. "You'll make an engineer yet. Tomorrow I want you to do exactly that."

"What will you be doing?" he asked.

"Sleeping, I hope."

8

JULIA WAS NOT HAPPY WITH MY FORAY into the underworld, but she was not as angry as I had feared.

"It was not wise to flout the customs of the Oracle and treat an ancient holy site like some Subura tenement. Iola is right to be furious and she will definitely have you charged with sacrilege when you step down from office." Of course I was immune from prosecution while I held office, but I was everybody's fair game as soon as I should step down.

"Now, Julia, don't we already know that this shrine is fraudulent? It looks like they've been using it for years to fleece the public, murdering some of them."

"We don't know anything. We have strong reason to suspect that at least some of the staff of the temple, at some time or other, have been using the Oracle for profit, and that murder may be involved. That doesn't make the site itself any less holy."

"Well, Hecate's a pretty poor goddess if she allows such goings-on in her own precincts. She's supposed to be fearsome. Why doesn't she sic her black bitches on the miscreants? They're the ones committing sacrilege, not I."

Despite my clearly sarcastic tone, Julia seemed to give this some serious thought. "The gods are not always swift to punish. They are immortal, time means little to them. They are content to bide their time and devise a fitting punishment. You recall a few years ago when Crassus took advantage of his position as one of the *quinqidecemviri* and falsified a prophecy in the Sibylline Books? Nothing happened to him at the time, but after he went to Syria, he met a catastrophe such as has befallen few Romans."

"That's pretty rough on the part of the gods," I said, "killing tens of thousands of Roman legionaries, plus thousands more foreign *auxilia*, just to punish one foolish old man."

"Immortality gives the gods a strange sense of proportion. Nevertheless, they won't be mocked or taken advantage of."

"Hecate is from Thrace. Do you think she even knows what is going on in Italy?"

"Honestly, Decius, you have the strangest ideas of what the gods are like, as if they were just oversized mortals with long lives and somewhat augmented powers. It's a concept suitable for primitives and ignorant peasants, not for an educated Roman of the ruling class."

"We can't all be philosophers," I said. My mind was not really on our conversation. I had a great many thoughts spinning around, looking for something to give direction to all I had learned. Murders and tunnels and ventilation slots in the ceiling and miniature arrows and rivalries going back centuries and a great general preparing for civil war and a subterranean river with a vicious current and a score of other things that made no sense but I was sure would, if I could just fit them together in the proper order, perhaps together with a few other missing pieces.

"Decius?" Julia was saying.

"Eh?" I answered brightly.

"You might as well be in Cappadocia," she said disgustedly. "I was just talking about Pompey."

"You were? I must have nodded off. Long day, you know."

"You were just ignoring me. I was just saying that having Pompey in these parts is changing the social scene. You are not the ranking Roman official now. Pompey's been consul twice and now he's proconsul with extraordinary powers in Italy—what are you chuckling about?"

"Sabinilla. I'll bet she's cursing herself for throwing that fantastic party for my benefit and wishing she'd saved it for Pompey. What's she going to do now to entertain him? She'd need months to put together another evening like that one."

Even Julia had to smile at that. "The poor woman. She must be pulling out her hair and throwing things and screaming fit to raise the dead."

"Assuming she has any hair to pull. I've seen nothing but her wigs."

We were taking our ease on a small terrace jutting from the base of the Temple of Apollo. Julia had fretted over my near drowning for perhaps three breaths and then had begun to berate me for my many lapses of judgment. I had expected far worse. The night was cool and pleasant, the noise from the encamped crowd no more than a distant murmur punctuated by an occasional tune played on a flute. We had just enjoyed a rare private dinner and now a pair of slave girls kept the air moving and the flies off us with huge ostrich-feather fans Julia had conjured from somewhere. There are worse ways to while away an evening.

"Do you know what surprises me?" I said.

"What is that?"

"That, so far, nobody has tried to kill me outright. With serious crimes under investigation, crimes that merit the death penalty, you'd think somebody would have had a go at me by now. They usually do."

She shut her eyes. "Don't talk like that. It tempts the gods. Just saying it makes it more likely to happen."

"Now you're being superstitious," I chided.

"Isn't everyone?" she said.

The next morning I was looking forward to my favorite activity, which is to have nothing to do at all. It was a day on which official business was forbidden, so no court. I was at a loss where to look next in my investigation, so no investigating. Hermes and a few of the other men had gone off to try the experiment with the rope, and there is nothing I like better than to delegate the work to someone else. I was back out on that terrace, enjoying the morning sun and about to open a letter from Rome when I heard pelting hoofbeats. I looked up and saw what had to be a messenger hurrying up the road from the south. I was certain that my perfect day was at an end before it had a chance to begin.

Yet, I reflected, it might have been worse. A messenger hurrying like that from the north would have had me in a cold sweat. That would have meant bad news from Rome. A few moments later, the messenger was pounding up the stairs. "Praetor Metellus?" I admitted that I was he, and the man handed me a leather scroll tube. "From the *duumvir* Belasus of Pompeii."

I opened the tube and shook out the scroll it held. While I was reading it, Hermes returned with his wet, knotted rope. "Just under three cubits," he reported. "Even closer than I'd thought. Of course, three cubits of solid stone is a lot of rock, but it's no wonder the Hecate cult figured the Apollo people were up to something. They must have heard a lot of scrapes and clinking over the years. Stone carries sound."

"Another little piece," I said.

"What do you have there?"

"A message from the *duumvir* of Pompeii. There has been a murder. The victim is a foreigner."

"Why is he writing you about it? You judge court cases involving foreigners. You don't get involved in every murder where a foreigner is involved until it comes to court."

"He thought I would want to know about it because the dead man, a Syrian, had a case on the docket, to be tried when I should go down to

133

Pompeii to hold court. It was to be the last town I was to visit before leaving Campania."

"And you were delaying it to stay in Campania as long as you could, eh?" Hermes said, grinning.

"Of course."

"Are you going to go look into it?"

"I might as well. It will put some distance between me and Pompey, anyway. Get some of the men together and get them mounted. I won't be holding court so the lictors can stay here. This will be a flying visit, I don't need any of my official regalia." I went inside to tell Julia, who was predictably put out.

"You just want to get away and have some fun," she complained.

"Anything wrong with that?"

"It's undignified. You can just send Hermes or one of the others."

"Then I wouldn't get to have any fun. I'll be back tomorrow or the next day." I left before she could marshal an argument.

Traveling on horseback and not slowed by a huge entourage and women carried in litters, we made Pompeii in a few hours. As always, the countryside was beautiful, the fine road lined with stately pines and excellent tombs.

Pompeii was another of those Oscan towns, once a part of the Samnite League, that had chosen the wrong side in the Social War and was besieged by Sulla. When the war was over, a large group of legionaries had been settled there and it now had the status of *colonia*. Latin had replaced the former Oscan dialect, and the inhabitants were now Roman citizens, the only sensible thing to be.

We approached the town from the northwest, but rather than enter through one of the northern gates, I swung around the city to the east and we rode along the wall until we reached the southeastern corner, where we came to a huge construction project. I had heard something of this and was curious to see it. It was a stone amphitheater, an architectural innovation pioneered in Campania. It was accomplished by, in essence, taking two ordinary theaters, getting rid of the stage, orchestra, *scena*, and so forth, and sticking them together face-to-face. The result was a huge oval of seats arranged in tiers, with an arena in the middle.

It had been begun almost twenty years previously by two local moneybags named Valgus and Porcius as a gift to the town, and had been in use for much of that time, but so great a project takes time and the finishing touches were just being completed. As I have said, Campania is gladiator-mad and the Pompeiians were determined to have the very best venue possible for their *munera*. In this they had succeeded handsomely.

We dismounted and walked over to tour the fabulous building. At this time Rome, a far larger and richer city, had no such permanent building. Until just a generation previously, we had held the Games, including *munera*, in the Forum, where temporary bleachers were erected. Men who wanted to stage especially splendid and extravagant spectacles built wooden amphitheaters, usually on the Campus Martius, which were to be torn down at the conclusion of the festivities. Up until this time, nobody had been willing to undertake the ruinous expense of erecting a stone amphitheater large enough to hold all the adult male citizens of Rome, and the citizens would want nothing less.

This new Pompeii amphitheater, by contrast, was far larger than the town needed. Since, unlike the chariot races, slaves, foreigners, children, and women were not supposed to attend the fights (although women got around that rule pretty easily), this place could absorb not just the locals but the whole countryside and several neighboring towns. This was source of huge pride for the Pompeiians, since it put such a large district under obligation to them. They attended the spectacles as the guests of Pompeii.

What we could see as we approached was a semicircular stone wall, perhaps thirty feet high, consisting of a series of high arches. It was impressive, but gave no true sense of the size of the place. A number of men were carving and painting decoration on the walls. A stairway slanted up the side of the wall and we mounted this. Its top ended in a platform. We crossed this and looked down. The tiers of seats stretched away from us in an enormous oval in a series of descending wedges separated by stairways. Each section was crossed by two walkways that allowed access to the other sections. The low walls of these walkways were themselves finely decorated with paintings of fighters, victors holding aloft laurel wreaths and palms and other symbols one associates with the Games. On the terrace where we stood were the masts that on the days of the spectacles would support a vast awning that could be adjusted to allow for the movement of the sun across the sky, providing shade on even the hottest days. Apparently the awning itself, which would consist of thirty or forty wedge-shaped pieces of sailcloth, was stored away someplace when not in use.

A master builder was there, supervising the placement of the last few blocks. We walked over to him and I complimented him on the incredible stonework.

"Truly, Praetor," he said, "it was finished years ago, but an earthquake last year damaged a lot of the stone and the decoration has weathered. This is really a restoration project, paid for by the *duumvir* Valgus."

"The original builder with his colleague Porcius?" I asked.

"His son, now holding the same office. Would you like to see the building?"

"Very much so. Please lead on."

So he took us through the whole wonderful structure, explaining how the designers and architects and engineers had solved numerous problems involving weights and stresses and the problems of getting twenty thousand spectators seated and out of the building as quickly and efficiently as possible. They had even had the foresight to plant plane trees all over the plaza separating the amphitheater from the town proper. These trees, now mature, were not only very handsome additions, they provided shade for the vendors who set up their stalls to supply the needs of spectators during intermissions in the shows.

Rome had larger venues: the Circus Maximus and the Theater of Pompey, for instance, but the Circus was not so well designed and the theater was no more than a very large Greek building of the ordinary type. This was something new and I could only wish that Rome had a structure as fine. I thanked the builder and we went back to our horses.

"Well," I told the men. "I wouldn't have missed that, but it isn't getting any work done, so let's go find this *duumvir* Belasus."

We rode along the south wall, through the Stabian Gate, and up a major street that traversed the town, then west along a cross street to the city forum. It was a beautiful city, but then it seems that all Campanian cities are, in contrast to Rome, which is a very large city with some very fine buildings, but lacking in overall grace and utterly unplanned, more like a cluster of villages crammed into walls that surround much too small an area. I love Rome, but I am not blind to her faults.

We found both *duumviri* in the town's modest basilica, just finishing up some public business. Belasus was a small, portly man, with a fringe of white hair and the look of a prosperous merchant. Porcius was tall, thin, and aristocratic, a much younger man. I complimented Valgus on his restoration of the amphitheater, and Porcius on his father's fine contribution to the city and to the district as a whole. Both seemed pleased.

"Now," I said, "tell me about this dead Syrian."

"His name was Elagabal, and he had an import-export business," Belasus said.

"Dealing in what?"

"He speculated in cargoes. He'd buy a shipload of oranges from Spain, for instance, and hold them hoping the price would rise so he could sell them at a large profit. He'd buy grain and send it to someplace where his contacts informed him that the harvest had failed, that sort of thing."

"It sounds like he ran a chancy business," I commented. "You can't hold on to oranges for very long, and anything that travels by ship is at hazard."

"We have reason to doubt that he made very much money that way," Porcius said. "But he made a lot of money anyway."

"And how did he do that?" I asked.

"Local rumor has it that he was a receiver of stolen goods," Belasus said. "His business was just a cover, and he could ship the stolen goods to places where they could be sold without raising suspicions about himself."

"Yet suspicions were raised," I noted.

"A fence can't work *alone*," Belasus said. "He must deal with thieves, and thieves talk."

"So they do. This court case he had pending, did it involve his nefarious activities?"

"Hard to say," said Porcius. "He had a citizen partner, as foreign businessmen must by law. He was a man named Sextus Aureus, a tanner. Aureus was bringing suit against Elagabal for defrauding him of his share of several years' profits from the legitimate business."

"You would think it would be Aureus who would end up conveniently murdered," I observed. "I'll want to speak with Aureus, but first I want to see the Syrian's body and his place of business."

"You want to see the body?" Porcius said. "Why?"

"You never know what you might learn from a dead body," I said. They looked at me as if I were a prize loon. It is a look I had grown used to.

"Very well," said Belasus. "If you will come with me, Praetor."

"I will have Aureus summoned and sent to you," Porcius said. "If there is any other way I can help you, please let me know."

We took our leave of Porcius and followed Belasus into the city. Its forum was long and narrow and we passed the local Temple of Apollo (that local Greek influence again) and a small but exquisite temple to the public lares. Past the forum we came to a district of more small temples, these dedicated to gods associated with death, as is the Temple of Libitina in Rome. Here we found the facilities of the undertakers. In Campania they don't wear the Etruscan costumes they wear in Rome. A man dressed like the rest in a black tunic took us to a table where the corpse of the Syrian lay covered by a shroud.

At my gesture the attendant threw back the shroud, revealing a lean, bearded man of perhaps fifty. Someone had thoughtfully arranged his features into an expression of serenity. Somewhat less serene was the wound in his abdomen, just below the sternum. He had been knifed.

"Any idea when this happened?" I asked.

"Probably the night before last," said the *duumvir*. "A man with business to transact went to the Syrian's offices and found him dead on the floor yesterday morning and reported it to the town watch, who sent a runner to inform me. When I remembered he was a defendant in a case coming up before you, I sent a messenger to inform you."

"Very thoughtful of you. I think we've learned all we are going to here. If you could lead us to his offices now I would be obliged."

As we made our way through the streets, I beckoned Hermes to my side. "Did that knifework look familiar to you?"

"Just like the girl at the temple," he said. "But it's a pretty common way to dispatch someone with a knife."

"If it was in Rome," I said, "I wouldn't give it a second thought. Although seeing two people in a quiet place like this, both killed identically, that makes me suspicious."

"A man like that Syrian," Hermes mused, "a professional criminal from the sound of it, used to dealing with thieves and worse—"

"What are you thinking?"

"To use a knife like that you have to get close. The man showed no signs of defending himself. Maybe the killer was someone he knew and trusted."

"It's likely. Of course, accomplices can always hold a man's arms while you stab him. Let's see what his office looks like."

The late Syrian's office occupied two rooms of no great size on the lower floor of a two-story building, flanked by a tavern and a wool merchant's shop. Inside, the main room contained a long table, a few chairs, a small desk topped by a tall, honeycomb scroll holder. Along one wall were some circular leather cases with wooden lids and these held yet more scrolls.

There was also a large bloodstain on the floor. Bloodstains are rather commonplace so I paid it little attention; the flies were giving it attention enough. The back room had obviously been the man's living quarters. It contained a bed, a low table with a basin and a large pitcher and a fairly clean towel. A niche in one wall held an image of some eastern god flanked by a pair of lamps. Before the image was a clay dish that held the ashes of some cheap incense There was a small wooden chest at the foot of the bed. I opened it and found a couple of tunics, an old belt, a pointed cap, and a striped woolen cloak. That was all. Obviously the man had done nothing in this room except sleep in it.

Back in the main room, we set to work. "Let's go over these papers," I said. "We're looking for names of contacts, lists of goods that may have been illegally acquired, letters, anything that might give us an idea of who would have wanted him dead."

"A fence?" said one of my men. "Who wouldn't want him dead?" This got a good laugh, even from Belasus. I stepped outside with the *duumvir* and we sat on a bench next to a fountain where water spouted from the carved face of Silenus into a basin carved in the shape of a seashell. We bought cups of wine from a passing vendor and settled down to talk. Naturally, the talk was about politics. I had other things to discuss with him but the proprieties had to be observed, and when two Italian politicians talked, the principal subject was always foremost.

"Well, Praetor," he said, "where's your money? Caesar, Pompey, the Senate? Some up-and-comer I've never heard about?" As if we were discussing Green against Blue at the Circus.

"Caesar," I told him bluntly. "Pompey's through. The Senate will go with the winner except for a few die-hard Pompey adherents who will probably end up in exile. Last time there was civil strife, this town backed the Samnite League against Sulla. Don't make the same sort of mistake again."

He stared at me, astonished. "Well, that's blunt enough. I thought your family backed Pompey these days. Then again, you're married to Caesar's niece, aren't you?"

"My family and my wife's have nothing to do with it," I assured him. "I know both men, I know their armies, I know the Senate. Caesar's the man, count on it."

"Very well then. But what's going to happen when Caesar's top dog on the pile, eh?" He had a self-made provincial's directness that I liked.

"I wish I knew that. It would make all the difference. Best would be if Caesar would reorder the Senate and the law courts, which are in need of reordering, set the calendar to rights, which is his job anyway as *Pontifex Maximus*, review the constitution, make adjustments where they're needed, and then step down, the way Sulla did. Only I hope he can do it without killing as many people as Sulla did. I know he wants to go to war against Parthia. Crassus was his friend and he wants to avenge him, get the Roman prisoners of Carrhae back, and retake the eagles Crassus lost. And, of course, add to his own laurels. If he'll just settle affairs at Rome to his liking and run off to his next war, Italy will have gotten off lightly."

"You think he'll be dictator then? Sulla broke the power of the Tribunes of the Plebs."

"He'll be dictator in fact even if he doesn't get the title voted by the Senate. And Tribunes can be obnoxious troublemakers, but we need them. Without them the people are at the mercy of the senators, many of whom are a pack of self-seeking thieves. Believe me, I know, being one of them myself. One of the better ones, mind you."

He laughed heartily at this. "Well, Praetor, you've answered me honestly, and now I'll tell you something that may be of use to you in the coming months. Pompey is a great favorite in this district. People like him. He's popular, and when he visits he's cheered and praised and we always throw a good banquet for him." Then he leaned close. "But nobody here is going to get in a war for him. Popularity is one thing. Loyalty unto death is another. We don't know Caesar very well down here, but we're not going to give him any trouble, either. Next time you see your wife's uncle, you tell him that."

"I will, and I appreciate the confidence. Now, tell me, do you know if this Syrian had any doings with the Temple of Apollo and Hecate's Oracle? You know I've been investigating the murders there."

"That I do and so does the whole countryside. It's the prime subject of gossip these days." He thought a while. "Rumor has it the man was thick with every thief, from bandit to burglar, for a hundred miles around. If anyone there was stealing, they may well have dealt with him. But men like him stay alive and in business by being discreet. Same for the thieves. I can't say his name was linked with anyone there, but then I don't get to hear the gossip in the lowest taverns."

Shortly after this we were joined by the tanner Aureus, the Syrian's citizen partner. He was a burly, tough-looking specimen, his hands stained brown by the noxious liquids of the tanning vats. Apparently, he didn't leave all the work to his slaves. The introductions were brief.

"Aureus, we can be pretty sure that your partner was a fence," I began.

"I can tell you he was a thief. That's why I was suing him."

"What caused you to be suspicious of him?"

"Well, to start with, he was a Syrian. They're all thieves."

"Yet you went into partnership with him."

"Well, a foreign businessman has to have a citizen partner. That's the law. So it only makes sense to partner with one. Doesn't mean you have to share his whole life. I only saw the man once a year, around Saturnalia, to settle accounts. Over the years I got suspicious, because he was living mighty high while he was telling me his business was barely clearing expenses."

"Living high?" I said. I nodded toward the office across the street. "It looks to me as if he was living with great austerity."

"That place? That's just where he stayed when he was in town doing business. Go visit his villa outside of town. It's better than the one the *duumvir* here owns."

I looked at Belasus. "I've never been there, but I've heard it's a fine place. He bought it about ten years ago, I think."

"So, you see? He was cheating me." Aureus shook his head. "Looks like I'll never get my money now."

"File a suit against his estate," Belasus advised. "I doubt the man has a relative to claim it. He was a foreigner and may never have filed a will. Praetor Terentianus will probably condemn the property and it'll be sold at auction. Get your claim in quickly and you should get a nice piece of the sale price."

The man grinned. "Thanks, *Duumvir*, I'll do that." I dismissed the man, telling him I might have more questions for him.

"There goes another vote for me next election," Belasus said contentedly.

Hermes came from the office with a scroll in his hand. "This was in one of the chests. It's an old one, going by the color of the papyrus. I'm not sure I understand everything, but some things look suspicious. See what you can make of it." He left it with me and went back inside. I puzzled over the abbreviations and eccentric spelling but it could have been worse. At least the man wrote in Latin, of a sort.

"As near as I can tell," I told my companion, "this says that he took delivery of some rings, some gold and silver plate, some gems, and a sword with an ivory hilt and sheath from one Sextus Porcius." I looked at him. "Any relation to your colleague?"

He shook his head. "That family's never used the name Sextus that I know of. Might be a distant relative. Porcius is one of the most common names in this district. There was a Porcius family when Pompeii was founded. By now their descendants and the descendants of the family's freedmen must number in the thousands."

"It's not exactly rare in the rest of Italy, either," I said. "My fellow senator Cato is a Porcius, and I think his family came from Etruria. No help there, then. But this inventory is standard burglar's loot: small items of high resale value, precious metals and gemstones and so forth. One sale could be legitimate, but I'll bet my men find more like this."

"Pretty foolish to put it in writing, don't you think?"

"Some people are fanatic record keepers. They can't help it. They always think someone is going to cheat them and have to keep track of every denarius. It's a sort of sickness."

As I had foretold, within the hour we had at least thirty more such records, all detailing the same sort of items. There were also records of the legitimate cargoes the man had bought on speculation and sold at a profit or, more often, at a loss, but the former outnumbered the latter by a great margin.

"No question about it," Belasus said with a sigh. "We have here the district's biggest fence. Well, good riddance to him. I, for one, don't plan to waste much time finding out who the killer might be. The man did a public service exterminating this wretch."

"I doubt you'll find the killer here, anyway," I muttered.

"Eh? What was that, Praetor?"

"Nothing. Just talking to myself, for which I have no excuse in such good company." I laid aside the scroll I had been reading. "It's getting too dark to read."

"So it is," Belasus said. "Come to my house for some dinner, you and your men. I'm a widower, my daughters are married, my sons are with the eagles in Macedonia, and I've nothing but room. We'll make a boy's night of it."

"That is the finest offer I've had in months," I told him, truthfully.

I called my men out of the office and the *duumvir* put an official seal on the door. We went to a market and stopped by a caterer's shop where Belasus ordered up a small banquet to be delivered to his house. The caterer was a man who knew the *duumvir*'s likes and dislikes and needed to be told very little. Belasus explained that, as an elected *duumvir* he did a good deal of entertaining, but didn't like to be troubled with a great staff of servants, so he had all his larger meals catered. This made eminently good sense to me. In the street we encountered some friends of his whom he invited to dinner in the usual fashion of politicians. "All bachelors and widowers," he confided to me, "and all good conversationalists. They won't bring along any women."

His house proved to be modest but very adequate for any reasonable need. It was in the old-fashioned design, just a square surrounding a courtyard with an atrium, a large triclinium for entertaining, and a dozen or so bedrooms, most of them now vacant. He ordered the servants to set up chairs and tables in the courtyard by the pool, and there we sat, drinking his excellent wine and snacking on nuts and dried octopus while the servants set up the triclinium and the caterer's people brought in dinner.

Our host, not quite formally, bade us all drink a health to the Republic, which really needed some drinking to that year. That done, we relaxed. The courtyard was of the usual design: a square with a pool in the middle. And in the middle of the pool was a pedestal supporting one of the most delightful sculptures I have ever seen. It was a dancing faun, no more than three feet high, its pose so lively and lifelike that its pedestal seemed inadequate to hold it.

"So, Praetor," Belasus began, "what's going on up there at the temple? I've been hearing the most lurid stories about the murders and the countryside's rife with rumors that there's a veritable battle of gods going on."

"Nothing as grand as that, I'm afraid." I gave him a bald outline of what had happened and what we knew and some of the things we had speculated about. This may seem unwise in the middle of an investigation, but I had often found that it paid to have the counsel of a person uninvolved in a case, who might look at the evidence with eyes unclouded by the prejudices and assumptions that clutter the thinking of those too close to the events under examination.

He whistled. "What a story! So you think there may be some sort of robbery ring operating up there?"

"I think that's a part of it, but I can't make a lot of things fit. The Hecate cult poses few problems. Foreign cults are always suspect, greed and larceny are everywhere. A number of things have me stymied. For one thing, how have they gotten away with it for so long? For another, what is the connection with the priests of Apollo? Granted Apollo is a foreign god, but the god himself, his worship, and his priests for centuries have practically defined respectability."

He thought about that for a while, taking an occasional sip of his own excellent wine. "Well, you know, a temple can fall on hard times, just like a business or a family. They don't live on the largesse of the god. They need patronage or they can go under. It wouldn't be the first time a temple got a bit underhanded to keep afloat. I'm told there's temples in the east that run whores and call them priestesses, just charge for their services right out front like any brothel."

"That's true," I said, pondering. The mention of patronage stirred up some thoughts. "What do you know about a family named Pedarius?"

"They live north of here. Don't see much of them, but they're patricians and they go all the way back to Aeneas, if you can believe them. Poor as hedgehogs, from what I hear, ashamed to show themselves around much, since they can't flaunt the style a patrician's supposed to have."

"Then why," I wondered aloud, "are they the patrons of the Temple of Apollo?"

"Couldn't say," said Belasus. "But if that family were my patrons, I'd steal, too."

Dinner was a fine, convivial affair. The caterer knew his business and laid on fresh fish from the bay, roast kid, suckling pig, and something rather rare in those days—beefsteaks. We tend to think of cattle as work animals too tough to eat except for the youngest veal, but some local farmer had a pampered herd of cattle that he never set to work but instead let them laze about eating grass and a special preparation of grain soaked in wine so that they put on flesh at an astounding rate. The very idea of tender beef may seem to be a contradiction in terms, but this was as tender as the finest lamb and had a subtle flavor such as I had never encountered. The Gauls and Britons eat a lot of beef, of course, but they boil the tough joints until they are nearly tasteless and only the broth is worth anything.

Anyway, the evening was a resounding success. We all ate and drank far too much, which men must do once in a while, or else the world gets out of balance. We kept the world well on an even keel that night.

As I went to bed in one of those vacant rooms that night, I knew that something was not quite right. Then it occurred to me. It was something that I had mentioned to Julia. Nobody had tried to kill me. That seemed wrong. In my career it always seemed that, when you looked into the wrongdoing of evil people, sooner or later some of them tried to kill you. It was only reasonable.

Despite this anomaly, I went to sleep easily. Nevertheless, the next day, when someone really did try to kill me, it came almost as a relief.

9

THE NEXT MORNING, HEADS RINGING and hands a bit shaky, we rode from Pompeii. The weather was no longer as fine as it had been, a drizzle had set in, but a little rain in the face was just what we needed. By noon, we were almost recovered. Every five miles along the road there was a pleasant alcove where travelers could rest. Each one had stone tables, a fountain of clear water, and plane trees for shade.

When we judged that the sun was at zenith (it was not visible, but the rain had stopped), we paused at one of these. We dismounted, put the horses to graze, and unpacked the luncheon Belasus had thoughtfully provided from the leftovers of the previous night's banquet. My men spread a cloth on one of the stone tables while I sat on the ground at the base of one of the trees. The morning's drizzle had not been heavy enough to penetrate the plane tree's dense foliage, and the ground was dry.

"Ready to join us, Praetor?" one of the men asked when all was ready.

"No, I like it here. Just bring me—" and at that moment I was struck by an arrow.

I've been wounded many times in my long and belligerent life. I've been speared, clobbered by slingstones, stabbed, cut, clubbed, bashed with fists, hit with stones and roof tiles, and even run over by a chariot, but this was the first time I had been struck by an arrow. I had never worried much about arrows. For one thing, Italians are, by and large, wretched archers. We specialize in close-in work with cold steel. The legions usually hire archers from places like Crete or the East where people favor the bow.

So here I was, in southern Campania, sitting beneath a plane tree, and out of nowhere an arrow flew through the remains of a morning mist and skewered me through the upper chest, just below my left collarbone. One second I was peacefully awaiting my lunch, mildly hungover but at peace with the world, the next I was looking down in amazement at the end of a feathered shaft protruding from my own all-too-mortal flesh. Sometimes life is just like that.

"Praetor!" shouted some of my men. They rushed over to me. All but Hermes, of course. He wasted no time in such foolishness. He had his sword out and was running toward the brush on the other side of the road, where the arrow had come from.

"Go help him!" I managed to get out. All of them did except one, a boy named Manius Silvius, son of a family ally. I had slumped over sideways and he gently raised me and leaned me against the trunk of the tree.

"You don't have much future in Roman politics, Manius," I managed to grate out, "if you'd rather nursemaid a soon-to-die praetor than chase a murderer, which at least holds an element of fun."

"You're not going to die, Praetor," he stammered with an utter lack of conviction.

"Why not?" I demanded. "Look. I've been shot through with an arrow. People die that way."

"But who could have shot you?" he asked.

"It might have been Cupid, but I doubt it. No women around, for one thing."

"What?" Sometimes I waste my best wit on such people.

Shortly thereafter, Hermes and the others returned without any trophies. "Let him get away, did you?" I said bitterly. "I'm going to die without the satisfaction of knowing that I'm at least avenged."

Hermes knelt, took out his knife, and cut my tunic away from the wound. He punched me rudely on the chest.

"Ow! What are you doing, wretch?"

"I'm seeing how bad it is. Asklepiodes taught me this." He took the arrow by the shaft and wiggled it. The world turned red before my eyes. He punched me lightly in the stomach and I began to vomit.

"No blood in your puke. Good."

"Good?" I raged in a very weak, strangled voice. "That's good? I'll have you crucified, you monster! I knew I never should have given you your freedom."

"Oh, be quiet. It missed your lung and your heart and your major pipes. We'll get the arrow out, and if you don't bleed to death inside and the infection doesn't kill you, you'll be fine. Just another scar to impress the voters at election time."

Somehow, I almost took comfort in this. "You're going to yank out that arrow, aren't you?"

"Unless you'd rather keep it," he said. Snide little bastard.

"Give me a gallon or two of wine and go ahead." Something occurred to me. "You know what? My hangover is gone." And that was the last I remembered for a while.

Sometime later I awoke and wished I hadn't. My chest and shoulders felt like molten lead. It hurt to breathe. I tried turning my head and my neck hurt; so did my head. I had the feeling that someone had just rushed from the room. At least that meant that I was in a room. I was in a bed, for that matter. I tried to look around, moving nothing but my eyes. They hurt, too. I recognized the wall paintings. I was in the villa Hortalus had lent us.

Julia came in. "You see what comes of talking about someone trying to kill you? Now they've tried and came within an inch of succeeding."

"So this is my fault, is it? How long have I been unconscious?"

"Three days. The physician had your wound treated and bandaged and he forced some drugged wine into you. That's why you've slept so long."

I had a horrible thought. "You didn't let him run a hot iron through the wound, did you?" I'd seen that done before and it's far worse than getting skewered in the first place.

"No, this physician doesn't favor such drastic methods; just drugs and poultices for wounds like yours."

"Better than some army surgeon, anyway. How is it healing?"

"It wasn't as red and swollen this morning as when you were brought in. But you won't be going anywhere for a while. Hermes has canceled all your court appearances and sent word to Rome that you've been attacked and wounded. Pompey sent his personal physician, but I wouldn't let him treat you. He's one of those who favor hot iron."

"That was good of Pompey and better of you. I want to sit up."

"You'd better stay as you are until the wound has healed a bit more."

"No, I'm not looking forward to it, but I'd better sit up. I've seen a lot of wounded men die from lying flat too long. Even if the wounds are healing, they get fluid in their lungs and soon they can't breathe."

"Very well, but it's going to hurt."

"I hurt anyway." She left and moments later was back with Hermes, a burly house slave, and one of her slave girls. Hermes and the man took me by the arms and hauled me up while Julia and the girl piled cushions behind my back. A great wave of red washed over me and I clenched my teeth to keep from crying out. I settled back against the cushions and the agony began to fade, but the sweat rolled down my face in torrents. Julia gave me a cup of heavily watered wine with ice in it (the Villa of Hortalus lacked no amenities) and soon I felt able to talk again.

"Have you learned anything?" I asked Hermes.

"I took the arrow to a fletcher and he said that it was locally made, but it's a common type used for hunting. I borrowed some huntsmen and their dogs and took them back to where you were shot, but you'll recall that it was raining that day and it rained hard that night. They were able to find where he crouched in the brush to shoot, but that was all."

"He must have followed us. Do you remember who was near us on the road?"

"There was a good deal of traffic but most was on foot. Whoever followed us must have been on horseback."

"He might have been in front of us and doubled back when we stopped."

"If it was a huntsman hired for the job," Hermes said, "he could have been keeping up with us on foot but off in the fields somewhere. We were just ambling along at no great speed."

"As usual," Julia said, "there are too many possibilities."

"This has not been a case distinguished by good luck," I noted.

When word got around that I had returned to the land of the living, I got a lot of visitors. All the head men of the towns showed up, as did the major landholders. Pompey dropped by to see how I was getting along and told me I should have taken the hot iron treatment, that it would make me heal faster. I didn't ask him if he'd ever tried it personally. Sabinilla visited, this time wearing a black wig. Porcia showed up with an armload of medicinal herbs from her own garden and she gave Julia careful instructions on how to prepare and administer them. I thanked her for her thoughtfulness, but I seemed to be healing well enough and didn't take them. Medical concoctions always taste vile.

Within ten days I was up and walking around and could breathe almost normally. By great good fortune the infection had been mild and had cleared up early. I had feared that infection would bring on months of convalescence. Not to mention death.

As soon as my chest and shoulder could bear the weight, I took to wearing armor beneath my clothes when I went out. It was a reasonable precaution and Julia insisted on it. My men now accompanied me armed at all times. I was nervous any time I walked past a clump of bushes. Indeed, I was as jumpy as a dog with piles. I had been attacked many times, but I'd always felt that I was a match for the situation, blade to blade. Yet there is something profoundly unsettling about being shot from a distance, by an enemy you don't even see.

Once I was well enough recovered, the physician prescribed a regimen of exercise. The villa had every sort of facility, and a gymnasium was among them, but I was a serving praetor and a man in public life is not supposed to shut himself away from the people, so I elected to use a public facility. Near Baiae there was a large, Greek-style palaestra that was used by the inhabitants of several neighboring towns. It had all the usual provisions for running, wrestling, boxing, and so forth, and this being Italy it had a field for arms training complete with practice weapons and shields, and targets for javelins and arrows. I vowed to keep an eye on those people with bows.

Since exercise was the order of the day, we did not ride there but walked and ran alternately. Some of my men insisted on carrying shields to either side of me. I thought this was a bit excessive and lacking in dignity, but then I thought of how that arrow had felt and indulged them. As we drew near the gymnasium, though, I had them fall in behind me. Couldn't have the people thinking the Roman praetor was scared, after all.

Because of the Greek influence, the Campanians are passionately fond of athletics, and the place was well attended with men and boys sweating mightily as they heaved balls, lifted stone or bronze weights, swung wooden clubs, jumped, sprinted, and otherwise exerted themselves. They went silent at sight of my heavily armed little troupe. "Hey!" some local wag shouted. "This is the palaestra. The *ludus* is down the road there!" This sally raised a general laugh and I acknowledged it with a wave.

I was already tired from the trek, but I gritted my teeth, doffed my toga and armor, and stripped to a *subligaculum*. I wasn't about to work out stark naked like a Greek. My multitude of scars drew whistles of admiration, especially the fresh, still-red one on my upper chest.

I began to run around the outdoor track, followed by my men like so many hunting dogs. I didn't last long, but at least I didn't disgrace myself either. When I'd had enough of that, I went to the target range and threw javelins for a while. I had always excelled at this art, but I found that I'd lost range and aim. Well, I was still recovering from a serious wound. I vowed to keep at it until I had my old strength and skill back. We sparred with wooden swords and wicker shields for a while. Hermes took great delight in whipping the other men one after another, but he took it easy on me. The *ludus* had taught him how to be a good trainer as well as a fighter.

By the end of all this I was half-dead from fatigue, so greatly had my wound sapped my energy. "I'm going to do this every day until I can run and fight all day long," I told Hermes.

"I've never known you to be in any condition that good," he said, "but we'll see what we can manage. Let's go get cleaned up."

So at last Julia was getting her wish. I was getting back in shape for the wars. She and the physician had conspired to curb my wine intake as well and she had threatened Hermes into going along with it.

In the exercise yard of the palaestra building we rubbed down with oil, then rolled in the sand and scraped it off with strigils, then went into the bath to soak. The bath needed no fire, as the water was piped in from a nearby hot spring. The sulfur-smelling water soothed away the soreness of my muscles and the lingering pain of my wound. Maybe this wouldn't be so bad after all.

While we lazed in the water, an unexpected visitor arrived: Gnaeus Pompeius Magnus came in and lowered himself into the water. Apparently he had put himself on a regimen like mine. He wasn't quite as corpulent as when he arrived in Campania, though he still had a long way to go before he would achieve soldierly fitness. He had almost as many scars as I had, too, but his were mostly on his arms and legs since he got them on the battlefield, wearing armor. I had won many of mine in the streets and alleyways of Rome.

"Well, you seem to be coming along nicely, Praetor," he said, as he settled in. "You'll be ready to serve with the eagles in no time."

"Whatever the noble Senate decides," I said evasively. "How goes recruiting?"

He made a sour face. "Oh, my veterans have flocked to the standards handsomely, but the youth of Italy are not what they were in my younger days. I've gone through all the cities and the country markets calling for volunteers, and I get a handful at a time, a dozen here, a dozen there. There was a time when I could raise ten legions from this area alone, stout young farm lads eager for a good war. I'd have to turn most of them away, there was never enough equipment to arm all the volunteers."

"Perhaps they don't smell much loot to be had in a civil war," I told him, "and there aren't that many farm lads left these days. The latifundia are worked by slaves, not peasants, and southern Italy is covered with latifundia these days."

"All the same, I should have more volunteers than I've been getting." He shook his head in disgust. "Have you managed to find out who put an arrow through you?"

Now it was my turn to shake my head. "If anybody knows, nobody is saying."

"It might have just been some local hothead, a Samnite out hunting who saw a chance to kill a Roman praetor and get away with it. There's still a lot of bitterness left over from the Social War in these parts."

"Somehow I don't think so. I've made myself very unpopular with some people in this district. They want to put an end to my investigation and the easiest way to do that is to put an end to me."

"Maybe you had better give it up, just pack up and move your court to Liguria or somewhere."

Instantly, I was suspicious. "Just a few days ago you wanted me to find the murderers, and quickly."

"A few days ago nobody was trying to murder you. Whatever this business is about, it's not worth the life of an important Roman, especially one I may need soon."

So he assumed that, because my family now supported him, I would as well. I thought it best not to disabuse him of the notion just yet.

"Actually, I'd been thinking of Sicily."

"Fine place," he commended. "Good climate, quiet natives. It's already been thoroughly looted, of course, but you could do far worse. I recommend it."

We talked of inconsequentialities for a while, then I dried off and returned to the villa. The next day I awoke stiff and sore, but I made myself take the same long trek back to the palaestra, and did the same on the days following. In an amazingly short time, I was running without breathing hard, hurling the javelin right on target, and even striking Hermes almost as many times as he struck me when we sparred with wooden swords. Before I knew it, I was very nearly in top shape and my wound scarcely pained me any more. Julia seemed pleased.

"I haven't seen you this tan and fit in years," she said. "Cutting back the wine has cleared up your eyes marvelously."

"I hadn't realized how sloppy I was getting," I admitted. Sometimes it was a good idea to admit that Julia had been right about something. "Almost being killed is a literally sobering experience."

Being wounded had one benefit: It gave me an excuse to stay in Campania longer than I should have. There came a day when Baiae celebrated an annual festival dedicated to one of the local gods, an equivalent of Bacchus whose celebrations were even wilder than those of the Roman god. This being shared some of the characteristics of Dionysus and I was eager to see what his adherents got up to. So I gave my lictors the day off, and Julia and I, along with numerous members of our entourage, set off for the city.

The road was crowded, with everyone from the countryside and nearby towns making for Baiae. Many of them were already decked out in wreaths of grape leaves and some carried *thyrsi*: wands tipped with pinecones. It was late morning when we got to Baiae, and the town was already rollicking. All its statues were draped with huge flower wreaths and more such wreaths hung from all the temples and public buildings. There were places where we walked through flower petals ankle-deep. Children ran about smashing eggs on people's heads. The eggshells were filled with perfume and the air smelled sweetly, not just from the perfume but from the incense that burned on all the city's altars. Sounds of pipe and tambourine and *sistrum* came from every part of town, and everywhere we heard the voices of people singing.

It was one of those days when almost all of the rules were suspended. Slave and free mingled on terms of equality, as at Saturnalia. Men and women partnered promiscuously, without regard to who was married to whom. There were women with their hair let down wearing only wreaths and loosely draped leopard pelts, waving their *thyrsi* or playing double flutes and dancing to their own wild music. Many people wore masks, and mask vendors were everywhere, doing a brisk business.

"No masks," Julia warned me sternly. "No fooling around with women, and no wine."

"Then what am I here for?"

"To show that the Roman praetor honors the local gods and customs. You can do that without acting like a purple-rumped baboon."

"Spoilsport."

So we made our way through the throng, leisurely and with impressive gravitas. There were tumblers and mountebanks of all sorts, fire-eaters I had last seen at Sabinilla's party, dancers, and musicians. There were many stages set up, where actors performed absurd and often obscene farces.

Of course I was quite aware that if someone wanted to kill me, this was the perfect place for it. Some masked assassin could easily step up to me, slip a dagger between my ribs, and be off into the crowd safely. However, I was wearing my armor and Hermes stayed close behind me, his hand always on his sword hilt, his eyes constantly scanning the multitude.

"Way for the praetor!" someone shouted. I thought they meant me, but then there came a roar of laughter from the crowd. Julia and I made our way toward the noise and we saw the crowd part and a procession of dwarfs approached, marching with exaggerated self-importance. First came six "lictors" who, instead of fasces, carried sponge-tipped sticks, of the sort used in public latrines. Behind them strutted the "praetor," a potbellied dwarf swathed in a purple-bordered toga and wearing a mask that was an unmistakable caricature of my own face, my long, Metellan nose drawn out to an absurd length. Just in case anyone was unsure who was being mocked, he had an oversized arrow protruding from his chest.

"Now, dear," Julia said, "hold your temper. It's all in fun."

"Of course," I said. "Have you noticed who's behind him?" The praetor was followed by a dwarf woman dressed in patrician white, her hair almost obscured by a huge, gilt laurel wreath, her mask bearing Julia's features, twisted into an expression of utter shrewishness.

"This is intolerable!" Julia hissed.

"Way for the proconsul!" shouted the same voice. Now the crowd parted and another procession came through. This time there were twelve dwarfish, obscenely equipped "lictors," preceding yet another dwarf, this one wearing a helmet and armor that almost reached his ankles. At his side hung a sword at least five feet long, its scabbard dragging along the ground behind him.

As the two processions met, the praetor's lictors lowered their latrine wipes, just as real lictors lower their fasces when they meet those of a superior magistrate.

"Hail all-powerful, wonderful, godlike General Gnaeus Pompeius Magnus!" shouted the "praetor."

"Greetings, Praetor Peregrinus Metellus, pursuer of evildoers, smiter of the wicked, target practice for archers, friend of the winesellers, and enemy of sobriety."

"And to you, glorious Pompey," cried the "praetor," "before whom recruits now flee as once your enemies did."

They went on in this vein for some time, bestowing fulsome compliments that were actually insults. At times it was hard to hear their act, so loud was the crowd's laughter. Seeing Pompey thus mocked took a bit of the sting out of being on the receiving end of the ridicule. Obviously, on this day, the people had license to lampoon anyone.

Throughout the day we saw more such ridiculous acts, featuring prominent locals, Caesar himself, and even a whole "Senate" made up of dwarfs, albinos, giants, and malformed persons of all sorts, debating all kinds of absurd issues such as war with India, economizing on the navy by building ships without nails, flying to the moon, and so forth. Every debate ended with the "Senate" awarding itself more lands, more money, or more power. This last was probably closer to the truth than most people there imagined.

We watched a troupe of Spanish dancers perform the famously salacious dances of that land, and attended a comedy by Aristophanes that was positively decorous compared with everything else that was going on. As evening drew on, the revelry only increased in its frantic pace, and Julia decreed that we must leave before the temptation to join in got the better of me. Reluctantly I agreed, and we made our way to the city gate, often having to step over unconscious and even unclothed bodies. Someday, I vowed, I'd contrive a way to come down to this festival without Julia.

"You've skipped a day at the gymnasium," Hermes reminded me cheerfully as we began our journey homeward. "Tomorrow you'll have to work twice as hard."

"Thank you for reminding me," I told him.

Back at the villa, Julia said: "We have to make some decisions. As much as I love this place, we can't stay here much longer. You've recovered from your wound and soon you'll have to take your court somewhere, whether Sicily or somewhere else."

"I know I can't dawdle much longer," I said, "but I hate to leave without catching whoever killed the priests and the girl at the temple, and, incidentally, the one who shot me with an arrow."

"It's awful to contemplate, but people get away with terrible crimes all the time. You may just have to admit that you've lost this one, swallow your pride, and go."

"If I do that, you know what my political enemies back in Rome will say. They'll say Metellus ran because he was frightened. That sort of thing can damage a political career."

"They'll lie about you anyway, you know that. Let them say what they want."

"Still," I groused, "they're going to make the most of it. Shot from ambush by an archer! It's disgraceful. Even Achilles suffered loss of honor when he was killed by an arrow shot by a coward."

"Are you serious? Does that actually bother you? It's too juvenile even for you!"

"I know. I just said it to annoy you. I'll give it a few more days. If I haven't found them in another four or five days, we're off to Sicily. I'll go ahead and send letters to the major towns and tell them I'll be holding court in Sicily soon."

This seemed to mollify Julia. Truthfully, I was not so certain. To me it seemed that the contending factions of the day were closing in on me like a great pair of blacksmith's tongs. I had not the luxury of remaining neutral. They would force me to choose sides in spite of myself. It was my great misfortune that the Republic came to such a pass just in the year when I was a praetor, wielding imperium and therefore a man to court, or to kill, as the case might be. Before, I had not been sufficiently important to merit the attention of the great men of the day. Should I survive my year, I might be inconsequential again. It would be some time before I should be given my propraetorian province to govern.

Perhaps I was deceiving myself. My family was one of the great ones, and I had at last achieved a standing and dignity that made me a power in that family. That made it difficult to maintain a pose of neutrality.

Still, one thing kept me focused on this corner of Campania, shutting out the distractions of a world about to plunge into war and chaos. I had to find out who had committed all these seemingly meaningless murders. It was just my nature.

At the end of the evening I went to bed, exhausted. When I woke in the morning, I thought I had the key to solving the riddle.

10

I AWOKE KNOWING THAT SOMETHING HAD come to me in the night. I know that I dream almost every night, but I rarely remember the dreams. They seem clear when I wake, but if I try to remember them in detail, they fade before me like a ground mist clearing in the morning sun. A few especially vivid ones stay in my mind, particularly those that seem to be sent by the gods. This one was not like that, but it was nonetheless compelling. Something, some voice or some sort of silent compulsion, was telling me that I had missed something, that there was a glaring factor that I had ignored or had not followed up on.

There is a certain dream that I have repeatedly, and sometimes remember. It has a number of variations. It always involves my trying to get somewhere, or trying to find someone, and always being frustrated. I recall one dream in which I wanted to go to the second floor of the Tabularium in Rome to look up something. I would climb the usual outside stair, but in some fashion it would not take me to the second floor, but instead I found myself on the third. I then took the internal stairway, but it bypassed the second floor and deposited me on the ground floor again. I stepped outside the building and I could see the second floor, but somehow I just could not get there.

Likewise, in another variation of the same dream, I sometimes found myself in the Forum, seeking some person I knew to be there, but always being frustrated in my goal. Some petitioner would always demand my attention just as I was about to find the person I sought. Or a procession of Vestals would come between me and my goal.

These are commonplace dreams, like the one in which you are a schoolboy again and the master has scheduled an examination in Greek, or Homer's poetry or the like, and you have not studied or prepared in any way and are in a panic. Everyone has these dreams, and they have nothing to do with the gods but are only a reflection of your own inner concerns. Such was my dream that night.

It had no coherent narrative or progression. It was just a repeated series of scenes in which I was in the tunnel of the Oracle, walking about tapping on the walls, trying to find hinges or hidden trapdoors or anything else that would help me solve the murder of Eugaeon and the others. In this dream, Hermes and the other men were not with me. I wandered alone in my bafflement.

In the dream, from time to time I would look up and see those vent slots. They loomed much larger that they had in real life. Somehow, they were trying to tell me something. In some fashion, they seemed to be important, even crucial. I heard sounds coming from them, not words but vague, inchoate sounds, like those I had heard on my first venture down the tunnel, when certain sounds had seemed to form words, if I could only hear them clearly enough.

In time I awoke and I knew where I should be looking. Julia noted my altered expression as we sat on a terrace outside our bedroom for a breakfast of the inevitable cherries, sliced fruit, bread, and honey.

"You look transformed," she said. "Did a god visit you in the night?"

"I don't believe so. I've had that sort of night vision, and in those cases it was pretty clear which god appeared to me, and what he or she wanted me to do. This was different. It told me something I had been overlooking, but there was no divine person communicating with me. It may merely have been that my own mind, unable to make sense of things in the waking state, sorted them out somehow in the dreamworld."

"What an interesting concept," she said. "And what did this vision tell you?"

"That the vent slots in the ceiling of the tunnel and the shrine are the key to what has been happening here."

"In what fashion?" she asked.

"That I don't know, but I intend to look into it." I sent for Hermes. He appeared within moments.

"Hermes, go fetch that master stonemason—what's his name?"

"Ansidius Perna."

"That's the one. Go find him and bring him to me at once."

"What is this about?" he asked.

"Why should I explain myself to you?" I demanded. "Go do as I bid you."

"Well," Julia said, "aren't we grand this morning. Why don't you tell him why you want to question the man?"

"Are you now taking sides against me with my freedman?" I demanded.

"Don't be ridiculous," Julia said. "Hermes, he's had some sort of insight concerning the ventilation holes in the tunnel of the Oracle. You know what he's like in times like this, he's not entirely sane or responsible."

This was the sort of respect I got in my own home. In any case, Hermes left to find the master mason. I chewed on my breakfast and mused. "That air is coming in from somewhere," I said. "But where?" Julia looked at me as if I were insane. Then I compounded her doubts. "So if air is coming in, what else might be?"

"What else *could* come through tiny little slits in the rock?" she demanded.

"Sounds," I told her. "Voices."

"But," she pounced, triumphantly, "you said that you found none of those vent slits in the chamber of the Oracle."

"They weren't needed there, if my thoughts are on track," I said. "I'm pretty sure now what they were used for, I just need to know where they came from."

By late morning, Hermes was back with Perna. "What does the praetor wish of me?" he asked.

"You will accompany me back to the tunnel of the Oracle." I said. "There are some questions about its construction that I wish you to clear up for me." I said these things in the tones of a Roman magistrate, tones leaving no scope for protest or debate, tones that allowed for nothing save obedience.

He knuckled his forehead. "As the praetor wishes."

A while later we were on our way to the temple complex. Besides Perna, Hermes and a dozen or so of my men rode with us, together with my lictors.

"What's this about, Praetor?" Perna asked.

"I want to know everything you can tell me about the ventilation system that provides air to the tunnel."

"Oh. I see." Of course he comprehended nothing, but knew better than to question me in my present mood.

We found the temple complex doing a fine business. The impromptu fair had dispersed, but there were plenty of petitioners seeking the advice of the Oracle. Iola emerged from the tunnel with her latest group and looked surprised to see me and alarmed at the size of my entourage.

"What may I do for the praetor?" she asked, approaching my horse. Behind her were a number of her acolytes, looking even more apprehensive.

"Iola, I must go into the tunnel again. There are some things I did not look into last time."

"Sir, we have many people who need the counsel of Hecate." She gestured toward the small crowd resting beneath the shade of the trees.

"They can come back another time. This is official business. It is business in which you should best not interfere."

She bowed. "Even the servants of the gods must yield to the authority of Rome."

I dismounted. "Perna, you and Hermes come along with me." We went to the tunnel and ignited the torches we carried. We didn't have to go far inside. I stopped at the first set of ventilation slots and held my torch up. The flame was drawn slightly toward the first slot.

"Perna, what lies above this tunnel? I know there must be some sort of channel to convey air into or out of the tunnel. What is its nature?"

Perna took a close look at the slot. "Well, there must be a tunnel up there, lying parallel to this one, following it down."

"How large would that tunnel be?"

He shrugged. "At least as large as this one. It couldn't be any smaller, or there'd be no room for whoever carved it."

"Where would that tunnel lead?" I asked him.

"I don't know of any tunnels surfacing anywhere near here. Of course, it might've caved in or got filled with rubble. But there's enough clearance for air to move, or everyone would suffocate down there." He pointed down the dimly lit descending tunnel.

"I need to know exactly where it leads. Perna, this is what I want you to do: I want you to go find some really good stone carvers. Bring them back here, equipped with their tools—and be quiet about it."

"What do you need them for?" he asked.

"I want them to carve a hole up there," I pointed to the slot, "large enough for us to get into the overhead ventilation tunnel. I want to know exactly where it leads, in both directions."

"But, Praetor," he said, "what about the goddess? She'll consider this a desecration, and from what I hear, she's a bad goddess to cross. I don't want to get on the wrong side of Hecate."

"Nonsense," I told him. "Temples get altered and augmented and restored all the time. The gods never take notice of a little chiselwork. We'll tidy it up nicely when we're done and I'll make a handsome gift for the goddess. Now go, and remember, not a word of what we are doing here."

"As you wish, Praetor." He left and we went outside.

"Do you think this is a good idea?" Hermes said.

"It's the only way we'll ever learn what's been going on here, and how it's been carried out. We can expect trouble from Iola and her colleagues. When the time comes, the lictors will have to take care of them. Go pass the word, but quietly. And they're to take note if any of the Oracle staff try to leave. I don't want them warning anybody, so be prepared to stop them."

"I'll see to it," he said.

While we waited for Perna to return, I walked about under the shade of the trees, pondering what I had learned so far and what more I needed to learn. This was where the woman Floria had unknowingly betrayed her master, and, as I thought of this, something else clinked into place like a stone in a well-made wall and I smiled slightly. Things were getting clearer now.

I left the trees and walked around the complex to the Temple of Apollo. There I went into the precincts and examined once again the ingenious trapdoor, recalling that that tunnel had no vent holes. Because nobody expected to be down there long enough to suffocate.

Then I went outside, to the stableyard. There I looked around the place where we had found the body of the slave girl Hypatia. She had come out here in the middle of the night to get away or to meet somebody. It must have been someone she trusted. Who? And why was she killed? She was pregnant. Was that significant? Perhaps she had a lover who might find himself embarrassed by her condition and had killed her to eliminate the problem. It would be a sordid sort of killing, but such were quite common, and it would have no bearing on the case. I had tinglings of imminent revelation, but nothing definite. I felt sure that her death was tied in somehow. I just had to put together the sequence of events that had led her out to this stableyard that night, and to her death.

My men followed at a discreet distance while I rambled about. Nobody had forgotten the hidden archer, least of all me. I was faintly amused by this. Hermes asked me why I was chuckling.

"Well," I said, "it just occurred to me that this would be a fitting place for whoever tried to kill me to have another go at it. After all, this temple is dedicated to Apollo the Archer, patron of bowmen. The god might help out and secure a fatal shot this time."

"Don't talk like that," Hermes said. "Remember what Julia said the last time you talked like this, and you were almost killed immediately after."

"You listen to Julia too much. She puts too much faith in the fates and godly interaction in mortal doings. You'll find that human beings will give you no end of trouble, with no involvement of the immortals whatever. The gods are just distractions when working out what has gone on here."

"If you say so," Hermes said dubiously. Despite being around me for so many years, he was born a slave, and a Roman slave at that. Such persons are usually inclined to superstition and to see supernatural forces at work everywhere. Especially if they are passionately fond of gambling, as Hermes was.

My podium still stood from the last time I had held court here, though my curule chair had of course gone with me on my travels. We sat on the podium and lunched on provisions we had brought with us, and by early afternoon Perna was back with four men who had tool bags slung from their shoulders. They wore workingmen's tunics, the sort that leaves one shoulder bare, and their hair was gray with stone dust. When Iola saw the chisels and mallets protruding from the men's bags, her eyes almost popped from their sockets. She came rushing over to me, black robes flapping.

"Praetor! What do you intend? You cannot allow the sanctuary of the Oracle to be harmed!"

"There will be no great harm done," I assured her. "The sanctuary of the Oracle will not be touched, nor the shrine and statue of Hecate. We are just going to make a small hole up here near the entrance. We'll plug it up again when we are done, if you like. You can even smear soot over it to hide any marks left behind." I was watching her, and when I mentioned soot she knew I was talking about the ceiling. From alarm and anger her expression turned to one of stark fear.

"I forbid it!" she shouted like a Tribune of the Plebs blocking legislation. "You cannot lay profane hands on the sanctuary! Hecate will curse you! She will send her black bitches to tear you to pieces! She will—"

"Be silent!" I barked. I didn't want the workmen to refuse to do my bidding for fear of divine retribution. I snapped my fingers and my lictors quietly surrounded Iola and her little knot of acolytes. "Confine these people to their quarters until I tell you to loose them. If any tries to get away, they are to be killed."

"You cannot do this, Praetor!" Iola screamed. "You have no authority!" One of the lictors stifled her protests by placing a broad hand over her mouth.

"I have all the authority I need. As I've told you before, if you have serious objections, you may go to Rome and take them up with the Senate."

They were marched away while the small crowd of petitioners and a few locals gaped. I addressed them. "You might as well go to your homes. The Oracle of the Dead is closed until I or the Senate decree that it is to be reopened. I rather fancy that that will be a very long time indeed." With looks of great disappointment they gathered up their possessions and left.

"Let's go," I said to Perna and his workmen. We entered the tunnel once more, and when we stopped at the first vent, Perna gave the men their instructions, which I could not follow very well because he spoke in the specialized language of stonecutters, using terms and abbreviations with which I was unfamiliar. He scratched a square on the ceiling with the corner of a chisel, and I had to admire the precision with which he drew, freehand and using a crude tool never intended for the task. I could not have drawn such a perfect square using a scribe and a compass to keep the corners true.

The cutters set about their work, two of them beginning at opposite corners of the square. The other two stood by. Perna explained that they would spell one another at intervals. There was not room for all four to work at once, and in any case when a man must work with his arms above his head, his hands and arms quickly grow numb and he has to lower them to get the feeling back before he can resume work.

Soon the air was full of stone dust and the sound of the mallets and chisels in the confined space became overpowering, though the workmen didn't seem to notice. I left them to it and went in search of breathable air.

"What do we do when they finish?" Hermes wanted to know.

"We go into the ventilation tunnel and see where it leads," I told him.

"I was afraid you'd say that," he said with a sour face. "More tunnel-crawling. I never want to see another tunnel as long as I live. There's something unnatural about descending into the underworld before you're dead."

"Well, this is good practice, since we all have to make that journey eventually."

"Cheerful thought."

In time I went back to check the work. The carvers were making progress, but they were carving, with great precision, an absolutely square hole, its sides as true and smooth as the altar of a temple.

"It doesn't have to be precise," I reproved them. "Just carve a hole up there I can get through. I don't care how ragged the hole is. This isn't for display." The carvers looked at me as if I were speaking Etruscan. Perna took me back to the entrance and explained.

"Sir, these men have been trained in fine stonework since childhood. They couldn't do sloppy work if you threatened them with torture. Besides, this way it will be easier to tidy up afterward; just cut a block exactly the size of that hole and you'll hardly be able to tell there was any carving done at all. They don't want to anger the goddess more than they absolutely have to."

I sighed, knowing when I was beaten. "Very well. Let me know when you have a hole I can get through."

"Right you are, Praetor," he said cheerfully.

I told Hermes about the problem and he, predictably, thought it was funny. "You'd have done better to get some convicts with sledge-hammers."

"I'll know better next time," I said, as if there would be a next time for this sort of work.

From time to time a workman would emerge with a bag of stone chips which he carried off to dispose of somewhere. These were truly men who believed in keeping their worksite tidy. At last, in late afternoon, Perna emerged from the mouth of the tunnel. "It's ready, Praetor."

Hermes and I went inside to view the work. We looked up an absolutely true, square, smooth-sided hole that went through about two feet of solid stone. Despite their fussiness, the carvers had cut stone fast. They had even swept the floor clean and the draft through the hole had sucked the rock dust out of the air. We were ready to begin our exploration. I sent the workmen and Perna out, but bade them stand by for further instructions. I didn't really expect to need any more stonework done. I just didn't want them heading for the taverns and blabbing about what we'd been up to here.

"This won't take many of us," I told Hermes. "Get two of the men and plenty of torches. I've no idea how far we'll have to travel and I don't want to do any of it in the dark."

Hermes went out and was back minutes later with two of the men, the ones he regarded as his best sparring partners. Both wore swords and one carried a bundle of torches. Hermes and the other man boosted the third up through the hole in the ceiling. He reached down and they passed him a torch. Hermes went next, then, with the two above pulling and the remaining man boosting, they hauled me into the tunnel overhead. Then the two reached down and hauled the other man up.

I held up a torch and had a look around. The tunnel was nearly identical to the one below. The chisel marks on the walls looked the same. It was probably carved out simultaneously with the main tunnel. This one hadn't seen much traffic over the centuries and its ceiling hadn't collected as much soot. But this one didn't follow the other all the way to the entrance. Instead, it ended right at the first vent slots. The only way to go was downward.

"All right," I said. "Let's go."

We followed the tunnel, examining everything as we had before. This time, naturally, the slots were in the floor instead of in the ceiling. The niches in the walls were not neatly carved in this tunnel, just rough alcoves for holding lamps. Undoubtedly, these had been for the benefit of the miners, since this tunnel was probably not intended to be used once it was finished. I counted the slots we passed, and when I came to one I thought was significant, I stopped and got down to peer through it.

"What's this one?" Hermes wanted to know.

"This should be the one that ventilates Hecate's shrine," I said. I couldn't see much through a slot carved through two feet of rock, but there was more light coming through it than through the others. I thought I could make out Hecate's altar below.

I stood up and raised my torch, taking a look around. This area was different from that we had come through. There was a pad like a thin mattress on the floor, and there were the remains of meals here and there; bread crusts, old cheese rinds, fruit pits, and so forth. There were a couple of pitchers for wine or oil. Someone had been accustomed to spend the better part of a day here. I bent and picked up a pit.

"Cherry," I announced. "Poor people don't yet have cherry trees in their orchards. This came from somewhere prosperous."

"Anyone can raid an orchard," Hermes said.

"So they can," I mused. "Someone has been visiting this spot for some time. They can lie on that pad, probably with one ear to the slot. When they hear their cue, they can utter the agreed-upon prophecy."

"Wait, that can't be right," Hermes said. "This is Hecate's shrine and altar. The Oracle speaks from the lower chamber, where the Sty— where that river goes through it."

"That's the way we got our Oracle," I agreed. "Still, something occurred to me. It was what the woman Floria said: that her master was given his prophecy *in the shrine of Hecate.* If at the time I thought about it at all, I thought it was a slip of the tongue, that she meant the chamber of the Oracle. But she had meant exactly what she said. You recall that she said he came back a second day. This is where the ones they intend to fleece get the Oracle that sends them to their death."

"So the Oracle of the Dead has more than one meaning," Hermes noted.

"Let's see where this leads," I said. We began walking. From this point the niches had lamps in them, most of them holding fresh oil. We lit some of these so we would have light on our way back, should we run out of torches.

The floor sloped up after the chamber of the shrine, and we climbed for a while. Then it leveled out. At intervals we found holes in the ceiling, these ones round and about six inches across, but these were either choked with rubble or else they had been deliberately covered over. Doubtless they had been intended to supply air to the miners when the tunnel was being driven.

"How far have we come?" Hermes asked after a while.

"About a mile as I figure it," I said.

"It seems like more than that," Hermes said, "but I suppose distances are deceptive underground."

"There's light ahead," I said.

"It's not much light if that's the exit," Hermes noted.

Indeed, the light that came through what I could now see was a doorway was rather dim. Surely we hadn't been underground long enough for night to overtake us. Then we were out of the tunnel and looking upward.

Overhead, the light of late afternoon streamed down through a round, stone-rimmed orifice about twenty feet overhead. We were at the bottom of a well.

"Now," I said, "where have we seen stonework like that?"

"The *mundus* on Porcia's property?" Hermes said.

"I don't know of any other within a mile of the temple," I said. "Then again, there's a lot I don't know about this district." I looked around on the ground. We were walking on a litter of leaf mold several inches deep. I wondered how long it would take to build up this mass from the leaves that drifted through the opening over the years and centuries. There was a path trampled through it that led from one side to the entrance of the tunnel.

"That's where they lower their ladder," I said, pointing to the end of the path opposite the tunnel. I looked around some more and spotted a rock lying in the path. It was about the size of my fist, black with streaks of green. "Unless I'm much mistaken, this is the stone I tossed in a few days ago."

"Then it's her *mundus* all right," Hermes said. "So it was a real *mundus,* of sorts, not a well. It leads to the underworld, though it takes a detour. So, do you think Porcia is involved?"

"I'll need more evidence before I can level an accusation," I said. "It's on her property, but she claims she never comes here and it would be hard to prove otherwise. She has a crowd of slaves and tenant farmers, and any of them might come here. The property isn't fenced, and with all the wildland she keeps, they could get here without being seen. We know that someone left offerings at that shrine to the *genius loci*. No. I can't bring charges against a very rich woman of this district on this alone. We'll need more."

"Praetor," said one of the men, "what are these?" He had been on one knee sifting through the leaf mold and now he showed me what he had found: a handful of miniature arrows. We looked around and found many more, and plainly some of them had been down there for centuries. We found many more points than complete arrows, their shafts and fletching having rotted away over the centuries. Some of these were bronze and we found a few tiny points made of finely flaked flint or obsidian. Once again, I felt the tremendous age of the place.

"Some of these are from before iron came to Italy," I said.

"When would that be?" Hermes asked.

"A thousand years ago, at least. Bronze was used for everything before that, which is why Homer's heroes fight with weapons of bronze. But this *mundus*, like the tunnel, couldn't have been carved without bronze tools. These stone points must date from a time when bronze was still too valuable to use for arrowheads, which are often lost. People still made arrowheads out of stone." I took a certain pride in that bit of deduction.

"Maybe Porcia was right," Hermes said. "You remember she said that the arrows might have been left by some hunter asking for luck in the hunt. Maybe in the old days that was what offers of arrows meant."

"Either that or there has been a huge amount of vengeance-seeking in these parts," I said. Just then, one more little piece clicked into place. It still wasn't enough, though.

"I wish we had a ladder," Hermes said. "Then we could climb out and go back by way of the road. It would spare us another tunnel trip and the people we left back at the temple wouldn't know what to think."

"Unfortunately," I said, "we didn't think to bring a ladder. So let's go back. We should be there well before nightfall."

So back we went. We extinguished the burning lamps as we passed them. We passed the litter where someone had lain speaking lying prophecies to doomed men. We came to the hole carved in the floor and lowered ourselves through it. We found ourselves out in the open air again just as evening was coming on. Perna and the workmen were sitting on the ground patiently.

"I'm afraid you men can't go home tonight," I told them. "I can't have anyone talking about what has been going on here today. There are good quarters here in the temple complex. Make yourselves comfortable. I will pay you handsomely for your time."

"It's all the same to me and these men, Praetor," Perna said. "As long as we get paid."

"It will be late by the time we get back to the villa," Hermes said.

"I'm not going back," I told him. "You are going back. Tell Julia to join me here tomorrow, and bring my curule chair. Tomorrow, I also want you to bring several people: the woman Floria, for one. You remember how I told you to find her home?"

"I'll find her," he said.

"Find her and bring her here, under heavy guard. I don't want her killed like poor Hypatia. Take as many men as you think you'll need, and send me the historian, Cordus."

"Done. Anyone else?"

"Not just yet. I will have you round up quite a few people when I settle things here."

He grinned. "We're getting down to serious business now, aren't we?"

I nodded. "Now it gets very serious indeed."

11

JULIA ARRIVED LATE THE NEXT MORN-
ing. With her was Antonia, who had been off visiting some friends in
Capua. Circe, it seemed, had returned to Rome. I had scarcely noticed
their absence, so preoccupied had I been. With them were most of the
entourage who had accompanied me south. Apparently Julia had decided that I was a praetor again, so she would see that I was properly attended.

"What has caused this sudden new enthusiasm?" she wanted to
know.

"Come and let's take a walk beneath these trees," I said. "This is
not for everybody's ears just yet." Antonia glared at being left out, but
of all the women in the world I wanted to confide in, the very last would
have been Antonia. She could no more keep a secret or resist gossiping
than she could have sprouted wings and flown to the moon.

As we walked in the grove, I told Julia of what I had found, and of my suspicions, and how I intended to wrap things up so we could pack up for Sicily.

"Infamous!" she said. "Defrauding people with a false oracle, then robbing and murdering them!" She paused. "But they wouldn't be able to do it very often, would they? How often would merchants going abroad carrying a lot of money have stopped by here?"

"More often than you'd think," I said. "People about to travel abroad often visit oracles and seek the help of the gods. We don't know how many confederates they had overseas, or whether they had men follow the victims and then choose a safe place out of Italy to kill them and dispose of their bodies. I also suspect that this was only one aspect of their depredations."

"What else do you think they've been up to?"

"Campania, with all its attractions, its Sibyl of Cumae and so forth, is always full of transients. The overseas killing must have been unwieldy and difficult to set up. I suspect that it was done only when local people were to be robbed. If they were killed here, they would be missed immediately and suspicion would naturally fall on people living in the district. It wouldn't be long before someone noticed that the last place they were seen was here at Hecate's Oracle. No, murder of locals could only be risked when they were away from Campania, preferably out of Italy altogether.

"But a great many people from other parts of Italy and from foreign lands come here to consult with the Oracle. They are far from home, they wouldn't be missed for a long time; without friends or relatives here, who would notice that the last place they were seen alive was here?"

She thought about this for a while. "But how would the killers know that these people had no local connections who might show up asking embarrassing questions?"

"They had slaves walking among the people as they waited to consult with the Oracle. People would let crucial information slip without noticing it. I'm not saying they did it every day. For one thing, the conditions would have to be perfect. It would be impossible if many people were present, but we know that sometimes there might only be one or two people here on a given day. When conditions were perfect, they might be given a false prophecy like Floria's master, or they might just be killed down there in the chamber of the Oracle. Knocked on the head or strangled, I would imagine. Blood is hard to scrub from coarse stone."

"But how would they dispose of the bodies?" Julia wondered. "That was the great convenience of killing a victim overseas. Or *at sea*. No corpse to explain away."

"Easily," I said. "A few days ago I almost got disposed of down there by accident."

"The river? What a hideous way to die, your body swept down beneath the earth without the proper rites." She shuddered at the horror of it.

"They were sent down—clothes, possessions, the lot. In an instant, there was nothing to connect their disappearance with the priests and priestesses of Hecate. Only sometimes they were not thorough enough. In our search we found a stylus, a sandal, a bone hairpin, and a necklace of Egyptian beads. They were lost when the bodies of victims were thrust under the water to be swept away by the current."

"How long has this been going on?" Julia asked. "The Oracle has been here for centuries."

"Not for that long, I think. I suspect that the operation has been running only in recent years. There was scarcely any soot on the ceiling of the ventilation tunnel."

"Very observant. But why, and how, were the priests of Apollo murdered?"

"That is the most difficult question, and I think that if we can put together just a few more facts, we'll have the answer to that, too, and we'll bag the lot of them. But I can't let anyone outside know how close we are to doing it. That would mean fleeings and undoubtedly more murder attempts. I personally don't want to be the recipient of a successful murder attempt. The bungled one was bad enough."

"How many people do you think are involved?"

"The entire staff of the Oracle, for certain. There must be at least a few outside partners, and maybe many. Although it would make sense to keep the outsiders to a minimum. Everybody knows that the more people involved in a crime, the greater the likelihood of being found out."

We went back out to the temple area and everyone had questions which I refused to answer. About noon, the historian Cordus arrived. "Has the praetor a task for me?" he asked, smiling. These were probably the happiest days of his life, employing his lonely work at the behest of the powerful. He'd be dining out on this story for years to come.

"Indeed I have, Cordus my friend." I took him by the arm and led him to a little table where, as before, I had laid out a generous repast. "Here, sit, refresh yourself. It's very good of you to come at such short notice." It never hurts to flatter the humble. They get it so seldom. "It's very important work indeed. But please, have something first."

For the sake of good manners he ate a little and drank some wine, but curiosity got the better of his appetite. "Please, Praetor, what can I do for you?"

"First," I said, "there is the matter of the slave girl, Hypatia."

"Is she the one that was murdered?"

"Precisely. She said that she was sold to the temple by an itinerant slave trader named Aulus Plantius. I am informed that he is a dealer in high-quality slaves and that he appears here once or twice a year. This would have been about three months ago. Can you find me a record of that sale?"

"I am sure that I can, providing all the legal forms were followed in the sale."

I sighed. "Legality is about the last thing I expect to encounter in this Gordian knot of a case, but see what you can turn up."

"I am at your service. Surely this is not all?"

"By no means. Would any records be kept around here concerning the priesthood of the Oracle? By this I mean names, the dates when each took office and left it, that sort of thing?"

"Naturally there should be records here at the sanctuary of Hecate. Have you looked for them?"

"I have. It seems there are no such records on the premises and the priesthood are not inclined to cooperate with me."

"I see. If there are such records to be found, I will locate them."

"Very good," I commended. "If you can do these things for me, and do them as quickly as possible, I will be forever in your debt."

"I shall do it at once, Praetor," he said.

"No, stay here and finish your lunch. It will be two or three days before I am ready to make my presentation. Will that be sufficient time?"

"A day should be sufficient, Praetor. The matter of the slave's sale should take little time. As for the priests, if such records are to be found at all, I should be able to turn them up quickly."

"Excellent." It was good to know that I could delegate a task to someone who knew his business and could be trusted to carry it out quickly and efficiently. I had often thought that it would be a good thing if the state could employ a permanent staff of such people to be at the disposal of the magistrates. Slaves could not be trusted to do the work. It would have to be done by free men, but who would pay them?

Shortly after the historian departed, Hermes rode in with the woman Floria, under heavy guard. She looked numbed with fright, not an uncommon thing in a powerless person who finds herself suddenly in the grip of the Roman legal system.

"I tried to tell her nothing is going to happen to her," Hermes said, "but she wouldn't believe me."

"Come down, Floria," I said. "You have nothing to fear. The guards are for your own protection. I just want you to repeat to a court what you told me."

"I just have to talk?" she said in a weak voice.

"That is all. You're free now, you can't be tortured."

"Of course she can't be tortured!" Julia said, pushing me aside. "Come, my dear, you're safe here. You will stay in our own quarters. Let me help you dismount." Julia and one of her girls helped the woman down, and already she looked vastly relieved. Julia had that way with people. She could put a man about to be crucified at ease.

So that was two tasks accomplished. I dictated a few letters to some people: to Belasus in Pompeii, asking him to come to my court and bring the letters and evidence we had found in the house of Elagabal the fence; and to Pompey, asking him to attend. I even gritted my teeth and sent one to Cato. Much as I disliked him, he had that horrible honesty. I was going to have to do things that might exceed my authority as *praetor peregrinus*, and I wanted someone I could trust to testify that I had done these things for good reasons, not because I was corrupt or tyrannical. My enemies in Rome would lying in wait for me as soon as I should step down from office and would charge me for what I did here. Cato was not afraid of them or of anybody else, and he would not lie about what he had witnessed.

When I had dispatched my messengers to their various destinations, I sat back, at loose ends for a little while. Things had been so hectic lately that this felt good. Then I got up and wandered out into the temple enclosure and thought, What were you up to, Eugaeon? Why were you murdered, along with your fellow priests? Were you just the last victims of this gang of murderers, or were you one of them?

These gloomy but important thoughts occupied me for a while, while I enjoyed my solitude. Not that I was perfectly alone. Several of my men hung off at a discreet distance, armed and bearing shields. Then there came a voice from behind me.

"Praetor, why aren't you with your suite? You shouldn't be wandering about alone out here in the dark." I turned to see that it was Sabinilla.

"Why, what brings you here? I thought you'd be plotting your next party, the one that's going to top even the one you gave for us."

"Oh, never fear, I'm putting together another. Word reached me that something has been happening here today and I yield to no one in my mastery of local gossip. I had to come see what was happening. I rejoice to see you are fully recovered from your wound. You *are* fully recovered, aren't you?"

"I am touched by your concern. Yes, I am as good as new, strength restored; the wound no longer even pains me." This was not quite true but it was beneath my dignity as a praetor to admit to pain from minor causes.

We walked back toward the terraces of the temple, where torches were ablaze. I saw that her wig was blue this time. Odd-colored wigs were just coming into fashion, and I didn't doubt she had one for every day of the year.

She stopped and turned to me. "Praetor, I—"

In that instant I heard a sound I had become all too familiar with. It was the whiz of an arrow, like the sound of a fast-moving insect. It went right past my ear and suddenly Sabinilla was standing there with an astonished expression, trying to say something, but nothing came from her mouth but a great gush of blood.

I wasted not an instant gaping. I hit the ground rolling, and the second arrow whizzed through the air where I had been standing and buried itself in Sabinilla, halfway between navel and sternum. It would have gone into my spine if I hadn't dived when I did. She was still upright, now trying to pull out the arrow that had gone through her throat. An arrow will not drop a person instantly to the ground the way a javelin or spear will. They don't have enough force. They pierce organs and cut blood vessels. I kept moving, and Sabinilla finally fell, as if she had just learned that she was dead.

I was shouting without being aware of it. My men were running toward me and I was still rolling, changing speed and direction constantly to keep from being an easy target. I had lost all interest in dignity. I was not going to catch another arrow if I could help it. In moments my men were all around me, shields up. I heard a final arrow glance from a shield, then quiet.

"Bring torches over here!" I yelled at the top of my lungs as I got to my feet. "Bring lots of them! I want you to fan out and find that archer. Bring him to me, alive if possible, but don't let him get away under any circumstances!" I am afraid that I lost my temper. Ordinarily I let little disturb me, but this was just too much. I railed at my men even as they went to search for the assassin.

"What is wrong with you?" I shouted at them. "Is it so difficult to keep a murderer armed with a bow away from here? Do all of my guests have to be killed before you bestir yourselves enough to notice that there is a man with a bow somewhere on the premises?"

Julia came running. "Come away from here now!" she ordered. "You're lit up like a statue at Saturnalia and the bowman is out there in the dark somewhere. Come inside immediately. Hermes has already taken charge of the search."

"But Sabinilla—" I began, gesturing toward the recumbent, bloody figure on the grass.

"She's dead. She'll be just as dead an hour from now. I'll have her body brought in, but first you have to be less of a target. Come along."

The rage went out of me. She was right, of course. We walked back to the temple with four men surrounding me with shields. Once inside, I sent them out to join the hunt. Then I poured myself a large cup of unwatered wine. This night, I felt I didn't need to observe my new regimen. Julia had wooden screens erected before all the windows.

"The assassin missed me with his first shot and hit Sabinilla instead," I told Julia. "I was moving by the time he drew his second arrow. It struck her too. The poor woman. She picked the wrong time to come visiting."

"Unless she was the target. The bowman may have tried to kill both of you with two arrows."

"Eh? Why?" The shock of the events had made me slow.

"She came here without sending word ahead and arrived unfashionably late. That woman was nothing if not fashionable. When she got here, she never came to the quarters to find me. She went straight out to where you were foolishly walking about in the dark. Perhaps she wanted to tell you something and the killer wanted to silence her."

"Yes, that could be how it was," I admitted. "I've said before that everyone is a suspect in this business. She may have been involved somehow. When she is brought in, I want her clothing searched. She may have brought something in writing. Who came with her? She wouldn't have come alone and she wouldn't have walked."

"I'll send to find out," Julia said. She went out and began to give orders. When Julia gave orders, they were obeyed quickly. A short while later she came back.

"She came in a litter carried by some of those Gauls of hers. She was accompanied by a bodyguard of her Gallic gladiators as well. The only other member of the party was this man." She snapped her fingers and a gray-haired man came in, carrying a small chest.

"Who are you?" I demanded.

"I am Eteocles, my lady's steward," he said. I vaguely remembered him from the party. "Praetor, is it true that my lady is dead?"

"I am afraid so. She was murdered in an assassination attempt on me." I saw no reason to burden him with my suspicions just yet. He gasped and turned pale. I allowed him to collect himself.

"Eteocles, your lady was traveling light when she came here. Did she usually travel with so few servants?"

"Why, no, sir. Ordinarily she traveled in considerable state, as befitted her wealth and position. Today she was in a great hurry and called for her swiftest team of bearers and a few guards and me."

"Why you?" Julia asked.

"Well, she told me to get this together"—here he raised the box in his hands—"and come with her and not allow it out of my possession. It was all very puzzling and she said nothing all the way here."

"What is it?" I asked.

In answer, he placed it on a table. It seemed so heavy he could barely hold it. Then he threw back the lid. The chest was perhaps a foot on a side and a foot deep. It was packed with gold coins, a considerable fortune.

"Leave us," Julia said peremptorily. The man bowed and backed out of the room. When he was well away, Julia turned to me and said, "What is this?"

I picked up a coin and looked at it. It was a beautifully struck

Alexandrian piece with the profile of Ptolemy Auletes on its front. I tossed it back into the box. "This, my dear, is a bribe. The woman came here to strike a deal with me. She learned that something was happening here and figured out that everything was about to come to light. She decided to get to me before anyone else could and bribe me to keep her out of it somehow."

"She must have had a low opinion of Roman praetors."

"For that much money, most praetors would have accepted gladly. I, however, am incorruptible. She merely got killed for her pains."

One of the servants stuck her head in the door and informed us that Sabinilla's body had been brought in. "Let's have a look at her," I said resignedly.

She had been lain on a table and nothing had yet been done to clean her up. The first arrow had gone through her windpipe and a jugular. In dying, she had lost almost all her blood. It covered the front of her gown as if it had been recently dyed red. The second arrow was no more than a gesture. She was dead within seconds of the first strike. Julia ordered two of her female slaves to search the woman's clothing. Reluctantly, they complied. They found nothing. Julia told them to go wash the blood off their hands and they ran out, gagging.

"I don't think we'll learn anything from her now," Julia said.

"Remove her wig," I ordered one of the slaves.

"Why?" Julia asked. "Do you think she hid something under it."

"No, I just want to know the true color of her hair." Julia snorted. The man lifted the wig which, thankfully, was unbloodied. Her hair was red, a striking shade. I wondered why she did not display it. Then again, red hair is often associated with bad luck, so perhaps she thought it best to hide it.

"She can go back home in the morning in her litter," I said.

Shortly after that, Hermes came in to tell us that the assassin had not been found.

"Somehow I am not surprised," I said. "This killer gets about like a phantom. Just flits from place to place to shoot arrows at me."

"I'll get the huntsmen and their dogs in the morning," Hermes said. "Maybe they can get a scent off the arrows."

"You can try," I said, "but I don't hold out great hopes. Whatever else he may be, this assassin knows what he is doing. I don't doubt he has taken precautions to confuse dogs."

So it transpired. The next day, the huntsmen arrived with their dogs. The animals sniffed the nock-ends of the arrows, where the shooter's scent should have been strongest, then they ran all over the temple compound, yipping happily.

"So much for that, then," I said.

"From now on, until this is settled," Julia said, "you will be indoors well before dark." I gave her no argument.

"Maybe we should just wait," I said. "The thieves are falling out now. They're afraid their confederates will betray them, so they are killing each other off. Soon there may be nothing left for me to do. They'll all be dead."

"Don't count on it," Julia advised.

I went outside, took a look around, and groaned. "They're back!"

Already, the mob was assembling: the vendors, the mountebanks, the vast number of gawkers. More murder. More fun.

"Why do they do this?" I inquired of no one in particular. "Don't they have anything else to do? This is southern Campania! There ought to be plenty of other diversions to occupy the idle." I received no answer from the gods or anyone else. There was no explanation. There is just a basic flaw in human nature that causes people to flock like vultures to a place where ghastly events have occurred. Doubtless they hope something equally ghastly will happen that they can actually witness. This was probably something that escaped when Pandora opened her box.

I sent Sabinilla's body home in her litter. I'd had undertakers come in so she was properly cleaned up and Julia had donated a gown so she wouldn't arrive looking as if the Furies had been at her. Whatever she had done, she was beyond the hand of justice now, and I felt the decencies should be observed. Needless to say, the gawkers lined the road to see the litter pass. I wondered what it was they expected to see. Just another of those inexplicable things, I supposed.

While I awaited the people I had summoned, who would not be likely to arrive before at least the next day, and the reports of those who were digging up evidence, I retired to a terrace that was away from the crowd and allowed me a broad vista. I was in no mood for appreciating the scenery, but it kept any archers from creeping within range. Just to make sure, I had stationed a lookout atop the Temple of Apollo. Young Vespillo was my choice, because he had exceptionally good eyesight.

I did not idle away my time, but began to write down my arguments and list my evidence, not all of which was gathered, but which I expected soon to have in my hands. I wrote out the events as they happened, in sequence. (I have that account by me now and it has been a great aid to my memory. It pays to keep all your old papers.) I organized my oration as I had learned from Cicero, in the fashion of the day, not neglecting the occasional character assassination, snatches of relevant poetry, and so forth. I knew I wouldn't be using all of it, but it helped to keep things orderly in my mind.

Around noon the next day Cordus arrived, and with him was a man of about thirty-five years, wearing a dingy, dark toga, his face unshaven. Accompanied by my guards, I went to greet them. "I believe I have found what you want, Praetor," Cordus said. "This is the distinguished Lucius Pedarius." Apparently "distinguished" was how the locals referred to genuine patricians. From his dress and grooming, it looked as if the family had fallen on truly hard times.

"Pedarius?" I said. "I wondered when some representative of your clan would see fit to show up."

"I do beg your pardon, Praetor. My household has been in mourning for my father." His Latin was impeccable. That explained the dingy toga, beard, and tangled hair. The Pedarius family still took the old-fashioned mourning practices seriously. In Rome, we usually just borrowed an old toga from a freedman, allowed a little stubble to show, and left our hair unbarbered but combed.

"I see. Well, why don't the two of you come join me for lunch."

I sent word to Julia that we had a patrician guest. She wouldn't want to miss this. She arrived with a small crowd of her servant girls, greeted Pedarius and Cordus, and set about arranging an informal lunch, which on this occasion included placing the guards where they would be unobtrusive but effective. Pedarius regarded these precautions with some apprehension, for which I could not blame him. Lunch with the praetor doesn't usually mean a visit to the war zone.

"Then it's true that your life is in danger, Praetor?" he said.

"Everybody is in danger around here," I told him. "I'm rather surprised to see that you are alive. Here, have some of this cured ham. It's excellent."

"Are you serious? Not about the ham, about my being alive. Am I in personal danger?"

"Serious as the gods' displeasure," I told him. "Can you tell me the circumstances of your father's death?"

Julia was annoyed. "Must you broach such a subject when we have just begun eating? Surely after lunch is the time for serious talk."

"Time is what we are running short of," I told her. "My apologies for my rudeness, but these are quite literally matters of life and death. Was there anything suspicious in the circumstances of your father's death, Lucius Pedarius?"

"Well, my father was in his fifty-sixth year, not young by any means, but quite vigorous and healthy. He rode and hunted most days when he was not preoccupied with overseeing our land. About three months ago, he began to complain of pains in his chest and abdomen. Very soon he could no longer ride and took to his bed. The physicians couldn't determine a cause for his decline and prescribed the usual purges, poultices, herbal infusions, and so forth. None of it did any good. His decline continued, slow but steady. This is why he could not call upon you as he wished to, and with his situation so precarious, I could not come in his place. Again, I extend my apologies."

"No need to," I assured him. "When did your father die?"

"Fifteen days ago. He had been getting weaker and thinner for some time, and could only take a little wine or broth. In time he lost consciousness and never regained it. Within one day of lapsing into unconsciousness, he was dead."

"I see. Tell me, did any new slaves join your household just prior to your father's illness?"

"Slaves?" He frowned, thinking. "Well, yes. My father came home with a slave woman just a few days before he fell ill. Why?"

"It's part of a pattern I've worked out," I told him. He looked at me the way people usually do when I say things like that. "Did he say where he bought her?"

"He said that he had acquired her from a neighbor."

"And this neighbor's name?" I asked.

"He never told me. He was not a very communicative man. I know there was a neighbor he visited from time to time, but he never took me with him, and he never mentioned names."

"Did that not seem odd to you?"

He shrugged. "Men often go visiting people they'd rather not talk about. I was too discreet to press the matter."

"And this slave. Was she young and pretty?"

"No, my father never bought slaves for decorative purposes. This was a stout, older woman. She was put to work in the kitchen."

"In the kitchen," I mused. "That is a strategic location. Is she there now?"

"Ah, no, Praetor," he said, his face flushing with embarrassment. "She disappeared a few days ago. I thought she was just another runaway. I hired slave hunters, but they have not turned her up. It never occurred to me to be suspicious. My father was poisoned, wasn't he? And the woman did it."

"I fear that is so. But don't feel that you are alone in being deceived. The person behind this is an expert in these matters." I looked to Cordus. "How is it that you came here with Lucius Pedarius?"

"After I found the slave sale document you wanted, I searched for records of the priesthood of the Hecate cult. I could find nothing in the public records, but it occurred to me that, as hereditary patrons of the Temple of Apollo, the Pediarii might have something. So, I went to call upon them and found a house in mourning, but Lucius Pedarius very kindly let me come in and look at his father's papers."

"I had just been going through them," Lucius said. "My father never took me into his confidence concerning business matters and rarely said anything about the temple, other than to complain about the expense of its restoration."

"Ah, yes," I said. "The temple has undergone some extensive renovations recently. Your family paid for that?"

"It was our hereditary duty as patrons," he said. "Of course our own patron, the great general Pompey," I noted that he said this without irony, "covered part of the expenses. I believe he would gladly have covered it all. Such sums mean nothing to him. But my father was too stiff-necked and proud a patrician to let someone else help out more than was proper."

"That was quite admirable," said Julia, predictably.

"Yes, well, it didn't make him happy about the necessity."

"I don't mean to pry into the finances of your family," I said, "but do you know how your father managed to pay for the restorations?"

He smiled sourly. "You mean since we Pedarii are notoriously penurious despite our patrician status? To be honest, I do not know. I thought that he had sold off some old family treasures that he had hidden somewhere. I began to think differently when I went through his papers after his death."

"When were the restorations undertaken?" I asked him.

"About nine years ago. It seems odd, now," he said.

"Odd how?"

"Because that was when he stopped visiting the temple altogether. You would think he would have taken pride in the task he had paid for. When men do that, they seldom omit to show themselves and accept the honors of the community."

"That is very true," I said. I had paid for such things myself, and I certainly would never have gone to the expense if it hadn't spread my fame and made people remember my name at election time. This is the traditional motivation that causes prominent men to undertake public works. So why did old Pedarius pay up and then avoid the place?

"I am going to want a look at those papers," I said.

"I've brought them, and, as my friend Cordus suspected, among the family records is a tolerably complete listing of the priests of the Oracle of Hecate. Although our association is with the Temple of Apollo, the temple and the Oracle for all practical purposes form a single complex. It seems that in centuries past they were not on a basis of mutual hostility and shared in the patronage."

I sighed. "Yes, much that appears terribly ancient here is of comparatively recent origin. Only the tunnel to the underground river itself, and the recently uncovered ventilation tunnel, are of great antiquity." This was the first Cordus and Pedarius had heard of the ventilation tunnel, but I was not yet ready to make that common knowledge. "I am convinced that this whole business has been about money."

Julia looked uncomfortable. She was ready enough to discuss these sordid matters in private, but she felt it improper to speak of matters as base as money in front of a fellow patrician.

"Now, my friend Cordus," I said. "About that slave sale."

"Oh, yes, of course," said the historian. "There was nothing at all difficult about its location. The town praetor's office keeps records of all such transactions. But there was one thing that threw me off the scent, so to speak, and caused quite a bit of searching. You said that the seller was one Aulus Plantius, an itinerant slave dealer . . ."

"That was the name given me by the girl herself," I told him. "It comes as no surprise that she lied, but she had been coached. My friend Duronius, who was my host that evening, confirmed that there was a slave dealer of that name, who sold him a cook."

"Yes, I ran across a record of that very transaction, which took place several days before the sale of the girl." He passed me his copy of the record of sale. I read the name of the seller and smiled. I passed it to Julia and her eyebrows went up. Then she looked at me.

"Gentlemen," I said, "I thank you. I will study the records Lucius Pedarius has brought later. I think I have everything I need now. I do hope you will accept my hospitality and stay for the—well, I won't call it a *trial,* but it will be a most damning presentation before the public."

"I would not miss it for anything," Cordus said.

12

THE DAY DAWNED SPLENDIDLY. IT HAD the sort of clear light spilling over the unspoiled countryside that the pastoral poets love to sing about. I detest pastoral poetry. To me the day was splendid because it put me one day closer to Sicily. As much as I loved southern Campania, I was anxious to be away.

At midmorning, Cato and his little band came clumping down the road, Cato giving the impression of wearing army boots despite his bare feet. He wore an expression of grim determination. Now that I think of it, that was the only expression he ever wore, with variations that included scorn, anger, and contempt.

"Hail, Praetor!" he shouted, saluting with upraised arm. "I take it you have things wrapped up here?"

"Just about," I said. I'd already sent a servant for copious wine and now we sat and she poured drinks all around.

"What do you want me to do?" Cato said, after he'd drained his cup and held it out for a refill.

"I want you here as a witness. I am about to do some things of questionable legality and I know that you will report to the Senate exactly what you have seen. There are few senators I can trust to do that."

He nodded. "Yes, there are no other senators who have my integrity." He said this with absolute sincerity and not a trace of humor. He was absolutely sincere about everything—and absolutely humorless. "How do you intend to proceed?"

I gave him a brief rundown of my plans. He nodded. "You will be exceeding your authority, all right, but I agree that the circumstances of this case are unique. Unique cases call for unique action. When Cicero condemned the Catilinarian conspirators to death without trial, he exceeded his powers as consul by a great margin, but I supported him because there was no other way he could have proceeded with sanity. When traitors are about to overthrow the constitution with violence, it is pure foolishness to give them the benefit of the constitution."

"Despite your support, which was admirable, Cicero ended up in exile," I noted.

He shrugged. "Sometimes a man must pay a price for his patriotic actions. At least he escaped death, which a good many senators wanted to inflict upon him."

"Things may get rough. I don't know for sure how many are involved in this and some may not come along quietly."

Cato gestured toward the men who followed him. They all looked supremely tough. So did Cato. "We don't object to a little bloodshed. Speaking of which, I heard you got shot with an arrow."

So I entertained him with the tale of my close brush with death. He and his men thought the whole affair was funny. I have said that Cato was humorless, but he did find amusement in things like pain and suffering. At the end he nodded with approval.

"That's the way to handle wounds: get back to the gymnasium as soon as you're back on your feet. A Roman on public service can't let something as trivial as being skewered by an arrow slow him down. You're just lucky that arrow wasn't poisoned."

I shuddered to think of it. "Apparently it didn't occur to my enemy to poison the arrows. About the only serious lapse in an otherwise excellent plan of mass homicide."

I sent for Hermes and he appeared within moments. "Hermes, take some men and go arrest the woman Porcia. Search her house thoroughly and bring back anything you find interesting. Put her under close guard in one of the rooms here. That means a permanent suicide watch."

He grinned. "So she's one of them after all, eh? I'm off!" He ran down the steps, calling out names, calling for horses. In moments he and a dozen other armed men were mounted and pelting down the road toward the villa. Then Cato surprised me.

"You've raised that one well. He'd make fine material for the army and even the Senate. It's too bad he's a freedman and barred from office. He's better quality than half the men in the Senate."

I was dumbfounded. For once, Marcus Porcius Cato had said something absolutely correct and sensible. "I'll tell him you said so. Coming from you, it will mean a lot to him."

"War is coming. When it comes, if you don't have a position for him, send him to me. I'll have command of at least one legion. I'll give him a centurionate." In those days it was still possible for an exceptional man to be appointed centurion without spending years in the ranks first.

"I will keep that offer in mind," I said, "but I expect that I'll have plenty of use for him."

Cato favored me with one of his rare smiles. "Of course, you'll be taking the field yourself." Cato always assumed that I was as military-minded as he was, and that I would look forward to wielding command. I had won a certain military distinction, but it was almost all against my own inclinations. He could never understand that. I certainly was not about to send Hermes to serve with Cato, no matter in what capacity. Not that Cato wasn't a good commander, but I knew he would sacrifice his army and himself over some point of principle that meant nothing to anyone else.

"All right," Cato said, "you've just taken your first extralegal step. I take it we are to expect more?"

"Far more," I assured him. He meant that I had no power of arrest here and the arrestee was not a foreigner.

"Good," Cato said.

Early in the afternoon, Pompey arrived. He was in full military fig and accompanied by a rather large bodyguard, around fifty mounted men. This was because of what I had written to him:

> *If you would like to see the end of this, come to my court as soon as you can. Bring some of your men. There may be trouble.*

He heaved himself from his saddle a little more adroitly this time, but he was still struggling with his weight. There was a two-inch gap between the front and back plates of his bronze cuirass. I took him to the terrace where our strategy session was still in progress. By this time I'd had a larger table brought out to accommodate our expanded numbers. He exchanged greetings with Julia, Cato, and some others. I gave him an abbreviated briefing on my findings and plan.

"I always thought it was unreasonable of Pedarius not to let me just go ahead and pay for the restoration of the temple," Pompey said. "I wouldn't have insisted on putting my name on the pediment."

"Poor men can be prouder than rich ones," I told him. "This one was so intent on preserving the dignity of his patrician name that it led him into some foolish choices."

"I hope he hasn't made me look foolish along with him," Pompey said ominously.

"You wanted this district to be quiet. When this is over it should be and you can concentrate on your recruiting."

"When do things start?" he wanted to know. "My time is limited."

"Almost everyone has arrived at my summons," I said. "We

should be able to begin tomorrow. If all goes well, it should be over to-morrow, too."

A prodigious crowd had gathered for the opening of my court the next morning. Actually, I use the word "court" advisedly. I was going to do something quite contrary to long-established Roman court practice. Perhaps if I had had more time and manpower, I might have called down some jurists from Rome to put it on a more conventional footing and make sure that the precedents were followed, but I had neither the time nor the resources.

A Roman praetor is not supposed to bring charges himself. He does not prosecute or defend. He presides in majesty over the arguments of lawyers and the deliberations of juries. He takes no part himself except to see to it that the proper forms are followed, that the jury's decisions are correctly arrived at, and at the conclusion he delivers his judgment in accordance with the findings of the jury. This was going to be very different.

My dais had been arranged so that Pompey and Cato sat beside me, my curule chair slightly elevated above theirs. Pompey had his own curule chair, spectacularly draped with tiger skins. Cato did not hold an imperium office and his chair was an ordinary one, slightly lower than Pompey's. My six lictors and Pompey's twelve made an impressive sight ranged before the dais, the polished wood and steel of their fasces shining in the morning sunlight. Just to add to the drama, Pompey had provided a pair of trumpeters with their great *cornus* curling over their shoulders.

I had Hermes make sure that everyone was present. It is always embarrassing to call a witness only to find that he is absent. It breaks the rhythm of the proceedings and makes the caller look foolish. He returned a while later to report that everyone was present. Just in front of my chair was a table, and it bore the documents I would need for my case.

In the forefront of the crowd were many of the most prominent persons of the district, and in the forefront of these were the various praetors, *duumviri*, dictators (yes, some towns called their elected headman dictator), and so forth of all the nearby towns. Ranged behind them were priests, guild chiefs, and other persons of consequence, many of them just plain rich. Those local lawyers looked at me with curiosity mixed with fear and anger. They knew that something here didn't smell right.

When I judged that the level of tension had reached the right pitch, I signaled the trumpeters and they blew a long, ringing blast. Instantly, the crowd fell silent. I stood and gathered my purple-bordered toga about me in the manner approved by all the best rhetoric instructors.

"Citizens!" I said, pitching my voice in outdoor-oratory mode, and flattering them somewhat since by no means all of them were citizens. "For some time now, this district has been afflicted by a most distressing series of murders. All the priests of the Temple of Apollo," here I gestured grandly toward that building, "a slave of that temple named Hypatia, a Syrian merchant of Pompeii named Elagabal, the wealthy widow Sabinilla, and now, I have learned, the patrician patron of the temple, Manius Pedarius, have been murdered!"

A murmur went through the crowd. Most of them had never heard of Elagabal, and this was the first proclamation that the death of the elder Pedarius had been a murder. They had a lot to murmur about.

"Not only that," I continued, "but I myself was nearly murdered, an arrow shot from ambush missing my heart by the breadth of a finger." This was something of an exaggeration for dramatic effect, but it had been close enough.

"These murders," I cried, "are only the latest and most public of a long line of homicides, going back many years, of which the people of this district were entirely oblivious. Consider this, citizens. Visitors have come to this area to consult with your oracles from all over Italy, from Greece and even from Ionia and beyond. They have come here, never to return to their homes. Murdered and robbed in your midst, their bodies disposed of, and you have known nothing of it. You have not even suspected that any of this was happening."

Those important dignitaries in the front row didn't like the sound of this. They depended on the transient trade. If people should get to thinking that this place was a death trap, those dignitaries stood to lose a good deal of money.

"Praetor!" one of them shouted. "These are outrageous accusations!"

"You will be silent while I speak," I proclaimed grandly. "As it happens, I have indeed marshaled a most incriminating host of documents and witnesses, sufficient to prove my charges accurate in the last detail." Then I gestured toward the two who flanked my chair. "Here to act as witnesses on behalf of the Senate of Rome are two of the most distinguished senators of our day: General Gnaeus Pompeius Magnus, most famous soldier in the world, propraetor of Spain and minister extraordinary of the grain supply, and the distinguished Marcus Porcius Cato, former praetor and the most incorruptible governor and minister Rome has ever produced." People cheered for Pompey and Cato. I hoped Pompey wasn't interpreting this as support for his military plans. Cheers cost nothing. "They will render to the Senate a full account of all that transpires here today."

I drew myself up. "Citizens, what has happened here was never the doing of a single murderer. It was the result of a conspiracy involving many persons, some of them active agents in robbery and murder, others passive accessories, who profited from their passivity and their silence."

They were quiet, half-stunned. "First of all, I charge Iola and the entire staff of the Oracle of Hecate!"

A local lawyer could stand no more. "It is no part of a praetor's duties to bring charges. This is an outrage and an example of Roman highhandedness and, dare I say it? Roman tyranny!" There were growls of agreement from the crowd.

"Don't arrest him or kill him," Pompey muttered in a low voice. "I need these people."

"Don't worry," I muttered back. I had expected exactly this accusation and had prepared for it.

"Citizens," I said with utmost scorn, "I would have been most happy to see some public-spirited local citizen come forward to indict these miscreants, but nobody has seen fit to do so. Nobody has raised a voice in the ten years that this outrageous conspiracy has existed! And it may go farther back than that. I felt it incumbent upon me to take up the task at which you have failed so miserably."

I switched to sarcastic, Ciceronian mode. "Of course, should one of you already have a case prepared and be ready now to come forth, I will be most happy to let you come forward, and I will resume my chair and preside." In a grand rhetorical gesture I cupped a hand to my ear and pretended to be listening. "What's this? Not a single voice to be heard?" I lowered my hand. "Then, if you will allow me to proceed." I turned to my lictors. "Bring forth the accused." The lictors marched off and returned with Iola and her crew, looking a bit the worse for a few nights in custody. At least they didn't have their dogs with them.

"Iola, I charge you and all your associates gathered here with the most heinous crime of murder, and not merely of murder but a whole series of murders. I charge you with sacrilege for falsifying oracles to lure your victims to their death, and with committing murder, and disposing of the bodies of the slain without the proper rites, in a place deemed holy for many centuries. How do you plead?"

She seemed to speak past some obstruction in her throat. "Not guilty, Praetor."

"I scarcely expected you to plead otherwise. Iola, stand with your other women over there, aside from the men." Mystified, she complied.

"Citizens," I went on, "I will now present you with the account of a crime typical of those perpetrated here. Ten years ago, there was an oil importer of Stabiae named Lucius Terentius. It was his custom to make voyages to consult with his suppliers overseas. Before undertaking a voyage, like many another traveler he would consult an oracle. On that occasion, he made the mistake of consulting the Oracle of the Dead, here at Hecate's sanctuary. I call the woman Floria, freedwoman of Terentius."

The woman was brought out and administered the terrible oath that calls down the vengeance of the gods on perjurers. Personally, I have never noticed anyone to suffer for committing perjury unless they were caught and couldn't bribe their way out of it. Still, I suppose the oath does no harm and scares some people into telling the truth.

"Floria," I said, "tell this court exactly what happened when your former master came to this place, and of what transpired afterward."

So she recited her story, much as I had heard it earlier. At first, her voice was weak, and I told her to speak up. When she finally understood that she would truly not be tortured or abused, she gained confidence and her voice steadied. It was actually far more effective than a rehearsed speech, and I could see that many of the onlookers were beginning to believe there was something to all this.

"Well done, Floria," I commended, when she was done. "Now, I want you to go over there"—I pointed to the knot of black-robed women—"and tell this court if you recognize the slave girl who so treacherously extracted crucial information about your master from you."

She walked over to them slowly. "I am not sure, Praetor. It was ten years ago."

"Just examine them carefully and see if you can recognize her."

The woman looked closely at them, one by one. Then she stopped and gasped. She pointed at Iola. "This is she, Praetor!"

"Are you certain, Floria? Be sure you are not mistaken."

"There is no mistake, Praetor! Now that I see her, I know her as if it was yesterday I saw her."

"Thank you, Floria. You are dismissed."

"So you see, citizens," I continued, "how they chose and deceived their victims. Those they picked were conducted to the shrine of Hecate, not the riverine Oracle chamber below, and given a false prophecy, which the victims believed to be the voice of Hecate herself. You will now learn how they performed this deception. I call the master stonemason Ansidius Perna." The man stepped forward and took the oath. "Perna, explain to this court the ventilation system that supplies fresh air to the subterranean tunnel."

Baldly, Perna explained how a second tunnel, above the first, provided ventilation. When he was done, I dismissed him.

"Ansidius Perna and his workmen cut me an access to the tunnel above. He did not accompany us on our exploration of this second tunnel. That was undertaken by myself and several of my companions. Directly above the chamber of the shrine we found lamps and litter indicating where Iola's confederate provided the false voice of Hecate. I would now like some of the distinguished men of this district to go and examine the ventilation tunnel and confirm that all I say is true. I have provided a ladder and my men will be there with torches. The more energetic of you may wish to travel the whole length of the tunnel, but it is a long walk, about two miles there and back."

As I had expected, quite a number of the prominent and less prominent people were eager to see this unprecedented marvel. While they were thus preoccupied, I decreed a recess, and most of the crowd headed for the vendors. I retired with Pompey and Cato to an inner room where we could drink without scandalizing anyone. Roman magistrates on court duty are supposed to abstain from food and wine for the duration. I had never seen this custom observed rigorously, but most officers tried to be discreet about it.

"Not much trouble so far," I said. "I expected more outrage."

"There would have been," Pompey said, "if we hadn't been here."

"True," I acknowledged. "The presence of heavily armed Roman soldiers has a remarkably calming effect."

Julia joined us. "I must say this is the strangest trial I have ever attended."

"The usual forms won't work in this situation," I told her.

"I am wondering," she said, "how you can get a verdict without empaneling a jury."

"Oh, I shall manage, my dear," I told her. She was not satisfied, but she knew better than to have at me in the presence of two high-ranking Romans. Roman wives, especially patrician wives, were not supposed to act that way, so she had to observe the proprieties. How she and all the other wives acted in private was another matter.

When we got word that people were returning from the tunnel, we went back out and I declared recess at an end.

"Are you satisfied," I asked, "that the circumstances of that tunnel are as I have described them?"

"We are, Praetor," said a man of distinction who appeared to be the spokesman for the group. "But we are at a loss how the false voice of Hecate reached the place above the shrine."

"When those who decided to go the whole length of the tunnel return, they will affirm that it ends at the bottom of what appears to be a deep and wide well, but which is in reality a sort of *mundus*. It is located in a remote area on the property of the woman Porcia, well known in this area." This raised a loud murmur from the spectators.

"Bring out Porcia," I said to my lictors. They tramped off and returned with the woman, who looked decidedly angry.

"Praetor!" she shouted before I could speak. "What is the meaning of this travesty? This is not a proper trial and you are charged only with hearing cases that involve citizens and foreigners. You have no right or authority to do this!" There were mutters from the crowd that she was right.

"As a matter of fact, Porcia, you are a woman of citizen status and she"—I pointed to Iola—"told me herself that she came here from Thrace. So she is a foreigner. I interpret this to mean that this matter falls beneath my purview. You will now take the oath."

Fuming, she did so.

"Very well," I said. "Now, Porcia, what was your father's name?"

"My father was Sextus Porcius," she said sullenly.

"I now summon Marcus Belasus, *duumvir* of Pompeii," I said. Belasus came forward, accompanied by a secretary. The secretary carried a satchel of the type used for holding papers. There was the usual oath taking and I continued. "*Duumvir,* will you tell this court the circumstances of my visit to Pompeii some days ago?"

Belasus explained about the murder of the Syrian Elagabal, and about my visit and what proceeded from it. He was a good public speaker, and threw in many embellishments and fine figures of speech. He left out the part about the party that evening.

"I thank you, *Duumvir,*" I said, when he was finished. The secretary took a paper and handed it to me. I held it up. "I have in my hand the first of many incriminating documents we found in the office of Elagabal the Syrian, supposedly a speculator in ships' cargoes, but in reality the most prodigious fence and receiver of stolen goods in all of Italy!" Once again, an exaggeration, but lawyers are expected to exaggerate. It is part of what makes a trial such a popular entertainment. I read off its list of goods. "These are typical robbers' and burglars' loot, and it was brought to Elagabal, something more than ten years ago, by none other than Sextus Porcius!" This went over well with the crowd. Many scornful looks were directed toward Porcia. Had she been well-born as well as rich, she might have drawn more sympathy, but she was a mere freedman's daughter, and her riches probably made her resented all the more.

"There are probably a hundred men named Sextus Porcius in Campania, Praetor!" she shouted. "Probably far more than that. This means nothing!"

"By itself, no," I agreed, "but it is only a small part of the evidence against you." I paused for drama. Then I held up a couple of the tiny arrows. "These, for instance. When we visited the *mundus* on your property and found some of these nearby, I asked what their significance might be, since they represented no Roman custom. You said that you didn't know what they were for. Yet I discovered that everyone else around here knows that they are used to petition a god for vengeance. Why this ignorance on your part, Porcia?"

"You think I know every detail about what people here believe? I'll bet there's lots you don't know about Roman religious practice.

Everyone's got more superstitions and beliefs than any one person can know about." The woman had a quick wit, I was forced to acknowledge.

"Yet," I said, "at the banquet held by my friend Duronius, whom I see in the first rank of those gathered here, you seemed to have a comprehensive command of local beliefs. And that *mundus* we visited, the one you said you thought was just a long-dry well that had been abandoned: That is the entrance to the ventilation tunnel." This last I spoke with the rising inflection employed by all lawyers and actors for making a major point. There came a collective gasp from the crowd.

"I told you I hardly ever visited there, and I spoke the truth!" she said. "You've seen my property. Anyone can go to that *mundus* without my ever knowing about it." I saw how Iola glared at Porcia. Iola sensed that she was doomed, but that Porcia might somehow get out of this. I was counting on her resentment.

"Yet the evidence is mounting against you, Porcia. You see, when I first suspected that the Oracle was faked, it occurred to me that whoever spoke as the voice of Hecate, a goddess, had to be a woman. You were the voice of Hecate, Porcia. On a day when a victim was to be fleeced by means of a false prophecy, you went down your *mundus*—we saw where you placed your ladder, by the way—and went down the tunnel to lie with your ear to the vent hole and listen for your cue like an actress about to go onstage. If it was going to be a long day, you took some refreshments with you. You left plenty of evidence behind."

"It wasn't me," she maintained.

"Iola, come over here," I said. Both women looked a bit startled, which was all to the good.

"Iola, you told me you came here from Thrace about seven years ago, but you were lying. According to the testimony of Floria, you were here ten years ago. You were a temple slave, or posing as one. Which was it?"

"The woman is lying. I was not here then and I was never a slave!"

"I believe you were here then, and that you were a slave, Iola. You see, the estimable Lucius Pedarius, whose family have been patrons of the Temple of Apollo for generations, has provided me with papers detailing the priests of Hecate as well as those of Apollo, their dates of accession and their deaths, providing some details of how they died. It also seems that there was a purchase of slaves twelve years ago including one young woman, unnamed, from Thrace. A lot seems to have started happening here right about that time."

"That was not I!" she cried, her voice trembling on the edge of hysteria. "The sanctuary has always had slaves, and many of them are from Thrace because that is the homeland of the goddess. I was born a free woman and I came here as a priestess!"

"Yet I believe you to be this Thracian girl in the records. There is no record of her manumission. You know what that means, do you not?" Iola went dead pale. As a noncitizen, a foreigner and a slave, she was subject to judicial torture.

"At the time you arrived, the priest was one Agathon. He died within a year of your purchase, displaying symptoms identical to those of the late Manius Pedarius, whom I am firmly convinced was poisoned by another slave recently arrived in his household. The position was then taken by one Cronion, who died shortly thereafter from an unspecified fall which resulted in a broken neck. Next to take up this hazardous office was Hecabe, a priestess, who lasted quite a bit longer, several years, before being found dead in her chamber from what appeared to be some sort of seizure: face blackened, eyes bulged and red, foam at the lips, and so forth."

"These were all natural deaths, Praetor," Iola protested.

"One such might not arouse suspicion," I admitted. "Even, perhaps, two. But three priestly deaths in a row that could easily be interpreted as violence or poisoning? This strains the limits of coincidence." Iola looked as if she was staring directly at her doom. Porcia, for her part, was glaring at Iola. She knew the other woman would break first.

"Oh, yes," I said, as if I had just remembered something, "there is a peculiarity about these records of the Pedarii. They go back for generations, kept by ancestors of the present generation of that family. They include fairly detailed records of their patronage of the Temple of Apollo. They also include much briefer records of the priesthood of the sanctuary of Hecate, since it seems there was a limited patronage of that cult, probably because both occupy essentially the same property. However, these record only such things as the accessions and deaths of the high priests and priestesses and, very occasionally, of large purchases of property such as slaves, this I presume because the Pedarii contributed some of the purchase money as partial patrons. These details of how the priests and the priestess died occur only in the records kept by Manius Pedarius, and only for the last ten to twelve years. Why do you think that might be?" I looked back and forth from Iola to Porcia. The crowd was utterly silent. I had them now.

"I will tell you what I think. I believe that Manius Pedarius was a man with a great deal of pride and very little money. His was once one of the great patrician families of Rome. They fell upon hard times, as have many other fine families, through no fault of their own but through bad luck or the malice of some god." Here I made one of the gestures to ward off the unwelcome attention of the immortals. It was repeated by everyone present, along with some local variants.

"Rather than continue dwelling in Rome as virtual paupers among the great families, they chose to remove to the south of Campania, where they prospered modestly and upheld the obligations of a patrician family through patronage of this unique double temple. It is not one of the great temples of Italy, but even its modest requirements strained the finances of the Pedarii.

"Some years ago, the priests of Apollo approached Manius Pedarius. The temple was in need of restoration. Could he undertake the costs incurred by this project? He could not, but he was too proud to say no. His patron and my friend General Pompey," here I gestured toward that resplendent figure, "very generously offered to underwrite the entire expense, and not even place his name on the pediment, the usual custom of one paying for such a project." There was applause for this largesse, which Pompey acknowledged with a slight inclination of his head.

"But Manius Pedarius thought it unfit that he should accept more than a fraction of the required money from his patron. Apparently, the priest of the sanctuary of Hecate knew of the proposed restoration and realized that this would put Pedarius in a very difficult situation. This was probably the priest Agathon, but I cannot be certain. He offered to cover the cost, but with a proviso: Pedarius was never again to visit the sanctuary, to take no interest in its doings. Naturally the man was suspicious, but he needed the money badly to save his honor. He stayed away, but he kept track of certain things, such as how the priests came and, more importantly, went. He had to be suspicious that the sanctuary had to have come by this wealth in some less than holy fashion."

"Praetor," Iola said, "this is pure speculation."

"Then call me a philosopher," I advised her. "My school of philosophy consists of collecting facts, even tiny facts that seem irrelevant, and building them into a picture of what has happened. With these facts and pictures, I can form a model, or to use the Greek word, a *paradigm*, of events as they are most likely to have occurred." I could see that nobody had the slightest idea what I was talking about. Well, I shouldn't have strayed into a field that I couldn't explain very well.

Pompey whispered behind me so only those on the dais could hear, "How far would this sophistry get you in a Roman court?" Even Cato chuckled.

"Thus," I said, getting back to business, "we can see that the illicit practices of the sanctuary of Hecate go back a number of years, probably before this woman Iola even came here. Perhaps they go back centuries, but we can do nothing about that. What is clear is that Iola brought a new scope to the proceedings—and I do not believe that she came up with the plan alone. Porcia was its creator."

"Prove that, Praetor," said the woman.

"In due time, Porcia. Be patient. We now come to the murder of Eugaeon and the rest of the priests of this venerable temple." Another grand sweep of the arm, toward the temple that stood above and behind me. A finely draped toga makes this gesture especially graceful and impressive. When the toga has a purple border, it can scarcely be matched.

"In earlier days, before the advent of the resourceful Iola and the devious Porcia, the practice at the sanctuary of Hecate had been to find petitioners who were from places far from here and who had no local friends who would notice their disappearance. They were taken into the chamber of the Styx and the Oracle"—I pronounced these heavily loaded words in my most solemn tones—"and there, instead of receiving a prophecy, they were murdered and their bodies thrust down into the river, where its powerful current swept them down beneath the earth, never to be seen again, their shades destined to wander forever because they never received the customary rites." My audience shuddered, their faces betraying horror.

"But Porcia," I pointed at her, "knew something that the clergy of the temple did not, or had long forgotten. You see, the tunnel and its grotto were here long before the Greeks or the Oscans came. It was already ancient even before they arrived. The cult of Hecate moved in and claimed it not knowing that the tunnel had a ventilation tunnel above it, and that the ventilation tunnel debouched at the supposed *mundus* on the estate of Porcia. At least, they didn't know until Porcia came and told them. But you didn't tell the whole staff, did you, Porcia? You told Iola first, and between you was hatched a long-range plan. The priests, Agathon or Cronion or whichever it was, would of course have leapt at a plan that promised such abundant booty with such safety. Nevertheless, you wanted to narrow the field. You would do away with the superiors until you had maneuvered Iola into the position of high priestess."

"I won't even protest this," Porcia said. "You have no power to condemn me. There is no jury here. Do as you like, I will take this all the way to the Senate at Rome."

Then Iola turned on her. "Of course he can do nothing to you. You are a woman of citizen status. I am a foreigner and have no rights here!"

Porcia glared at her. "Be still!"

Yes, they were definitely falling out. Time to work on Iola again.

"It was a cozy arrangement. Porcia provided the false Oracle. You picked the victims and committed the murders, except for those that had to be carried out at a distance by confederates, whom you will name for us later. Elagabal and probably others fenced the goods for you, and Manius Pedarius kept his mouth shut and stayed away. There was only one factor you did not have under control: those pesky priests of Apollo upstairs. They have been living side by side with you, only in a vertical fashion, for centuries. They just had to have noticed that there were odd doings going on down below."

Now I addressed the assembled audience in sorrowful tones, "I would like to believe that Eugaeon was threatening to denounce the Hecate cult as criminals and mass murderers, but it is also possible that Eugaeon wanted in on it and demanded a cut for himself. Which was it, Iola?"

"You have no proof!" she said desperately.

"That's a weak objection. No matter. Doubtless Apollo and Hecate will judge which of these people betrayed their trust, and in what fashion. Both are reputed to have terrible punishments in store for those who would violate their most sacred oaths." Porcia looked unimpressed, but Iola was clearly terrified.

"Once Eugaeon approached her, for whatever purpose, Iola and her confederates began to plot his death and those of the other priests. Murder had always been a simple business for these cultists: a rap on the head or noose around the throat, rifle the bodies, and send them down the river to the underworld. Or else leave it to professionals overseas. Either way was eminently safe. This was different. The priests of the Temple of Apollo were persons of public importance, known locally by everybody. They would be immediately missed, even if you could kill them all quickly and dispose of the bodies down the river. It had to be planned carefully, so that no suspicion could fall on you. You had to know the schedules and routines followed by the priests, and exactly when they would be most vulnerable. There was only one way you could accomplish this: plant a spy in the temple.

"Whatever their other austerities, the priests of Apollo are no less captivated by feminine beauty than are other men. To this end you acquired the girl Hypatia, a remarkable beauty, intelligent, and a good actress. You taught and coached her carefully, then you presented her to Eugaeon at an outrageously reasonable price. Smitten, he complied at once. Once in the temple, she commenced her true duties. I suspect that you already knew all about the other tunnel, that it had no ventilation and that the priests stayed down there only a short time. Hypatia told you the days and hours during which the priests descended to their crypt, and that they stayed only a short time, during which all other persons were barred from the temple. It was perfect. The girl would simply shut the trap behind them and they would suffocate quickly because they took numerous lamps or torches with them. A day was appointed on which to carry out the deed." I stood back and paused. Everyone was eager to hear what I had to say next.

"It would have worked, Iola, but two things happened that you could not have included in your calculations. First, a Roman praetor showed up and wanted to consult the Oracle. There was no way you could refuse. Second, when Eugaeon lost consciousness, he fell into the river and surfaced literally at our feet. Do you think it was the gods taking a hand in mortal matters to see that you suffer a horrible death in this world?"

"I never sold that girl to Eugaeon," Iola maintained. "There cannot be a single witness to say I did!"

"Quite right," I said to her. Then I pointed to Porcia. "You did."

"Liar," she said succinctly.

"One of the most gratifying things about criminal conspirators," I said to the audience in the tones of a teacher, "is that they rarely think of the evidence they leave behind in the form of papers. The written word can condemn as efficiently as the spoken word. Witness the lapses of these murderers, who otherwise planned their actions so admirably. They killed the fence Elagabal, but did not think to take his papers. They did away with Manius Pedarius, but left his papers for his son,

and consequently myself, to peruse at leisure. Here is another paper."
Again I held one aloft.

"When I questioned the girl Hypatia after the discovery of the dead priests, she said that she was sold to the temple by Aulus Plantius, a traveling slave dealer familiar to many here. When my suspicions were aroused and I began to put together my own explanation of what happened, I consulted with the distinguished historian Lucius Cordus and he generously found for me the relevant document." I gestured to where Cordus stood in the crowd and he basked in the attention.

"This is a praetor's office document for the sale of a slave girl named Hypatia to the Temple of Apollo. The seller is not identified as Aulus Plantius. The seller is named as Porcia, daughter of the freedman Sextus Porcius." There were great sounds of outrage from the crowd. "Her father was indeed that same Sextus Porcius who had dealings with Elagabal. She followed her father into the business."

At last Porcia saw the trap closing around her. "You two are guilty, and many others with you," I told the two women. "You might as well come clean. I remind you that you stand condemned to the complete satisfaction of these people here assembled. Only the presence of these soldiers keeps them from tearing you apart right now. I may decide to withdraw that protection. Talk, and you may live to bribe your way out of this. Decide now."

"She came to me with the proposition," Iola said, while Porcia looked disgusted. "She showed me the tunnel from her *mundus* to the chamber of the shrine. She said she'd found it when she was a little girl playing in the fields."

"And together you plotted out your future, but recently things went sour, as they usually do when too many people get involved with a criminal enterprise. It was time to eliminate most of your accomplices. You got rid of Pedarius, who was superfluous anyway. You got rid of Elagabal. There were plenty of other fences, ones who didn't know quite so much about you. Why was Sabinilla killed?"

"Her husband," Iola said, "the one we poisoned for her, was a partner of Sextus Porcius. She had overheard too many of his conversations with Porcius. She was stupidly extravagant and always in debt, always borrowing money from us. When you came here and she made such a point of cultivating you, we knew she would sell us out to you to escape prosecution for her involvement."

"I see. Well, now to a relatively minor matter: the attempt on my own life. Porcia, when you were arrested, my men searched your house and among other interesting things they found this." I gestured and Hermes handed me a very fine bow, made of layered wood and ibex horn, the sort a professional hunter would use. "You know, I had quite forgotten that, on our trip to the *mundus,* you had said that you enjoyed hunting. You didn't even have to hire an assassin, did you? You shot me yourself."

Finally, she gave up. "I hadn't practiced in too long."

"How did you ambush me? It was quite well done."

"I knew you were in Pompeii. When you left the town, I was well ahead of you in a litter. My Gauls can keep pace with slow-pacing horses easily. When you stopped, I took them off the road and went back through the brush with my bow. Pity my aim was off."

"Pity, indeed. And no wonder we didn't find you when you tried again and killed Sabinilla. My men were searching the countryside all around, but you arrived by way of your tunnel, where we had thoughtfully made you a door to the temple grounds, and you returned the same way. The dogs couldn't track you because your scent was all over the place, so often did you visit."

Porcia shook her head. "That stupid bitch." I knew she wasn't referring to Iola.

"Yes, I was about to ask about that. Why did poor Hypatia reveal to us where the bodies were hidden?"

"The little slut went and got herself pregnant by one of the younger priests," Porcia said. "It meant nothing to me. All the priests had to die. But she felt"—she searched, as if for an unfamiliar word—"she felt *guilty* or something. She thought if she showed you where the bodies

214

were, she might get off if the whole story should come out. Another night, and we'd have gotten them disposed of, down the river. We never thought you'd set up your court right here and move in. It made things awkward."

"So you sent word to her to come join you in the stables, that you'd take her to safety. Then you stabbed her just as you stabbed Elagabal. I have to hand it to you, Porcia, you don't delegate the dirty work."

"Like you said, Praetor, it's not a good idea to have too many people in on an extralegal operation."

"So it is." I drew myself up and faced the crowd. "For crimes of multiple murder too numerous to enumerate and, I might add, including poisoning which carries extra penalties, I condemn all these people to death. I'll think up some really nasty way to do it."

The crowd was stunned by my abruptness. They had expected a summation, a great speech, something they could repeat in the bars, but some of the more legal-minded detected certain flaws in my actions.

"Praetor," said a *duumvir* of Cumae, "while there can be no doubt that these vile creatures deserve the worst of punishments, you are still not authorized to carry out summary executions. There has been no true trial by a jury, no arguments, only the results of your own investigation, which all here must agree has been superlative. We must observe the legalities."

"We must?" I said. "Well, I suppose you're right. I'm done here. You can all go home." I looked at the accused. "You're dismissed. It looks like I can't have you executed after all."

"Praetor!" Iola said, looking around with bugged-out eyes at the surrounding crowd. "They will rip us apart!"

"Oh, I don't think so," I said. "What's about to happen will be the most celebrated trial in Italy. Whoever prosecutes you will be famous. His legal reputation will be made. He can move to Rome and maybe win a seat in the Senate." I pitched my words so that all could hear and already I could see the lawyers and politicians cutting deals.

"People of Campania," I cried, "I have truly enjoyed my stay here and I hope to see you all again someday. Now, I'm off for Sicily!"

Of course, everyone knows what happened in the next years. Caesar crossed the Rubicon and the war came. Pompey perished miserably in Egypt and Cato died nobly in Utica. I tried to keep my head down and attached to my shoulders. My Julia died many years ago. Every December I sacrifice to her shade, hoping it brings her some comfort. I will know soon enough.

These things happened in Campania in the year 704 of the City of Rome, in the consulship of Lucius Aemilius Lepidus Paullus and Caius Claudius Marcellus. We did not know it then, but it was the last year of the true Republic.

GLOSSARY

(Definitions apply to the year 704 of the Republic.)

Aborigine, Aboriginal   In Roman legend, the earliest inhabitants of
Italy, before the arrival of Aeneas from Troy.

arms   Like everything else in Roman society, weapons were strictly
regulated by class. The straight, double-edged sword and dagger of the
legions were classed as "honorable."

The *gladius* was a short, broad, double-edged sword borne by Roman soldiers. It was designed primarily for stabbing. The *pugio* was a
dagger also used by soldiers.

The *caestus* was a boxing glove, made of leather straps and rein-
forced by bands, plates, or spikes of bronze. The curved, single-edged
sword or knife called a *sica* was "infamous." *Sicas* were used in the arena
by Thracian gladiators and were carried by street thugs. One ancient

writer says that its curved shape made it convenient to carry sheathed beneath the armpit, showing that gangsters and shoulder holsters go back a long way.

Carrying of arms within the *pomerium* (the ancient city boundary marked out by Romulus) was forbidden, but the law was ignored in troubled times. Slaves were forbidden to carry weapons within the City, but those used as bodyguards could carry staves or clubs. When street fighting or assassinations were common, even senators went heavily armed, and even Cicero wore armor beneath his toga from time to time.

Shields were not common except as gladiatorial equipment. The large shield (*scutum*) of the legions was unwieldy in narrow streets, but bodyguards might carry the small shield (*parma*) of the light-armed auxiliary troops. These came in handy when the opposition took to throwing rocks and roof tiles.

augur An official who observed omens for state purposes. He could forbid business and assemblies if he saw unfavorable omens.

autochthenoi Greek word meaning literally "sons of the earth," i.e., being decended from natives who inhabited the land from time immemorial.

auxilia *See* **military terms.**

basilica A meeting place of merchants and for the administration of justice. Among them were the Basilica Aemilia (aka Basilica Fulvia and Basilica Julia), the Basilica Opimia, the Basilica Portia, and the Basilica Sempronia (the latter devoted solely to business purposes).

bustuarii The earliest gladiators. The name comes from *bustuum,* a funeral pyre. These gladiators fought at the pyre or tomb site of the deceased dignitary to propitiate his shade.

client, pl. *clientele* One attached in a subordinate relationship to a patron, whom he was bound to support in war and in the courts. Freedmen became clients of their former masters. The relationship was hereditary.

colonia   Roman colonies were originally established as military out-posts. At this period of the Republic, *colonia* were lands given to vet-eran soldiers as a reward for service.

crucifixions   The Romans inherited the practice of crucifixion from the Carthaginians. In Rome, it was reserved for rebellious slaves and insurrectionists. Citizens could not be crucified.

curule   A curule office conferred magisterial dignity. Those holding it were privileged to sit in a **curule chair**—a folding camp chair that be-came a symbol of Roman officials sitting in judgment.

duumvir, **pl.** *duumviri*   A duumvirate was a board of two men. Many Italian towns were governed by *duumviri*. A *duumvir* was also a Roman admiral, probably dating from a time when the Roman navy was com-manded by two senators.

eagles   The standard of a Roman legion was a gilded eagle. The eagle was the tutelary deity of the legion and came to embody the legion it-self. Thus, a Roman on military service was "with the eagles."

eques, **pl.** *equites*   These were originally "kinghts" who fought on horseback. At this time during the Republic, they were a social class below the patrician Senate and above the plebeians. *See* **orders.**

families and names   Roman citizens usually had three names. The given name (**praenomen**) was individual, but there were only about eighteen of them: Marcus, Lucius, etc. Certain praenomens were used only in a single family: Appius was used only by the Claudians, Mamer-cus only by the Aemilians, and so forth. Only males had praenomens. Daughters were given the feminine form of the father's name: Aemilia for Aemilius, Julia for Julius, Valeria for Valerius, etc.

Next came the **nomen.** This was the name of the clan (gens). All members of a gens traced their descent from a common ancestor, whose name they bore: Julius, Furius, Licinius, Junius, Tullius, to name a few. Patrician names always ended in *ius*. Plebeian names often had differ-ent endings. The name of the clan collectively was always in the femi-nine form, e.g., Aemilia.

A subfamily of a gens is the **stirps.** Stirps is an anthropological term. It is similar to the Scottish clan system, where the family name "Ritchie" for instance, is a stirps of the Clan MacIntosh. The **cognomen** gave the name of the stirps, i.e., Caius Julius Caesar. Caius of the stirps Caesar of gens Julia.

The name of the family branch **(cognomen)** was frequently anatomical: Naso (nose), Ahenobarbus (bronzebeard), Sulla (splotchy), Niger (dark), Rufus (red), Caesar (curly), and many others. Some families did not use cognomens. Mark Antony was just Marcus Antonius, no cognomen.

Other names were **honorifics** conferred by the Senate for outstanding service or virtue: Germanicus (conqueror of the Germans), Africanus (conqueror of the Africans), or Pius (extraordinary filial piety).

Freed slaves became citizens and took the family name of their master. Thus the vast majority of Romans named, for instance, Cornelius would not be patricians of that name, but the descendants of that family's freed slaves. There was no stigma attached to slave ancestry.

Adoption was frequent among noble families. An adopted son took the name of his adoptive father and added the genetive form of his former nomen. Thus when Caius Julius Caesar adopted his great-nephew Caius Octavius, the latter became Caius Julius Caesar Octavianus.

All these names were used for formal purposes such as official documents and monuments. In practice, nearly every Roman went by a nickname, often descriptive and rarely complimentary. Usually it was the Latin equivalent of Gimpy, Humpy, Lefty, Squint-eye, Big Ears, Baldy, or something of the sort. Romans were merciless when it came to physical peculiarities.

fasces   A bundle of rods bound around with an ax projecting from the middle. They symbolized a Roman magistrate's power of corporal and capital punishment and were carried by the lictors who accompanied the curule magistrates, the *Flamen Dialis* (*see* **Priestheads**), and the proconsuls and propraetors who governed provinces.

First Citizen   In Latin: *Princeps*. Originally the most prestigious senator, permitted to speak first on all important issues and set the order of debate. Augustus, the first emperor, usurped the title in perpetuity. Decius detests him so much that he will not use either his name (by the time of the writing it was Caius Julius Caesar Octavianus) or the honorific Augustus, voted by the toadying Senate. Instead he will refer to him only as the First Citizen. *Princeps* is the origin of the modern word "prince."

forum   An open meeting and market area.

freedman   A manumitted slave. Formal emancipation conferred full rights of citizenship except for the right to hold office. Informal emancipation conferred freedom without voting rights. In the second or at least third generation, a freedman's descendants became full citizens.

games *ludus*, **pl.** *ludi*   Public religious festivals put on by the state. There were a number of long-established *ludi,* the earliest being the Roman Games *(ludi Romani)* in honor of Jupiter Optimus Maximus and held in September. The *ludi Megalenses* were held in April, as were the *ludi Cereri* in honor of Ceres, the grain goddess, and the *ludi Floriae* in honor of Flora, the goddess of flowers. The *ludi Apollinares* were celebrated in July. In October the *ludi Capitolini;* the final games of the year were the Plebian Games *(ludi Plebeii)* in November. Games usually ran for several days except for the Capitoline games, which ran for a single day. Games featured theatrical performances, processions, sacrifices, public banquets, and chariot races. They did not feature gladiatorial combats. The gladiatorial games, called *munera,* were put on by individuals as funeral rites.

genius loci   The spirit of a particular place. An altar to the *genius loci* was typically a squat pillar with a serpent wrapped around it.

gravitas   The quality of seriousness.

gymnasium, *palaestra*   Greek and Roman exercise facilities. In Rome they were often an adjunct to the baths.

imperium   The ancient power of kings to summon and lead armies, to order and forbid, and to inflict corporal and capital punishment. Under the Republic, the imperium was divided among the consuls and praetors, but they were subject to appeal and intervention by the tribunes in their civil decisions and were answerable for their acts after leaving office. Only a dictator had unlimited imperium.

Lapis Niger   A very ancient monument in the Forum, consisting of a block of basalt carved with words in extremely archaic Latin. It was already ancient during the late Republic and only a few words were recognizable. It bears to this day the oldest example of written Latin.

legion   Legions formed the fighting force of the Roman army. Through its soldiers, the Empire was able to control vast stretches of territory and people. They were known for their discipline, training, ability, and military prowess.

libitinarii   Rome's undertakers. Their name comes from Venus Libitina, Venus in her aspect as death goddess. Like many other Roman customs associated with the underworld, the funeral rites had many Etruscan practices and trappings.

lictor   Bodyguards, usually freedmen, who accompanied magistrates and the *Flamen Dialis,* bearing the fasces. They summoned Assemblies, attended public sacrifices, and carried out sentences of punishment.

maiestas   A crime against "the majesty and dignity of the Roman people." Not quite treason, but still a serious offense, it became a catch-all charge to use against one's political enemies in the late Republic.

Master of Horse   In Latin *Magister Equitum.* A dictator's second in command. In times of emergency, the Senate could appoint a dictator who would have absolute imperium. The dictator would appoint a Master of Horse who would carry out his orders. Marc Antony (Marcus Antonius) was Julius Caesar's Master of Horse.

military terms   The Roman legionary system was quite unlike any military organization in existence today. The regimental system used by all modern armies date from the Wars of Religion of the sixteenth century. These began with companies under captains that grouped into regiments under colonels, then regiments grouped into divisions under generals. By the Napoleonic wars they had acquired higher organizations such as corps, army groups, and so forth, with an orderly chain of command from the marshal down through the varying degrees of generals, colonels, majors, captains, sergeants, corporals, and finally the privates in the ranks.

The Roman legions had nothing resembling such an organization. At the time of the SPQR novels the strength of a legion was theoretically 6,000 men, but the usual strength was around 4,800. These were divided into sixty centuries. Originally, a century had included one hundred men, but during this period there were about eighty. Each century was commanded by a **centurion,** making sixty centurions to the legion. Six centuries made a cohort. Each centurion had an *optio* as his second in command. The centurionate was not a single rank, but a complex of hierarchy and seniority, many details of which are obscure. We know that there were first-rank and second-rank centurions. The senior centurion of the legion was ***primus pilus,*** the "first spear." He was centurion of the first century of the first cohort and outranked all others. Centurions were promoted from the ranks for ability and they were the nearest thing a legion had to permanent officers. All others were elected or appointed politicians.

Legionaries were Roman citizens. They fought as heavy infantry, fully armored and armed with the heavy javelin (***pilum***), the short Spanish sword (***gladius Hispaniensis***), and the straight, double-edged dagger (***pugio***). They carried a very large shield (***scutum***) that at that time was usually oval and curved to fit around the body. Besides holding the center of the battle line, legionaries were engineers and operated the siege weapons: catapults, team-operated crossbows, and so forth.

Attached to each legion were usually an equal number of ***auxilia,*** noncitizen troops often supplied by allies. These were lightly armed troops, skirmishers, archers, slingers, and other missile troops, and cavalry. The legion had a small citizen cavalry force but depended upon the *auxilia* for the bulk of the cavalry. Through long service an auxiliary could earn citizen status, which was hereditary: his sons could serve in the legions. *Auxilia* received lower pay and had lower status, but they were essential when operating in broken terrain or heavy forest, where the legions could not be used to advantage. In battle they often held the flanks and usually, with the cavalry, were charged with pursuing a broken and fleeing enemy, preventing them from re-forming or counterattacking.

There were other formations within a legion, some of them obscure. One was the **antesignani,** "those who fight before the standards." Already nearly obsolete, they were apparently an elite strike force, though how it was manned and used is uncertain. It seems exceptional bravery was required for assignment to the *antesignani.*

In Decius's time the legions were still formed as a unit, served for a number of years, then discharged collectively. Even when on many years' service, they were ceremonially disbanded, then re-formed every year, with the soldier's oath renewed each time. This archaic practice was extremely troublesome. When a few years later Augustus reformed the military system, legions became permanent institutions, their strength kept up by continuous enlistment of new soldiers as old ones retired or died. Many of the Augustan legions remained in service continuously for centuries.

The commander of a legion might be a **consul** or **praetor,** but more often he was a **proconsul** or **propraetor** who, having served his year in Rome, went out to govern a province. Within his province he was commander of its legions. He might appoint a **legate** (*legatus*) as his assistant. The legate was subject to approval by the Senate. He might choose a more experienced military man to handle the army work while the promagistrate (proconsul, propraetor, proquaestor, or procurator) concentrated upon civil affairs; but a successful war was important to a political career, while enriching the commander. For an extraordinary command, such as Caesar's in Gaul or Pompey's against the pirates, the promagistrate might be permitted a number of legates.

Under the commander were **Tribunes of the Soldiers,** usually young men embarking upon their political careers. Their duties were entirely at the discretion of the commander. Caesar usually told his tribunes to sit back, keep their mouths shut, and watch the experienced men work. But a military tribune might be given a responsible position, even command of a legion. The young Cassius Longinus as tribune prosecuted a successful war in Syria after his commander was dead.

mundus, **pl.** *mundi*   Literally, "mouth." A cave or opening in the ground believed to lead to the underworld and used to contact the dead.

munera   Special games, not part of the official calendar, at which gladiators were exhibited. They were originally funeral games and were always dedicated to the dead.

offices   The political system of the Roman Republic was completely different from any today. The terms we have borrowed from the Romans have very different meanings in the modern context. "Senators" were not elected and did not represent a particular district. "Dictator" was a temporary office conferred by the Senate in times of emergency. "Republic" simply meant a governmental system that was not a hereditary monarchy. By the time of the SPQR series, the power of former Roman kings was shared among a number of citizen assemblies.

Tribunes of the People were representatives of the plebeians, with power to introduce laws and to veto actions of the Senate. Only plebeians could hold the office, which carried no imperium. **Tribunes of the Soldiers** were elected from among the young men of senatorial or equestrian rank to be assistants to generals. Usually it was the first step of a man's political career.

A Roman embarked upon a public career followed the **cursus honorum**, i.e., the "path of honor." After doing staffwork for officials, he began climbing the ladder of office. These were taken in order as follows:

The lowest elective office was **quaestor:** bookkeeper and paymaster for the Treasury, the Grain Office, and the provincial governors. These men did the scut work of the Roman world. After the quaestorship he was eligible for the **Senate,** a nonelective office, which had to be ratified by the censors; if none were in office, he had to be ratified by the next censors to be elected.

Next were the **aediles.** Roughly speaking, these were city managers, responsible for the upkeep of public buildings, streets, sewers, markets, brothels, etc. There were two types: the **plebeian aediles** and the **curule aediles.** The curule aediles could sit in judgment on civil cases involving markets and currency, while the plebeian aediles could only levy fines. Otherwise their duties were the same. The state only provided a tiny stipend for improvements, and the rest was the aedile's problem. If he put on (and paid for) splendid games, he was sure of election to higher office.

Third was **praetor,** an office with real power. Praetors were judges, but they could command armies, and after a year in office they could go out to govern provinces, where real wealth could be won, earned, or stolen. In the late Republic, there were eight praetors. Senior was the *praetor urbanus,* who heard civil cases between citizens of Rome. The *praetor peregrinus* (praetor of the foreigners) heard cases involving foreigners. The others presided over criminal courts. After leaving office, the ex-praetors became **propraetors** and went on to govern propraetorian provinces with full imperium.

The highest office was **consul,** supreme office of power during the Roman Republic. Two were elected each year. Consuls called meetings of the Senate and presided there. The office carried full imperium and they could lead armies. On the expiration of their year in office, ex-consuls were usually assigned the best provinces to rule as **proconsul.** A proconsul had the same insignia and the same number of lectors as a consul. His power was absolute within his province. The most important commands always went to proconsuls.

Censors were elected every five years. This was the capstone to a political career, but it did not carry imperium and there was no foreign command afterward. Censors conducted the census, purged the Senate of unworthy members, doled out the public contracts, confirmed new senators in office, and conducted the *lustrum,* a ritual of purification. They could forbid certain religious practices or luxuries deemed bad for public morals or generally "un-Roman." There were two censors, and each could overrule the other. They were usually elected from among the ex-consuls.

Under the Sullan Constitution, the quaestorship was the minimum requirement for membership in the Senate. The majority of senators had held that office and never held another. Membership in the Senate was for life, unless expelled by the censors.

No Roman official could be prosecuted while in office, but he could be after he stepped down. Malfeasance in office was one of the most common court charges.

The most extraordinary office was **dictator.** In times of emergency, the Senate could instruct the consuls to appoint a dictator, who could wield absolute power for six months, after which he had to step down from office. Unlike all other officials, a dictator was unaccountable: he could not be prosecuted for his acts in office. The last true dictator was appointed in the third century B.C. The dictatorships of Sulla and Julius Caesar were unconstitutional.

orders The Roman hierarchy was divided into a number of orders (*ordines*). At the top was the **Senatorial Order** (*Ordo Senatus*) made up of the senators. Originally the Senate had been a part of the Equestrian Order, but the dictator Sulla made them a separate order.

Next came the **Equestrian Order** (*Ordo Equestris*). This was a property qualification. Men above a certain property rating, determined every five years by the censors, belonged to the Equestrian Order, so named because in ancient times, at the annual hosting, these wealthier men brought horses and served in the cavalry. By the time of the SPQR novels, they had lost all military nature. The equestrians (*equites*) were the wealthiest class, the bankers and businessmen, and after the Sullan reforms they supplied the jurymen. If an *eques* won election to the quaestorship, he entered the Senatorial Order. Collectively, they wielded immense power. They often financed the political careers of senators and their business dealings abroad often shaped Roman foreign policy.

Last came the **Plebeian Order** (*Ordo Plebis*). Pretty much everybody else, and not really an order in the sense of the other two, since plebeians might be equestrians or senators. Nevertheless, as the mass of the citizenry they were regarded as virtually a separate power and they elected the Tribunes of the People, who were in many ways the most powerful politicians of this time.

Slaves and foreigners had no status and did not belong to an order.

patrician   The noble class of Rome.

pedagogues   Greek for a slave who accompanied children to school.

Pomerium   The sacred boundary of the City of Rome.

popular assemblies   There were several of these. They were non-senatorial and had varying powers. The *Comitia centuriata* included the entire citizenry. The *consilium plebis* was restricted to the plebeians. The *comitia tribute* consisted of the citizenry organized in "tribes" (voting groups.)

praetor peregrinus   *See* **offices.**

priesthoods   In Rome, the priesthoods were offices of state. There were two major classes: *pontifexes* and *flamines*.

Pontifexes were members of the highest priestly college of Rome. They had superintendence over all sacred observances, state and private, and over the calendar. The head of their college was the ***Pontifex Maximus,*** a title held to this day by the pope.

The *flamines* were the high priests of the state gods: the *Flamen Martialis* for Mars, the *Flamen Quirinalis* for the deified Romulus, and, highest of all, the *Flamen Dialis,* high priest of Jupiter.

The *Flamen Dialis* celebrated the Ides of each month and could not take part in politics, although he could attend meetings of the Senate, attended by a single lictor. Each had charge of the daily sacrifices, wore distinctive headgear, and was surrounded by many ritual taboos.

Another very ancient priesthood was the ***Rex Sacrorum,*** "King of Sacrifices." This priest had to be a patrician and had to observe even more taboos than the *Flamen Dialis*. The position was so onerous that it became difficult to find a patrician willing to take it.

Technically, pontifexes and flamines did not take part in public business except to solemnize oaths and treaties, give the god's stamp of approval to declarations of war, etc. But since they were all senators anyway, the ban had little meaning. Julius Caesar was *Pontifex Maximus* while he was out conquering Gaul, even though the *Pontifex Maximus* wasn't supposed to look upon human blood.

Princeps (First Citizen)   This was an especially distinguished senator chosen by the censors. His name was first called on the roll of the Senate, and he was first to speak on any issue. Later the title was usurped by Augustus and is the origin of the word "prince."

scena   A building or backdrop for a play.

The Sibylline Books   Very ancient books of prophecy, kept by a priesthood called the *quinquidecemviri;* (board of fifteen men). In uncertain times, the Senate might order a consultation of these books to discern the will of the gods. The language was very archaic and obscure and the interpretation doubtful.

sistrum   A percussion instrument consisting of a handheld frame to which small metal deses are attached, rather like those on a tamborine.

Social War   A war fought from 91 to 88 B.C. between Rome and its Italian allies. It is call "Social" from *socii*, Latin for "allies." It is also called the Marsic War (from Marsi, the most prominent tribe). Unrest developed among Rome's allies when Rome stopped sharing wartime plunder. A political solution was first sought that citizenship. However, when Marcus Livius Drusus, who was the chief sponsor of the measure was assasinated war broke out. Rome won in the field, but wound up giving citizenship to the allies, thus a share in war plunder plus voting rights.

SPQR *Senatus Populusque Romanus*   The Senate and People of Rome. The formula embodied the sovereignty of Rome. It was used on official correspondence, documents, and public works.

subligaculum   The Roman loincloth. Typically worn during athletic activity.

thyrsus* pl. *thyrsi   A wand wreathed with vines and tipped with a pinecone. It was part of the regalia of the rites of Dionysus/Bacchus.

toga   The outer robe of the Roman citizen. It was white for the upper class, darker for the poor and for people in mourning. The ***toga candidus***

was a specially whitened (with chalk) toga worn when standing for office. The *toga praetexta,* bordered with a purple stripe, was worn by curule magistrates, by state priests when performing their functions, and by boys prior to manhood. The *toga trabea,* a striped robe, was worn by augurs and some orders of the priesthood. The *toga picta,* purple and embroidered with golden stars, was worn by a general when celebrating a triumph, also by a magistrate when giving public games.

triclinium   A dining room.

triumph   A ceremony in which a victorious general was rendered semidivine honors for a day. It began with a magnificent procession displaying the loot and captives of the campaign and culminated with a banquet for the Senate in the Temple of Jupiter, special protector of Rome.

Vestal Virgins   Virgin priestesses, chaste like the goddess Vesta; six of them served for thirty years, and any violation of the vow of chastity was punished by burial alive. Vesta's shrine was the most sacred object of Roman religion.